Some Glad Morning

A Novel

Some Glad Morning

—Irene J. Steele—

AS/IS Press
Huntsville, AL

Some Glad Morning © 2007 Irene J. Steele

Printed in the United States of America
Set in Goudy Old Style
Designed by Scottie Designs

Publisher's Cataloging-In-Publication Data
(Prepared by The Donohue Group, Inc.)

Steele, Irene J.
  Some glad morning : a novel / by Irene J. Steele.

  p. ; cm.

  ISBN-13: 978-0-578-33709-8
  ISBN-10: 0-9772515-1-9

1. African Americans—Civil rights—History—20th century—Fiction. 2. African Americans—Illinois—Chicago—History—20th century—Fiction. 3. Chicago (Ill.)—History—20th century—Fiction. 4. Political campaigns—Illinois—Chicago—Fiction. 5. African American women—Fiction. I. Title.

PS3619.T44 S66 2007
813/.6
2006933099

ACKNOWLEDGMENTS

Grateful acknowledgment is extended to the songwriters and music publishers for permission to reprint selected lyrics from the following works.

"Four-Day Creep" by Ida Cox © 1961 by Vogue Music. All rights administered by Universal—Songs of Polygram International, Inc./BMI. Used with permission. All Rights Reserved.

"Gimme a Pigfoot (And a Bottle of Beer)" © 1933 by Wesley "Six" Wilson, courtesy of Universal Music.

"I'd Rather Go Blind," courtesy of Arc Music Group. Used with permission.

"I'll Fly Away" by Albert E. Brumley © Copyright 1932 in "Wonderful Message" by Hartford Music Co. Renewed 1960 by Albert E. Brumley & Sons/SESAC (admin. by ICG). All rights reserved. Used with permission.

"I Never Make My Move Too Soon" © 1970 by Will Jennings. Used with permission.

"Take Him Off My Mind" by Porter Grainger © 1940 by Peer International Corporation, Copyright renewed. International Copyright secured. Used with permission. All Rights Reserved.

Portions of this novel have been published previously as "A Movement of the People" in *West Side Stories* © 1993 City Stoop Press and *Guildworks: Writings by the West Side Writers Guild* © 1996 Blacksmith Press.

For Tony: "...The voice of my beloved! Behold, he cometh leaping upon the mountains, skipping upon the hills..."
        —Song of Solomon, 2:8, King James Version

To: My mother, Juanita Smith, who instilled in me the love of literature.

To: Pastor Robert J. Brown, Jr. Thank you for your encouragement.

To the memory of Shaun Westbrook.

EASTER SUNDAY, CHICAGO, ILLINOIS, 1984

THE CONGREGATION IN WISDOM SEAT Baptist Church was hushed. All eyes were focused on a four-year-old brown-skinned girl in a red-and-white ruffled dress.

Trembling, the child looked out upon the congregation and reached down to scratch her knee. Twisting her hands together, she looked at the front pew as if for reassurance. Then, taking a deep breath, she said, "I don't know why you all are looking at me; I didn't come to stay. I just came to tell you that today is Easter Day."

The congregation clapped and cheered loudly. Mothers smiled as the little girl ran to sit down. "Who was that?" Mildred whispered. "She sure is cute."

"That's Nikki Anderson's little girl Jamila."

Aunt Rose held her fan in front of her face as she talked to her niece. "You've seen Nikki and Dwayne—they live in Mrs. Patillo's building. Dwayne works at the Greater Foods over on Kedzie, and I think Nikki stays at home." She began to fan vigorously.

The organist began to play the first bars of "Blessed Quietness." The congregation fell silent as they waited to receive the Word. Reverend Giles slowly approached the pulpit, pausing every now and then as if to ponder some divine inspiration. His long flowing purple robe shimmered with each step, and the grave expression on his face told all that this would not be a happy sermon.

"Good morning," he whispered, shaking his head at the seriousness of his task.

"Good morning," the congregation murmured back as they prepared themselves for their fall from grace.

"I have," Reverend Giles cleared his throat, "a serious message to lay on you today. Amen. The Lord pressed this upon me last night, and I struggled with it all night long, church."

Some of the parishioners nodded as if they, too, had experienced this same dilemma. "Preach it," a few called out.

"Talk, Pastor," a young woman urged.

The organist played a few tentative bars. "The Lord wants me to talk to the womenfolk today," the reverend intoned. Aware that he had the congregation's full attention, he leaned back and folded his arms over his protruding stomach.

"The family unit is being destroyed!" he thundered. "Young women today think there's something wrong with staying at home and taking care of their families, Amen. They beat their husbands getting up and going to work, letting someone or something else raise their kids!"

Reverend Giles searched the faces for confirmation. Mildred stared blankly ahead. Aunt Rose bobbed her head and waved her fan.

"They don't want to cook; they don't want to clean..." Reverend Giles punctuated each point by jabbing his finger at members of the congregation. "They just don't want! But they do want to spend your money," he shouted.

Mildred leaned toward her aunt. "Is this directed at us or at Mrs. Giles?" she whispered.

"They want to buy shoes and bags from Gucci and Lucci," he continued. A few teenagers giggled in the back of the church. Reverend Giles focused in their direction. "They want to walk around with all kinds of face paint on." He began to strut back and forth in imitation. "They want to go out and drink and shake and shimmy," his voice began to escalate as he performed his version of a young girl's dance. "And you can't talk to the mothers about them!" He screamed, "Help me, church! Because the mothers are out there on the floor shaking with their daughters!"

The organist struck up a lively tempo, and people began to witness. Reverend Giles collapsed into his high-backed chair and wiped his face before continuing his sermon.

* * *

Aunt Rose sat in front of the window in her rocking chair, watching the neighborhood. Mildred lay on the floor in front of her, reading.

"Mildred Walker," Aunt Rose whispered to herself and chuckled. Mildred glanced up and wondered what story Aunt Rose was reliving about herself and Mildred Walker. "Mildred Walker." Aunt Rose said the name belonged to a woman that folks were still talking about in Crayton, Tennessee. Mildred Walker didn't take nothing from nobody. She stood up for what she believed in, and if she thought you were right, she stood up for what you believed in, too. Aunt Rose often turned to her niece to say, "My greatest compliment to her, and my gift to you, was to give you her name. Wear it proudly and take it to her on Judgment Day"—she always stopped and fixed her eyes on Mildred at that point—"unstained."

"Unstained Mildred Johnson," Mildred called herself privately. The only thing that stopped her from saying it out loud was that maybe someone would hear it and take it up like a chant, and then before you knew it, everyone would be saying it over and over: "Unstained Mildred Johnson! Unstained Mildred Johnson!"

"Mildred, are you listening to me?" Aunt Rose's voice broke the silence.

"Yes, Aunt Rose."

"If you want to meet a nice boy, just go to church."

"I was just there today, remember? I didn't see anything extraordinary there other than Reverend Giles," Mildred said dryly.

"I noticed Wilbur Spencer eyeing you from across the pew," Aunt Rose said hopefully. "What's wrong with him?"

Mildred looked up. "You mean the one who drools all the time? Are you serious?"

Aunt Rose pressed her lips together. "Nobody's perfect, Miss, not even you. Could be the Lord wants you to take Wilbur and clean him up? Make him what you want him to be."

"Believe me," Mildred returned to her book, "the Lord don't want that."

"You know what we used to do in my day?" Aunt Rose persisted.

"What?" Mildred continued to read.

"If you saw a nice boy in church, first you just stared at him awhile and let him stare back at you. Then, when you knew he was looking at you, you opened your pocketbook quietly and snapped it closed real loud."

Mildred looked up at her aunt incredulously.

"That's all it took, and if you ask me, that's enough. You don't need to walk around with your face all painted and showing every single thing God gave you. It don't take all that."

Mildred knelt down in front of her aunt. "Yes, it does. It takes all of that plus a good personality, intelligence, and charm. You have to know what to do in the kitchen and in the bedroom." She smiled innocently up at her aunt.

Aunt Rose chose to ignore that last comment. "Mildred, you make the best lemon meringue pie in Chicago."

"But what about all those other things?"

"What about them?"

"Aunt Rose, look at me."

Mildred inched up until her face was right before her aunt's. "I mean really look at me."

"I am looking at you, baby, and you're a good-looking girl." Aunt Rose took Mildred's face between her hands and kissed it. "You're my baby, that's what you is."

Mildred smiled resignedly at her aunt and stood up. She walked over to the hall mirror and stared at the taller-than-average, thinner-than-average, and plainer-than-average 27-year-old reflection.

Her nondescript face was accentuated by a nose that was a tad too wide, matched with lips that were slightly too thin. This—aided by a shyness that only Aunt Rose was able to penetrate—was Mildred Johnson.

Mildred carried her book into her bedroom to read.

Aunt Rose's memories about growing up in Crayton, Tennessee with Mildred Walker could go on for hours. Her stories had no beginning, middle, or end; they were woven together in a warm, colorful tapestry like the patchwork quilt that covered her bed.

Mildred often wished that she'd been born during that era. Maybe if she'd been surrounded with the "down-home" feeling of the Southern people and the easygoing atmosphere, she would be able to relax and open up more. As things stood now, her contribution to most conversations and encounters consisted of nods of the head or shrugging of her shoulders.

Although Aunt Rose assured her that that was more than enough for most conversations these days, Mildred would have preferred to be more of a bluesy, gutsy woman like Aunt Rose or Mildred Walker.

She sighed, flopped down on her bed, reopened her book, and returned to where she had left off.

One

MILDRED ENTERED THE EL car with her head down and eyes averted. She scanned the aisles as though looking for an empty seat, but she was secretly canvassing the El car.

It was a game she played often. She memorized the faces, mannerisms, and actions of people she encountered during the day. If anything ever happened, or if something "big" were to go down, Mildred, and Mildred alone, would be the one to call on. She would be able to vividly recall to the police on the scene:

"He was wearing a plaid coat with a yellow, dirty handkerchief in his pocket on his right, no left side... Officer, she was a gray-haired, stoop-shouldered woman with a topaz ring on her third finger..."

She would be on Ted Koppel's *Nightline*, explaining her method of total recall. Oprah would invite her on her show and hug her, saying, "Girlfriend, how do you do that?" Mildred would only smile enigmatically and shake her head. Some gifts could never be shared or explained. Then she would wink at Aunt Rose, who'd be smiling proudly in the front row of the studio audience.

Mildred slid into an empty seat while making a mental note of the snake charm on the neck of the man in front of her. She stared out the El window and watched the platforms and people whiz by. The El slowed to a stop and she read, "Cathy sucks good ____!" She felt herself blushing. She could just imagine Aunt Rose riding with her and watching her aunt's mouth drop open in shock. "What's the world coming to?" Mildred could hear her saying. Still grinning to herself, Mildred was soon lost in thought.

"Hey, sister, what's putting that smile on your face? Who are you thinking about? Or should I say, what are you thinking about?"

A tall, slender man with dreadlocks slid into the seat next to Mildred. She could smell a faint trace of incense on him. Incense and maleness. A sweet, musky combination.

"When someone tries to bother you on the El, don't look at them," Aunt Rose *cautioned her. "If you on the bus or El, look out the window and shake your head a little; that'll let them know."*

Mildred turned her head to the window with a slight shake.

"What's that shake mean? 'No, I'm not smiling about somebody' or what?" he persisted.

As he slid closer, she could feel his warm breath in her ear. She stared at the platforms and people whizzing by.

"You got a name?" he asked.

Mildred continued to stare.

"Baby, am I that ugly that you can't even look at me?"

She turned slightly toward him to prove that he wasn't that ugly. And he wasn't. He had a red, black, and green skullcap pulled down over his dreadlocks. His eyes were bright and laughing at her from smooth, brown skin. His mustache and beard were sprinkled with gray, and the V-neck of his multicolored dashiki revealed a hairy chest with more sprinkling.

"My name is O'Kanta," he said, smiling at her. "And yours?"

"Mildred," she whispered.

"Uh, Mildred, listen." O'Kanta slid his arm across the back of her seat. She could feel it tickle her neck. "Do you think me and you can get together sometime?"

7

She snapped her head back to the window.

"I told you."

The El slowed to a stop, and O'Kanta looked out of the window.

"Oh wait, this is my stop! Here," he jumped up and took a leaflet out of his pocket and dropped it on her lap. "You can reach me here...and keep smiling, okay?" He gave her a wicked grin and was gone.

"Don't touch it," Aunt Rose warned. *"Leave it right there."*

Mildred waited until he'd gotten off and the El was speeding away before she curled her fingers around the paper and slid it into her pocket.

Getting off at her stop, she floated down the El steps at Pulaski and bought a $2.50 bunch of carnations for Aunt Rose. She smiled at the toothless flower man and held her head up as she walked the two blocks home. When she came into sight of the brown brick two flat, she reached deep into her pocket to feel if the paper was still there. It was.

She unlocked the four deadbolts that Aunt Rose insisted would protect them from the scum of the streets.

"Millie? Is that you?"

"Yeah, Aunt Rose, it's me."

Mildred walked into the front room and saw her aunt at her favorite post—sitting in front of the window, watching the comings and goings of the neighborhood.

"Look what I bought you," she said as she handed the flowers to her aunt. Aunt Rose smiled as she took the carnations and stood up as Mildred bent down for their customary greeting. Aunt Rose always kissed on the forehead or on both cheeks. She believed firmly that once a child passed the age of eight, she should never be kissed on the mouth by anyone other than a spouse.

"My goodness child, why did you go and do this?" She sniffed the carnations and then held them away from her to examine them.

"I don't even think I'm dressed fancy enough for these."

Mildred left her talking foolishness and went into the bedroom to change. She wondered if she should read the paper now or wait until later when she was in her nightgown and could appreciate it the most.

8

She decided to wait.

"I fried some chicken and opened up a can of cream-style corn. It's on the stove," Aunt Rose said.

Mildred came out and went into the kitchen. "I don't like cream-style corn."

"Yes you do."

"No, I don't. You like cream-style corn. I like whole-kernel corn."

Mildred wondered how many times the two of them would have this discussion.

"How anybody could like that dry whole-kernel corn is beyond me," Aunt Rose said. "Cream style is better for you and that's a proven fact."

Mildred knew where her aunt got her facts. She made them up. She went into the pantry and got out a can of whole-kernel corn.

Aunt Rose came into the kitchen holding the flowers and got a tall vase out of the cabinet.

Mildred turned to her. "Do you want me to make a salad to go with it?"

Aunt Rose nodded absently as she arranged the flowers in a vase. She sat the vase in the middle of the kitchen table and turned to watch Mildred reproachfully as she opened the can of whole-kernel corn and poured it into a pot.

"I met a man today," Mildred said offhandedly.

Aunt Rose's head turned excitedly toward her niece. "Where? At the bank?"

"No, I told you that tellers can't talk to the customers." She went back to the refrigerator and pinched out a hunk of butter with her fingers. Aunt Rose normally could not stand for this, but she was just curious enough about the man to let it pass. She dropped the butter into the pot of corn and put a lid on it.

"Well, you can talk to some when you're cashing their check, can't you?" Aunt Rose persisted. "You can give him change and smile, can't you?"

Mildred went back into the refrigerator and took out lettuce, tomatoes, pickles, and cheese. "Do you want to hear this or not?"

9

Aunt Rose propped her elbows on the table. What's his name?" she said warily.

Mildred stared at her. In her excitement her aunt seemed to be forgetting her table manners entirely. "Well, you don't have to sound so excited." She rinsed the vegetables in the sink and smiled.

"Where did you meet him?" Aunt Rose ventured.

"On the El."

"I told you not to talk to nobody on the El. Nobody but a bunch of fools ride the El."

Mildred got two bowls out of the cabinet. "I ride it."

"I'm talking about men, as you well know, Miss Fast. What's his name?"

"O'Kanta."

"What? O' What?"

"O'Kanta," Mildred said nonchalantly as she placed the two bowls of salad on the table and turned the corn off.

"What kind of name is that?" she asked suspiciously.

"What kind of salad dressing do you want?"

"What kind have I been using for twenty years?"

"I don't know; I didn't ask him." Mildred got out the French and Italian dressing.

"What was he, drugged out or something?"

"What do you mean 'drugged out'?" Mildred turned to face her aunt with her hands on her hips. "Does he have to be drugged out to talk to me?"

"You know what I mean." Aunt Rose got up to get the plates.

Mildred sat down and wondered why she could fix salad, corn, or cook anything under the sun, yet Aunt Rose would never permit her to fix her own plate.

Aunt Rose uncovered the platter of fried chicken on the stove and got out a wing and a thigh for Mildred and a back and neck for herself. She spooned out cream- style corn on her plate and whole-kernel for Mildred.

"He asked me out," Mildred offered.

"Well, I hope you told him 'no.'" Aunt Rose placed the two plates on the table and sat down heavily.

The last evening rays of the western sun filtered into the Johnson kitchen window and reflected on their two heads bowed in prayer.

"Precious Lord, we thank You for the food we're about to receive for the nourishment of our bodies in Jesus Christ's name," Aunt Rose prayed.

Two

MILDRED QUIETLY CLOSED THE DOOR of her bedroom. She slowly walked over to the closet and pulled out her brown winter coat. Fumbling in both pockets, she found the wrinkled square of paper and smiled. Curling one foot under her, she sat on the bed and closed her eyes. She summoned up the handsome face that had sat next to her on the El, breathing in his sweet scent and remembering the way his eyes smiled at her. She unfolded the paper.

"*Brothers and Sisters, let us become united in our struggle against racism. Let us educate ourselves economically and politically. Let us come together as we show our love and concern for each other. The Center for Black Awareness is open as a means towards achieving these ideals. Classes are offered in GED preparation; counseling is available for job assistance; and forms are here for voter registration—*"

"Millie!" Mildred jumped up guiltily and ran into the front room. Aunt Rose sat in her chair in front of the television and pointed at the television screen.

"What is it?" Mildred asked.

"Ssh," Aunt Rose waved her hand impatiently and leaned forward.

"Sources in the black community are offering the name of Raymond Williams as a possible candidate for the upcoming mayoral primary. Williams, currently Congressman of the 22nd District, could not be reached for comment. Political pundits say that if there is a large enough black voter turnout, Williams could become a viable candidate in the primary. Here now with the weather..."

Aunt Rose relaxed and turned to Mildred.

"Did you hear that, Mildred Johnson?" she asked softly as she rocked back and forth in her chair. "Did you hear that, baby?"

"Aunt Rose, what are you getting yourself so worked up about?" Mildred asked. She thought about O'Kanta waiting for her in her bedroom and wriggled her toes in anticipation.

"Turn the TV off baby, and sit down. Patience. Patience," Aunt Rose repeated. "Now that's something that you young people don't know nothing about. But I know about it. I know about it, and Mildred Walker knew about it, too."

She closed her eyes and began to rock.

"I'm talking about the kind of patience that makes you smile when a young white boy calls you 'Auntie.' About the patience that makes you wait in line until everybody in the whole store is gone and then a little girl, a girl you used to watch, mind you, says 'Hurry up, Auntie, I ain't got all day to wait on niggers.' I'm talking about patience, child."

"Don't go getting yourself all worked up now, Aunt Rose," Mildred said.

"Patience will help you to weather many a storm, baby. Patience lets you look at white men down South and wonder if they had anything to do with the bombing of your church. Now that kind of wondering really used to tear me up inside."

She turned to look at Mildred. "But I wanted to know if I was cooking food for the same men that raped my neighbor. I'd serve the fried chicken, fried corn, and okra and think...was it you? Uhhh, uhhh, uhhh." She shook her head back and forth as memories seemed to march before her eyes.

Watching her rock and hum, Mildred was struck by how old her aunt suddenly had become. "You want me to make you some hot tea,

Aunt Rose?" she suggested.

"Tea!" Aunt Rose's eyes flew open. "Baby, we gonna have something stronger than tea with the celebratin' we gonna do tonight."

She grunted as she got up from her chair and walked over to the china cabinet that housed all of the Johnson family heirlooms, and took out two heavily designed lead-glass cups.

"What are we celebrating?" Mildred asked as she watched her Aunt Rose reach for the dusty bottle of Mogen David wine.

Aunt Rose turned to her niece. "Didn't you hear a word I said? What are you doing just standing there? Put the record on!"

Mildred walked over to the ancient console and slid open the side door that held her and Aunt Rose's prized collection of blues records. She pulled out the favorite that serviced all of their wedding, funeral, and party needs. Wiping the album gently, she remembered for the 99th time that it was time to get another copy. She wondered if O'Kanta liked the blues. Nothing else was played in the Johnson household. She placed the record reverently on the turntable.

"Here, baby." Aunt Rose brought her a glass of Mogen David.

"Do you think we can at least drink David's share too?" Mildred teased.

"This is quite enough," Aunt Rose stated. "Have you got the record on?"

Mildred turned to her aunt and raised her cup.

"Patience," her aunt answered.

They both stared solemnly at each other as they turned their cups up. Mildred walked over and started the record.

"I've been from Spain to Tokyo, from Africa to O-h-i-o,
I never tried to make the news, I'm just a man who plays the blues."

Mildred started out with her shuffle. Head bent and eyes closed, she folded her arms across her chest and slid across the floor, stopping only to slowly rock down to the floor.

"I take my loving everywhere, I come back and they still care...
One love ahead, one love behind, one in my arms and one on my mind
...but there's one thing they knew—I never make my move too soon..."

Mildred turned to Aunt Rose who, never moving from one spot, was doing her shimmy. Staring straight ahead with her lips pursed together tightly, both hands were planted firmly on her hips as she swayed from side to side. At periodic intervals, she would slowly shimmy down to the floor. Taking her left hand off her hip, she touched the tip of her index finger to her tongue and touched the hardwood floor, whispering, "Caldonia, why is your head so hard?"

Mildred slid over to her aunt and they continued to dance until the record went off. She opened her eyes. "Do you want to hear it again?"

"No, baby, we got planning to do." Aunt Rose sat down heavily in her chair and reached for the cardboard fan from Wisdom Seat Baptist Church that she used to cool herself off.

Mildred went into the kitchen and opened the icebox to pull out a jug of ice water. She poured a tall glass full and carried it into the front room.

"Oooh, thank you, thank you, Jesus," Aunt Rose murmured as she drank.

"If you get that worn out after one record, maybe you'd better leave the shimmy alone," Mildred teased. "I could always teach you my dance," she volunteered.

"Don't worry none about my shimmy," Aunt Rose snapped. "Any fool can shuffle across the floor." She motioned for Mildred to sit down beside her chair.

"We gonna help get Raymond Williams elected," she stated.

"What do you mean we gonna help get him elected? You don't know anything about him. Are you just gonna vote for him because he's black?"

"Do you think I'm a complete fool?" Aunt Rose shouted. "Don't you think I'd know a charlatan if I saw one?" She paused and took a long

15

breath. "Look, baby, I know that you think that I don't do too much of anything all day. You think that all I do all day is sit in this chair, looking out of that window, and rock. Or maybe do word puzzles and watch game shows." She held her hand up to silence Mildred's protests. "And I do sometimes. But I just don't sit and watch kids playing, women switching, and men cussing. I watch people, and that's a big difference. I watch the looks on their faces when they think that nobody's looking. I watch the children's faces light up when they mamma comes home from work. I watch when they eyes get big when they hear the ice cream truck coming down the street. Do you know that that's a completely different look? I see the beaten-down look in a man's eyes when he comes home after looking for work all day, only to come up empty." She closed her eyes and rocked. "I see plenty, baby. I see the stuff that makes character. And I'm not crazy."

"And you see all that in Raymond Williams' face? I'm not saying you're crazy, Aunt Rose," Mildred interrupted. "But can't we just vote for him? We can do our part by voting for him, can't we?"

"I just told you that I see something in his face, didn't I? We are not just going to vote for him, we're going to help him get elected."

"What do you mean?" Mildred asked suspiciously. "I don't know anything about him and I don't have your powers of face reading. I'll have to read something in print before I cast my vote." Mildred stood up and started to go back to her room to be alone with the piece of paper from O'Kanta.

"Well, while you're reading about him you're gonna be going around with me, knocking on doors and doing whatever we have to do to get him elected."

"What are we going to say when people answer the door?" Mildred turned around and looked at her aunt in amazement. "Are you going to tell them about the character lines on his face?"

"Well, since you're so smart, I guess we'll be telling them about whatever you find out."

"Aunt Rose, he didn't even say he's going to run. The reporter just announced that his supporters were offering his name for consideration. I mean, he's already a congressman, right? Maybe he'll just stay there. What fool would want to get involved in the politics of this city anyway?"

"He's gonna run. He's from here, so he already knows how messed up things are. Trust me, he'll run," Aunt Rose said smugly.

Mildred walked over to her. "Aunt Rose, you know that I can't talk to strangers," she whispered. "Please don't ask me to."

"Baby, you don't have to. I'll do all the talking. You just stand behind me and back me up with all the information," Aunt Rose said decisively.

"And where are we supposed to get this information?"

"That's what I haven't figured out yet. But there's got to be some folk out there behind him. Otherwise his name wouldn't have been thrown out here. You know, some kind of group to help us get started." Her voice trailed off as she looked up at the ceiling, thinking aloud. "I know there's somebody out here besides me that believes in this man. Somebody who's got the facts."

O'Kanta began to itch inside of Mildred's jeans pocket. She reached in and pulled out the warm, wrinkled paper. "Maybe we could start here..."

Three

"YOU SHOULD HAVE SEEN MISS SHARON tipping around to the side of that car like it was hers. Ten o'clock in the morning, mind you, and she's stepping out with Mrs. Robinson's husband. You know how long she's been making eyes at him?"

"Uh-uh." Mildred parted a section of Aunt Rose's hair and began to scratch the dandruff out.

"She's been making eyes at him for over a month now. Switching pass him in that red dress she likes so much, knowing good and well that he's married. I sat right in that window watching her. Then she had the gall to look up at me and say"— Aunt Rose turned to Mildred, demonstrating—"'How you doing today, Miss Rose?'"

Laughing, Mildred smoothed a thin line of pomade on her aunt's scalp and rubbed it in. "Now didn't you feel funny with her catching you watching her and Mr. Robinson?"

Aunt Rose leaned back into the kitchen chair and propped her feet up on a brown hassock. "Why should I feel funny? Now if they feel funny with me watching, then maybe they shouldn't be doing what they doing out there where everybody can see them."

Mildred grunted, parted another section, and began to scratch. "So are you going to tell Mrs. Robinson when she comes up here to use the telephone?"

"Don't scratch so hard, Millie. You know I'm—""tenderheaded," Mildred finished.

"Yes, tenderheaded. You parting my hair like there's no tomorrow. No, I'm not going to tell Sandra Robinson about Miss Sharon. That poor woman's got enough on her mind without me adding to the list. If there's anything anybody can say about Rose Johnson, it's that she minds her own business."

Mildred decided to let that pass and concentrated on the next part.

"Turn the news on, baby."

Mildred turned on the twelve-inch black-and-white set on the kitchen counter. Harry Phillips, the local reporter, stared at Mildred and Aunt Rose with a pained expression. *"Raymond Williams has just confirmed that he will run as a Democrat in the mayoral primary in February. Going now to the Williams headquarters..."*

Raymond Williams stood in front of a cheering crowd of supporters and smiled broadly at the camera. Mildred and Aunt Rose smiled back.

"Friends and supporters, we are the participants in a movement. A growing movement that seeks to encompass all of this city's disillusioned and downtrodden. This city is a city divided. A city where citizens are treated unequally and unfairly. A city in decline."

Mildred began to massage Rose's scalp as she watched the TV screen.

"I visualize a city that runs well, in which services are provided as a right, not as a political favor."

"Look at him, Millie. Just look at him. Preach, Mr. Williams," Aunt Rose motioned to the television screen. "Preach. Look at his eyes, Mildred; read his face."

19

"*We seek out the poor white who has been downtrodden.*" Williams continued. "*We reach out to the Latino community and say to them, come into the mainstream of this city.*"

The cameras returned to the grave expression of Harry Phillips.

"Well," Aunt Rose leaned back into her chair. "Well," she repeated.

Mildred picked up the brush and began to brush her aunt's hair. She studied the blend of silver and black strands glistening with oil. "Do you want two cornrows or one?"

Aunt Rose smoothed her hair back with both hands. "I think I want you to press it for me. I want to look extra fancy tomorrow."

Mildred went into the pantry and got the straightening comb. "Where are you going tomorrow?" she asked as she placed the comb on the burner and turned the fire on low.

"Tomorrow we're going to go down to that center that was on that paper you showed me," Aunt Rose said.

Not trusting herself, Mildred turned the burner off. "You know, Aunt Rose, I've been thinking." She walked around the kitchen table and sat down facing her aunt. "You know, we really don't know much about this place, do we? Maybe we should wait awhile before we go there. It could be some kind of hangout for gangs or a dope den for all we know." She looked at her aunt hopefully. "I mean, I just found that leaflet on the El; anybody could have dropped it."

Aunt Rose waved away Mildred's protests with her hand. "Don't worry about the center. I already had it checked out."

"What do you mean you had it checked out? You didn't ask me anything."

"How could I?" Aunt Rose's voice rose. "You claimed you found it. So how could you know anything about it?"

Lost for an answer, Mildred traced a pattern on the kitchen table. "So who did you ask?" she said quietly.

"I had Clarence check it out for me."

"Clarence the garbage man?" Mildred jumped to her feet. "Aunt Rose, he empties garbage, for Christ's sake! What could he possibly know?"

"Mildred Johnson, if you don't sit down and watch your mouth, we can just stop this conversation right now," Aunt Rose said with authority.

Mildred sat down.

"Yes, Miss. Clarence is a garbage collector. Did I raise you into thinking that something is wrong with that? I asked him because he's the one person who would know. Don't you know that the things people throw away tell more about them than what they keep? Take you, for instance. When I empty that trashcan in your room, I throw out all of those magazines that you like to read. I look at those pieces of poems that you decided weren't good enough to keep. I look at all of the clothes that have gotten too small or too old. Right there in the garbage I see what you like to read, what you think about, and I can tell how you dress. Don't you think that tells me something about you?"

"I guess so," Mildred muttered, vowing to herself to start burning any and all poetry that she decided to throw away in the future.

"If you looked in my garbage," Aunt Rose continued, "you'd see that I like word puzzle books, Hershey's Kisses, and that I make quilts. So I had Clarence collect about a week's worth of their garbage and bring it to me."

"You mean you have their garbage?" Mildred got up. "What did he find?"

"Clarence didn't have time to look through it. He brought it to me, and I put it on the back porch. But he did tell me that the folks who run that center are real nice. Clarence said that they never have any beer bottles or wine bottles in their garbage. He said they make sure the bags are tied up real nice and neat in those plastic garbage bags."

"I don't believe I'm having this conversation," Mildred turned to her aunt. "Clarence just did all of this for you out of the goodness of his heart?"

Aunt Rose got up and walked into the pantry. "Well, I did promise him that you would make him one of your lemon meringue pies." She threw the words over her shoulder.

"Well you can just *un*promise him," Mildred returned.

21

Aunt Rose came out of the pantry with two pairs of plastic gloves. "Clarence has always been sweet on you. What's wrong with you making him a pie just to show our appreciation?"

Mildred took the gloves. "Appreciation for what? For bringing us somebody's filthy garbage? And what's this *'our'* stuff? I wasn't in on this plan. You make the pie."

Mildred went out on the back porch and saw a gray bulging garbage bag. Torn between disgust and amusement, she untied the bag, wrinkling her nose to fend off the smell. Clarence spared her. There was none. "Thank you, Clarence," she whispered.

Aunt Rose stood over her. "Millie, you know my lemon meringue pie don't hold a candle to yours," she said while putting on her gloves.

Four

MILDRED LOOKED AT THE RED and yellow flashing neon sign that read: ay's Li ors. "Do you think it's supposed to say Ray's Liquors?" she asked, turning to her aunt. "Or Jay's Liquors?"

"Who cares?" Aunt Rose looked disdainfully at the blinking lights. "Are you sure this is the right place, baby?"

Mildred pulled her coat closer to her body and shivered. "No, I'm not sure," she snapped. "This is you and Clarence's thing. I'm not even sure why I'm here."

"Really?" Aunt Rose focused on Mildred. "If you're really that confused, why don't you think of this as a mission to find out why the name O'Kanta was on so many of them pieces of paper we found in the garbage? Maybe that'll clear it up for you."

Mildred walked a few steps away from her aunt and pretended that she was all alone. She looked up at the building and at the people who were loitering outside that were curiously watching her and Aunt Rose.

What should she do if she saw O'Kanta? Would he expect some kind of recognition from her? Would he even remember her? Maybe she could slip in sort of nonchalantly as if she'd been there before. She'd walk in and throw her coat on a hook and start stuffing envelopes or something. Her outfit was probably all wrong, though. Was her corduroy skirt and sweater too 'establishment'? Aunt Rose wouldn't hear of her wearing jeans this morning. What if she took her coat off and everyone laughed? O'Kanta would probably help her out of her coat and back away in horror..

."Let's go into the store and ask them how to get to the center," Aunt Rose suggested.

"*You* want to go into the liquor store?" Mildred raised her eyebrows. She held out her hand to her aunt. "I guess we could always pick up some Mogen David," she teased.

Aunt Rose squeezed her hand. "I should say not. We've got more than enough at home. If we run out, we can always ask Dwayne to bring us some from Greater Foods."

Hand in hand, Mildred and Aunt Rose crossed the street and opened the door to Ray's Liquors. Aunt Rose walked past the lottery line and went up to the man behind the cash register.

"I think we should get in line," Mildred whispered.

"Why should we?" Aunt Rose's voice rang out over others. "We don't want to buy anything."

Mildred hurriedly stepped away.

"Excuse me, son," Aunt Rose put her hand on the arm of a customer waiting in line to pay for a bottle of Jack Daniels. "Would you mind if I asked this gentleman how to get to the Center for Black Awareness? My niece and I want to help get Raymond Williams elected," she explained.

Mildred turned and began to browse through the racks of potato chips.

"Say!" A heavyset woman in the lottery line turned around. "Did he say he was going to run?"

"Yeah, baby." The man whom Aunt Rose butted in line flashed a toothless grin. "My man was on the news the other night, and he said he was gonna run. That is one heavy brother," he nodded confidently.

"I thought Williams was the congressman from the 22nd District?" The cashier stopped and leaned his elbow on the register.

"Yes, that's right," Aunt Rose broke in happily, "but he's going to leave that job and run for mayor."

"Hold on, and wait just one minute."

A man of about sixty waved his hand at Aunt Rose. Turning back to the cashier, he mumbled, "454, a dollar straight, and a dollar box."

He turned to Aunt Rose, "Let me tell you one thing," he said while stopping to tuck his shirt into his pants. "These white folks here ain't never gonna let a black man become no mayor."

"Now that's our problem," the heavyset woman in the lottery line broke in. "We can't wait for white folks to let us do nothing. If we want it, we gonna have to take it." She pointed to the man in front of her. "You are our biggest problem. Old Negroes like you who are scared of change."

"Well, I really don't think that age has anything to do with it," Aunt Rose said huffily. "I think—"

"Sho you right," the old man broke in, addressing the heavyset woman. "I am your biggest problem." He turned and faced the line. "Every one of you women out here screaming politics is going home to an empty bed. Frustrated, that's what you is. Trying to be the man, trying to lead."

He shook his head as he took his lottery tickets and turned to leave.

The woman laughed along with the cashier. "Oh, is that our problem?"

A young man sitting on a stool in the corner raised his hand as if asking for permission to speak.

"They gonna kill him," he stated. "And we gonna set this city on fire when they do. Aaron, you better get you some fire insurance," he said to the cashier as he looked around the store.

Mildred stood in front of the potato chip aisle, wondering what she would do if O'Kanta walked up to her at that moment. She wondered if he was a vegetarian. She seemed to remember people with dreadlocks and dashikis being into health foods. She casually moved over to the display of nuts.

The cashier grinned and picked up the bottle of Jack Daniels. "I ain't worried 'bout nobody coming up in here. They gonna have to *bring* something to *get* something." He turned to Aunt Rose. "Lady, if he becomes mayor, I'll give you a bottle of my best champagne-on the house." He picked up a toothpick and laid it on his bottom lip. "You can get to the center through that back door over there."

Mildred looked up. "You mean we have to come in here to get to the center?" she asked.

"That's right." The cashier bagged the bottle of Jack Daniels. "I let them use my basement." He looked at Mildred. "You don't mind coming in here to get there do you?"

Aunt Rose smiled and held out her hand. "Not when we have the pleasure of holding such a pleasant conversation." She turned to Mildred. "Come on, baby."

When they reached the door, they both looked back with a questioning expression on their faces.

"Go on. It's open," he hollered. "I know y'all not scared, are you?"

Aunt Rose opened the door to a flight of stairs. Walking down slowly, she turned back to see her niece still standing at the top. She held out her hand. "Come on, baby," she said reassuringly. "Let's go show them the Johnson stuff."

Mildred gripped the handrail and walked down one step at a time.

The basement was filled with crates of beer and wine bottles. Boxes of potato chips and pretzels were stacked up against one wall. Located on the adjacent wall was a door posting the same leaflet that O'Kanta had given Mildred on the El. Aunt Rose studied the leaflet. "Well, this is it." She turned to Mildred who, poised for flight, was eyeing the staircase.

Aunt Rose took her hand and knocked confidently on the door.

A little girl of about four or five opened it.

"Well hello, Jamila," Aunt Rose exclaimed. "How are you, sweetie?"

"Fine," the child answered and promptly stuck her two middle fingers into her mouth.

"Jamila, take your fingers out of your mouth." A young black woman with a short-cropped natural and smooth, dark skin reached down and pulled the offending fingers out of the child's mouth. She had on a faded Bob Marley tee shirt and a blue jean skirt. Looking up, she smiled in recognition. "Hi, Miss Johnson! What are you doing here?"

"Well, hello, Nikki," Aunt Rose smiled and tugged on her skirt. "I'm fine. You remember my niece Mildred, don't you?"

Nikki smiled at Mildred and held out her hand.

"I've seen you around the neighborhood, but we've never talked. How are you?"

"Fine," Mildred whispered.

"Do you work here, child?" Aunt Rose beamed at Nikki.

"Kind of." Nikki reached down and removed Jamila's fingers from her mouth. "I run the day care center here for women who come to the GED classes. What are you two here for?"

"We're here to help Raymond Williams get elected," Aunt Rose said. "Can you help us?"

Mildred found a peppermint in her pocket and flashed it at Jamila.

"That's fantastic," Nikki said, smiling. "I wish more of us would get involved, including Dwayne. You know, I think O'Kanta is organizing people into groups to go out and talk to voters, getting them registered and stuff. Let me go find out. Jamila, do you want to come with me?"

Jamila looked conspiratorially at Mildred and shook her head. Nikki disappeared into the back, humming.

Jamila looked at Mildred and held out her hand.

"Take the fingers out," Mildred said, handing her the peppermint.

Jamila took the peppermint and placed it and her two fingers in her mouth, grinning at Mildred.

Mildred looked around her. She and Aunt Rose were standing in a makeshift front office. There were two battered file cabinets in the corner. On top of one was a drooping plant. There was a table in the other corner with pamphlets and fliers strewn over it. A poster faced them outlining the center's goals and guidelines. Mildred closed her eyes and smelled the scent that had clung to O'Kanta.

27

Aunt Rose turned to Mildred. "Your boyfriend O'Kanta is in charge of this whole operation. What do you think about that?" she said, winking.

Jamila took her fingers out of her mouth, "Is 'Kanta your boyfriend?" she asked.

Mildred watched in horror as Jamila ran off calling,' Kanta, Kanta!"

Nikki came back with Jamila in tow.

"A session is going on now. You're lucky. Just come with me." She led Mildred and Aunt Rose into an open room that held five rows of metal folding chairs. Approximately seven people were seated facing the speaker.

O'Kanta looked over and smiled, "Welcome, sisters. We were just beginning. Please," he gestured, "have a seat."

Aunt Rose, staring at O'Kanta's hair, pressed her pillbox hat more securely on her head and took a seat. Mildred followed her, refusing to look up.

"What we're discussing, for those of you who just joined us, are the ways in which we can galvanize the black community behind the candidacy of Raymond Williams."

"Yes!" Aunt Rose witnessed and bobbed her head.

"Uh," O'Kanta, somewhat taken aback, continued. "We have figures, which show that approximately forty percent of the black voters on the West Side are not even registered."

"Well?" Aunt Rose stated.

Mildred, still looking down, reached over and pinched her aunt's arm.

"We need to start out in our neighborhoods with the people that are familiar to us," O'Kanta continued. "Tell them the importance of being registered. Don't criticize them because they are not registered. Explain to your neighbors and your families that we need each other now."

"Yes we do!" Aunt Rose agreed.

"Will you stop it?" Mildred whispered.

"We don't want to be exclusive," O'Kanta folded his arms across his chest. "We want to be *inclusive*." He opened his arms wide.

Mildred bravely glanced up and saw the bright oranges, reds, and browns of O'Kanta's dashiki. His dreadlocks were tied back with a string, and as he gestured with his hands, she could see the muscles ripple in his chest.

"For those voters who are already registered," O'Kanta continued, "talk to them about Raymond Williams. If you are not familiar with his record, we have the literature available. Williams is a man whose record speaks for itself and, more importantly, he's from here. So let us fellowship with each other and share the good news that this candidacy has to offer. After you have talked to your families and neighbors, come back here and we'll designate certain recruitment areas so that we don't overlap each other, and so that all areas are covered. Are there any questions?"

Aunt Rose looked around, smiling.

"Good," O'Kanta smiled. "The literature is on the table."

The group began to file out.

"I'm going up there to talk to your O'Kanta," Aunt Rose whispered.

"He's not *my* O'Kanta," Mildred muttered. "Just don't drag my name into it. I'll get us some information from the table." She walked over to the table and picked up a variety of pamphlets, each of which featured the smiling face of Raymond Williams. She opened one and read.

"*Received his bachelor's degree in political science, president of the senior class... Received his law degree in 1970 and then went on to become...*"

"...One of the most sought-after legal counsels in the city," O'Kanta finished.

Mildred jumped and dropped the pamphlet that she'd been holding.

"I'm sorry, I didn't mean to scare you." O'Kanta smiled. "I've read those pamphlets so many times that I could recite them in my sleep."

"Uh, that's okay." Mildred bent down to pick up the literature. "I was just taking these to my aunt," she continued speaking to the floor. As she stood, she turned to find Aunt Rose.

"Hold on a minute." O'Kanta held her elbow. "Did you really think that you could come in here with your head down, looking at the floor,"— O'Kanta held his head down and shuffled his feet in imitation— "and I wouldn't remember you?"

"Don't make fun of me," Mildred whispered.

O'Kanta gently lifted her chin. "I wouldn't do that for anything in the world," he said softly. "You know I've thought about you over these few months and wondered if I'd ever see you again."

Mildred shoved the pamphlets into her coat pocket and shrugged her shoulders.

"Tell me this," O'Kanta pulled her hand out of her pocket. "How is someone as shy as you are going to recruit voters for Raymond Williams?"

Mildred smiled. "Aunt Rose said she'd do all the talking."

"Now that I believe," O'Kanta laughed. "Your aunt is truly dedicated. I wish we had more like her." He smiled at Mildred and touched the heart-shaped locket around her neck. "You know, I like this. You don't see many women wearing lockets anymore. I thought it was no longer considered in vogue. Do you have a picture inside of?—"

"O'Kanta!" Nikki yelled. "It's time for the next group."

"Well." O'Kanta gave Mildred a mock salute. "I'm off to give my speech again. But I'll see you next Saturday at seven o'clock sharp." Turning to leave, he turned back as if in an afterthought. "How did you know that lemon meringue pie is one of my favorites?" He winked and left.

Mildred turned to see Aunt Rose smiling triumphantly at her.

"How could you?" Mildred whispered. "How could you?"

The two of them walked in silence to the bus stop. Once there, Aunt Rose turned to Mildred. "I only asked him to dinner because I need to talk to him about my strategy in this voter registration. You saw how busy he was at the center, didn't you?" Getting no response from her niece, she added defensively, "I did what I had to do!"

"Fine," Mildred said. "Then I guess you won't mind if I don't join this little tête-à-tête of yours. I'll be more than happy to leave the two of you alone."

"What do you mean?" Aunt Rose put her hand on Mildred's arm. "Where are you going?"

Mildred shook her arm off. "The bus is coming."

"I'm not getting on that bus until you explain what you mean by saying that you're not going to be home for dinner on Saturday." Aunt Rose folded her arms across her chest and pursed her lips.

"Then I guess I'll see you at home," Mildred snapped.

"Just tell me this. What did I do that was so wrong?" Aunt Rose raised her arms in confusion. "I asked him for pointers on how to deal with our neighbors. He tried to talk to me, but every five minutes somebody came up to him with a question. He's a very important man, your O'Kanta. So he said, 'Look Miss Johnson, is there some way that we can get together to talk about this?'" Aunt Rose opened her arms beseechingly. "I said that my niece and I don't really get out much — just to the store, church, and a movie sometimes. Then," Aunt Rose touched Mildred's arm for emphasis, "he said, 'Is that your niece?'" Aunt Rose puffed herself up. "I said 'yes' you were my baby, and you should have seen the smile that came over his face."

Mildred grunted.

"Then he kind of leaned back on his legs and pulled on his beard a little bit. Of course I knew that he was trying to think of a way to talk to me and see you at the same time." Aunt Rose looked knowingly at Mildred. "But I knew you didn't want me to say nothing, so I didn't." She folded her arms across her chest. "I licked my lips and I waited." She rocked back and forth on her heels, indicating to Mildred how patiently she'd waited. "Then he said, 'I really wouldn't like to impose,' real enthusiastic like, 'but perhaps I could come and visit with the two of you?' Then I said only if he promised to do it over dinner. So you see?" Aunt Rose flourished her arms and stepped regally onto the bus.

Mildred paid the two fares and wondered how much of the truth could be siphoned from Aunt Rose's story. She slid into the seat next to her aunt.

"What do you think we should have to eat?" Aunt Rose turned to Mildred. "What are his favorite foods?"

"I have no idea," Mildred returned dryly.

"Well, I found out that he likes lemon meringue pie," Aunt Rose informed her. "So make it one of your best. Put a lot of meringue on top."

"Do you want to make it?"

"No, no," Aunt Rose said hastily, laying a reassuring hand on her niece's arm. "What about fried chicken? Or maybe pot roast?" Aunt Rose began to check off menu ideas.

Sighing, Mildred turned to the window.

Five

AUNT ROSE AND MILDRED STOOD on the steps of 2911 W. Jackson Boulevard and rang the bell marked 'Patillo.'

"Maybe she's not at home," Mildred suggested.

"She's there."

Aunt Rose stared up at the second-floor window. "I saw that window shade move a little bit."

"Well, maybe she doesn't want to talk to us. Maybe she thinks we're going to ask her for some money."

"Not when she sees you with that basket. Just don't drop it."

"Why do we have to bring cookies anyway?" Mildred shifted the basket to her other hand. "Am I going to have to bake every time we visit someone?"

"I told you that the cookies are going to lay the groundwork for my speech. Hush now, here she comes."

Mrs. Patillo slowly opened the front door. She was wearing a bright red housedress and her hair was rolled in brown paper twists. Esther

Patillo was in her early fifties and casually admitted to having a slight weight problem. Mildred was positive that she weighed over 300 pounds. Mrs. Patillo had one of the prettiest complexions she had ever seen. Smooth, black skin that held no wrinkles or blemishes.

"Why, hey, Miss Johnson, Mildred. I looked out my window and saw the two of you standing on the porch and I thought, now what are they doing paying me a visit?" She looked at the basket in Mildred's arm. "Am I dying?"

Aunt Rose laughed and nudged Mildred, who managed to clear her throat. "Go on with you, Esther," she kidded. "My baby and I just came to visit and sit with you a spell. We brought you some cookies that Millie made."

Esther Patillo pulled her housecoat closer together. "What kind of cookies?"

Aunt Rose smiled at Mildred.

"Chocolate chip," Mildred whispered.

Esther grinned. "Well, come on in. I must say, chocolate chip cookies sure have a weakness for me. Come right on in, but y'all have to excuse this house. I wasn't expecting company."

Following Esther into the house, Aunt Rose said teasingly, "Don't you mean that you have a weakness for chocolate chip cookies, Esther?"

Esther turned around and faced Aunt Rose. "No, I don't, Rose. The only weakness I have is for Jesus Christ. I don't have the time or inclination to be weak for anything else."

"Well, uh, yes," Aunt Rose stammered. "Yes, of course."

Aunt Rose and Mildred followed Esther into her front room. The room was spotless and housed two floral-print love seats covered in plastic. One end table held an ornate Bible and a large crucifix hung on the wall over the mantel.

"I'll go and get us some milk to go with these cookies," Esther smiled as she held out her hand for the basket. "You all have a seat."

Mildred sat down on the love seat and smiled at Aunt Rose. "I guess she told you. She does not have time to be weak for anything else.

34

Do you still want to do all the talking?"

Esther rolled in a serving cart with a platter that contained about half of the cookies and three glasses of milk. She smiled at Mildred.

"I put the rest of the cookies up so they wouldn't get stale." She reached down and took a handful and settled herself on the love seat facing Aunt Rose and Mildred. "Now what are we going to talk about?"

Aunt Rose smiled and tugged at her skirt. "Well, Esther, it's like this. My baby and I are tired of being divided in this city and trodden down. We want to swell ahead and come into the main!" She flashed a triumphant grin at Mildred.

Esther stopped chewing. "What?"

Aunt Rose smiled apologetically. "What I'm saying, Esther, is that Raymond Williams is running for mayor. A black man with more degrees and clout than even we" she opened her arms– "know about. My baby and I want to know if you are gonna come out and vote for one of our own. I can't think of any one man who can turn this city around other than him." She smiled at Esther. "Can we count on you?"

Esther picked up another cookie and bit into it. She stared at Aunt Rose thoughtfully while she chewed. When she finished she took a large swallow of milk and walked over to the mantel.

Mildred looked at Aunt Rose questioningly.

Esther turned around. "You say that you can't think of any other man who is able to turn this city around?" She pointed to Aunt Rose. "Have you thought of Jesus Christ?" she shouted.

Mildred jumped and stared at Mrs. Patillo.

Esther stood before Aunt Rose and Mildred. "Let me give you my personal testimony. She placed both hands on her breasts.

"I was saved on February 2, 1972 and filled with the Holy Ghost. Even though I was saved, praise the Lord, I still kept putting my faith in people. I was living in a one-bedroom apartment on 18th and Pulaski. I was out of work with no heat and my lights were about to be cut off. My landlord had given me a two-week eviction notice because I was two months behind on my rent. I went to my pastor, Reverend Otis Simpson of the

New Faith of God and Christ Church—do you know him?" She turned to Aunt Rose and Mildred.

They both shook their heads.

"I said, 'Pastor, please help me find a place to live.' I told him that I didn't have any heat and I was going to be evicted in a couple of weeks.

"Pastor Simpson sat behind that big desk in his office going, 'Uh-huh, uh-huh.' Then he said, 'Sister Patillo, I sympathize with your situation and so does the Lord. I'm going to pray for you, and if I hear talk of a place, I'll let you know.'

"I went home and I prayed," Esther raised both arms in the air. "I said, 'Lord, you have saved me and filled me with the Holy Spirit. What am I to do'?"

She turned to Mildred. "I waited for my pastor, and he didn't do nothing!

"Then that next Saturday I saw my mailman Sam outside, and I went downstairs to get my mail. Sam got saved about a year before me at How Great Thou Art Apostolic Church. Anyway, I came downstairs to get my mail and Sam saw how down I looked and asked me what was wrong. I told him that I was about to be evicted and I didn't have a place to stay. Sam asked me why, and I told him. He asked me if I had a job, and I told him I was going to start at Neiller's Drugstore in three weeks.

"And you know what? He said that his brother owned a two-flat over on Ashland Avenue and he was looking for a Christian person to rent out the second floor to."

"Yes!" Aunt Rose broke in. "So you see what happens when we can come together—"

"I'm not finished, Rose," Esther interrupted. "I went home and I thanked God because He sent me that apartment. Then I said, 'But God, how am I going to move? I don't have any money for a security deposit and no money to move with." Esther went over to the cart and got another cookie.

Mildred and Aunt Rose exchanged looks.

Esther took a deep swallow of milk and wiped her mouth. "Like

I said, God had gotten me the apartment, but I didn't have any money. I was lying down thinking about it later on that night when my neighbor, Mrs. Greenwood, came upstairs and told me that I had a phone call. It was my family from down South. My two sisters and three brothers were over to my Uncle Melvin's house. My one sister Lorraine had told the rest of them about my situation."

Esther turned to Aunt Rose and raised her hand. "The next day I had $500.00! Each of them wired me $100.00 to help me out in my time of need. I'm here to tell you that I didn't get it by putting my faith in no man. Praise God. I got it by putting my faith —Thank you, Jesus — in the Almighty Father! Esther Patillo can testify to you here today— Amen— that you don't get anywhere by putting your faith in man but that you can get everywhere by putting your faith in the Lord Jesus Christ!"

"Well, I see..." Aunt Rose seemed at a loss for words.

Esther stood in front of the mantel and stared up at the large crucifix.

Mildred motioned to her aunt for them to leave.

"Esther?" Aunt Rose walked over to Esther and put her arm around her. "That's a mighty powerful testimony. Millie and I are going to be going now, but we'll leave you some literature in case you change your mind."

Esther nodded.

Mildred and Aunt Rose left quietly.

"Well, I guess I didn't do so good." Aunt Rose shook her head as she and Mildred walked back home. "Now O'Kanta, he could have turned her around."

"I don't think Raymond Williams could have changed her mind." Mildred put her arm around her aunt. "You did fine."

"No," Aunt Rose shook her head. "I should have been able to change her mind somehow. I should have showed her that this is the time for us to come together."

"I don't think anything short of a brick could have changed Mrs. Patillo's mind."

"Don't be judgmental, baby. Esther's got a right to stand up for what she believes in. Maybe I just didn't talk to her right. How did you like my speech?" She looked up at Mildred.

Mildred chose her words carefully. "I think the beginning part may have gone over her head. Maybe you should save that part for later."

"Could be you're right," Aunt Rose nodded. "Esther did look right confused at first. What about the second part?"

"Oh you smoked on the second part. I was ready to run out and vote." Mildred squeezed her Aunt.

"I still wish I could have convinced her, though. Esther was our first one, and we couldn't get her."

Mildred reached in her pocket for her key. "The only thing that reached Mrs. Patillo was those chocolate chip cookies."

Aunt Rose grinned at Mildred. "Are you saying that she has a weakness for chocolate chip cookies?"

Laughing, Aunt Rose and Mildred climbed the steps of the brownstone.

Aunt Rose stopped on the second step and rubbed her stomach. "My stomach is feeling kind of peculiar. I wonder how fresh Esther's milk was. Did you have any of it?"

"Nope," Mildred jingled her keys. "That cart was too close to Mrs. Patillo for me. She parked that cart next to her like she didn't want nobody to come near it." She looked at her aunt searchingly. "I was going to run over to the Chicken Shack to pick up some dinner. Can you eat anything?"

Aunt Rose's face brightened. "Yes. Get me a three-piece dark with a side order of corn and mashed potatoes. We can split an order of cole slaw."

Mildred laughed. "Are you sure your stomach can handle this?"

Aunt Rose bristled. "I'm going to take some seltzer when I get upstairs. My stomach should be fine by the time you get back."

Mildred skipped down the stairs. "I should hope so." She looked over her shoulder at her aunt. "Is this what's called 'laying the groundwork'?"

Aunt Rose opened the door. "I'd say. And don't worry none about my stomach, Miss Fast. Just you be careful in the Chicken Shack."

"I'm always careful," Mildred muttered as she walked down Jackson Boulevard. "That's my problem. I'm too careful."

Aunt Rose stood on the steps watching until Mildred was almost out of sight. Then, as if on cue, Mildred turned, waved, and continued down the street.

Six

MILDRED WALKED THROUGH THE apartment, criticizing every cushion, chair, table, and picture. She nervously rearranged the twice-arranged knickknacks on the coffee table.

Aunt Rose walked into the living room from the kitchen and wiped her hands on her apron. "You're going to make yourself sick in one minute. Baby, why don't you sit down?"

Mildred fell into the brown recliner. "I'm sick right now," she moaned. "I don't believe I agreed to this. I must have been out of my head."

"What's that? What on earth is that!" She jumped up and ran to the corner end table and peered underneath. "Oh," she got up from the table. "It's just a cobweb." She turned and looked at her aunt's strange expression. "What's the matter with you?"

Aunt Rose stared at her niece. "I think you ought to go and lie down for a while. O'Kanta won't be here for two hours."

Mildred began to pace the living room floor. "You know what I just thought of?" She turned abruptly to face her aunt. "What if we're talking here in the front room about the mayoral election and a roach crawls across the television screen?"

Aunt Rose stood up to her full five-foot-three-inch height. "Mildred Johnson! We do not have roaches in this house!"

"But what if one crawls across the television screen? What should we do?"

Aunt Rose looked at her niece as one would look at a child. "Well, I reckon we would kill it."

Mildred threw up her arms in frustration. "But can't you see? I just can't walk over there and smash it," she demonstrated. "He'd think that I've been killing roaches all of my life."

"Well, what are we supposed to do? Just stare at it?"

"Maybe." Mildred rubbed her temple. "I don't know what we should do, Aunt Rose."

Aunt Rose walked over to her niece. "Baby, don't worry yourself sick over this. He's the one who invited himself over, remember? We've got fried chicken, corn, okra and stewed tomatoes, cornbread, and lemon meringue pie. If we don't like his company, we'll feed him and throw him out." Aunt Rose demonstrated how she would throw O'Kanta out.

Mildred rested her head on her aunt's shoulder and giggled. "Promise me that you won't leave me alone with him?"

Aunt Rose looked up in surprise. "Where will I go?"

"I'm serious, Aunt Rose. Promise."

"Well, what if I have to go to the bathroom?"

Mildred turned to go into her bedroom and looked over her shoulder. "Go now."

* * *

Mildred closed her bedroom door and leaned against it. She walked over to her mirror and stared at her reflection. She shook her head sadly. She longed to see a dark, exotic, confident woman staring back at her. A woman who was witty and sassy and whose personality would keep O'Kanta in stitches.

41

She shook her head again and lay across the bed. Thinking and dreaming about O'Kanta was one thing—looking at him across the dining room table was quite another. She closed her eyes and wished she were five years old again, sitting in Aunt Rose's lap.

Little Boy, Little Boy
Yes Ma'am?
Did you feed my horse?
Yes Ma'am.
What did you feed him?
Oats and Rye.
What did you feed him?
Oats and Rye.
Little Boy, Little Boy
Yes Ma'am?
Did my horse die?
Yes Ma'am.
How did he die?
He died all over.
How did he die?
He died all over...

She yawned and closed her eyes.

The dining room was bathed in candlelight. Mildred sat in Aunt Rose's rocking chair in front of the window waiting for O'Kanta. "Moody's Mood for Love" wailed on the stereo. Mildred took a long, deep drag from her cigarette, arched her neck back, and blew out a plume of smoke ceilingward. She reached down and picked up her glass of Mogen David and curled her long, red-lacquered nails around the glass. Tensing, she sensed her lover's footsteps on the stairs. She slowly rose to her feet and slinked to the door as her lover knocked...

"Millie! Millie!" Aunt Rose knocked on the door. "O'Kanta's gonna be here in a half hour. Are you getting ready?"

Mildred pulled herself up with an effort and sighed heavily.

Aunt Rose opened Mildred's bedroom door and stepped inside.

"Wow!" Mildred sat up and grinned at her aunt.

Aunt Rose had on a black, satiny straight dress with black fringe on the bottom. She strutted in front of Mildred and let her admire the outfit.

The dress had a belt with black tassels on the end. On her shoulder was pinned a ladybug broach that Mildred had given her when she was in the eighth grade. A string of pearls graced her throat.

Mildred bent down and felt the fringe on the bottom of her aunt's dress. "You look like you should be *going* out to dinner instead of *cooking* it."

"Nonsense," Aunt Rose twirled her belt. "Gladys wears dresses like this all the time when she's entertaining."

"Gladys is on a soap opera," Mildred reminded her.

Aunt Rose shrugged her shoulders. "What are you wearing?" She looked in the mirror and tugged at her dress.

Mildred pointed to her outfit hanging on the back of the closet door.

Aunt Rose walked over and picked up the brown corduroy pants and beige sweater. She turned to Mildred. "Are you serious?"

Mildred walked over to her dresser and began rummaging through her jewelry box. "Yes, I believe I am. What's wrong with it?"

"Nothing, if you're wearing it to work."

Aunt Rose opened Mildred's closet and pulled out a gold-silk blouse. "How about wearing this with the pants?" She walked over to the dresser and picked up a gold chain that she'd bought Mildred for her 21st birthday. "Here," she handed the blouse and chain to Mildred. "Hurry up and change. Don't forget to put on a pair of stockings and your brown pumps. And don't wear knee-hi's."

Mildred held out the gold chain for Aunt Rose to fasten around her neck. "What's wrong with knee-hi's? O'Kanta won't know the difference."

Aunt Rose fastened the chain and leaned back with her hands on her hips. "He may not know the difference, but *you* will. There's nothing like walking into a room and feeling the sensation of your dress as it rubs against your stockings." She winked at Mildred.

Mildred shook her head. "I think you've been watching too many soap operas." She turned to her aunt. "Here, put this on."

Aunt Rose looked at the red tube of lipstick and backed away. "No, baby, I already put on some face powder. I don't need that."

Mildred opened the tube. "If you don't put a little of this on, I'm gonna wear my corduroy pants, wool sweater, and oxfords."

Aunt Rose leaned forward and let Mildred apply the lipstick. "That's enough, that's quite enough." She began to rub her lips back and forth.

Mildred laughed, "If you keep doing that, you'll rub all of the lipstick off."

Aunt Rose looked in the mirror, "Jump back, Sally! I haven't had on lipstick this red since me and Mildred Walker kicked our heels up on a Saturday night!"

A loud knock sounded at the door.

Mildred jumped and turned a frightened face to Aunt Rose.

"He's too early, Aunt Rose! It's not seven o'clock yet!"

Aunt Rose looked in the mirror and gave her dress a final tug. "He's prompt, baby. One of the first signs of a true gentleman." She looked at Mildred's face and took her hand. "Now I'm going to go out there and entertain our guest while you get ready. Right?" She searched her niece's face.

"Right," Mildred whispered.

Another knock sounded at the door.

Aunt Rose hugged Mildred and hurried out of the room.

Mildred leaned on the dresser, not knowing whether to laugh or cry. She stared at her face in the mirror and tried a weak smile.

Aunt Rose burst back into the room. "Here, baby." She set a can on the dresser. "Put a little bit of my face powder on. If you gonna wear that red lipstick you might as well go all the way." She hurried out.

Mildred looked at the can of Café Au Lait face powder that she was sure was at least ten years old. She heard the front door open and hurriedly reached for a cotton ball.

Mildred opened her bedroom door to the familiar sounds of B.B. King. Each twang of the guitar seemed to pull her into the living room.

Aunt Rose was showing O'Kanta their collection of blues records.

"Yes, B.B.'s good," O'Kanta agreed, "but he is not the king of the blues. The king of the blues is, without a doubt, Muddy Waters."

O'Kanta had on a pair of black corduroy pants with a red and black dashiki. His dreadlocks were secured by a red rubber band. He was arguing good-naturedly with Aunt Rose and smiling.

Mildred stared and felt a pang of jealousy at their closeness.

"No, no," O'Kanta shook his head. "If you really want to hear the true Mississippi blues, you have to listen to Muddy Waters."

Aunt Rose flipped her hand in a gesture that Mildred knew so well. "I don't know where you heard that. Don't you know what 'B.B. King' stands for?"

O'Kanta shook his head.

Aunt Rose put her hands on her hips. "There is only one Blues Buster King," she stated matter-of-factly.

O'Kanta threw back his head and laughed, catching sight of Mildred. "Well, hello," he said as he rose to his feet.

"Hello," Mildred whispered as she stood in the entrance of the living room, wondering how to move. She looked into O'Kanta's eyes and slowly stopped breathing.

O'Kanta smiled at her.

Her stomach began to flutter.

O'Kanta smiled at her.

Her throat felt dry.

O'Kanta smiled at her.

Aunt Rose smiled at Mildred, "My, don't you look nice?"

"Yes, she does," O'Kanta agreed quietly.

Aunt Rose looked at Mildred's face. "Baby, would you help me set the table?"

Mildred moved quickly to the safety of the kitchen.

She put her hands on the kitchen sink and began to take deep breaths. Was O'Kanta really sitting in her living room listening to records? Sitting on a couch that she, herself, had sat on only an hour ago?

"Hand me the plates in the pantry," Aunt Rose's voice broke in.

Mildred floated dreamily into the pantry.

"Not *those* plates," Aunt Rose hissed. "Get the good plates that I got with my Greater Foods bonus stamps."

"Oh, excuse me," Mildred said as she went back into the pantry and got the correct plates.

"Mildred?"

"Hmmm?" Mildred set the plates on the counter and went back for the glassware.

"I want to know what your strategy is going to be tonight."

"What?" Mildred turned to face her aunt.

"Lower your voice," Aunt Rose whispered. "I want to know what your plan is." She leaned toward Mildred conspiratorially.

"I don't *have* a plan," Mildred retorted. "This dinner"— she waved her arm in the air— "was your idea, if I remember correctly."

"Yes, it was my idea," Aunt Rose snapped. "I had to get him over here, didn't I? And now that he's here I want you to act as if you're glad to see him."

Mildred grabbed her aunt's arm and pulled her into the pantry. "Just what am I supposed to do, Aunt Rose? Fling myself across the table at him?" Mildred began to pace back and forth in the pantry. "Just what did you have in mind?"

"Talk to him," Aunt Rose whispered as she looked over her shoulder toward the dining room. "Let him know you're interested in him."

"I can't talk to him," Mildred moaned. "You know that."

"Well, then use your eyes on him," Aunt Rose decided.

"Use what?"

"If a young lady isn't able to converse with her gentleman, she can let him know her every thought by the expression in her eyes," Aunt Rose recited.

"Where did you read that?" Mildred asked. "*True Confessions?*"

"Don't worry about where I got it," Aunt Rose snapped. "It makes good sense. I want you to look at him and smile every once in a while."

She demonstrated how Mildred should look and smile.

"Are you quite finished?" Mildred asked.

"Yes," Aunt Rose put her hands on her hips. "Now what are you going to do?"

Mildred walked around her aunt and out of the pantry. "Eat," she threw the word over her shoulder.

Aunt Rose's platter of golden fried chicken was placed near the end of the dining room table. A bowl of fried corn and a bowl of okra and stewed tomatoes were at the other end. A heaping plate of cornbread patties graced one corner. A vase of wildflowers was placed in the center of the table.

Aunt Rose shook her head, "This is a mighty fine-looking table."

O'Kanta picked up the edge of the intricately designed white-lace tablecloth. "This is beautiful. Where did you get it?"

Aunt Rose fingered the tablecloth. "Yes, it is beautiful, isn't it? Millie bought it for me to replace one that I had many years ago."

Mildred watched the shadows pass over her aunt's face. Her hands reached out instinctively to comfort, to protect..... .

"Let's eat," she suggested.

O'Kanta held out a chair for Aunt Rose.

"Thank you. I must say I truly feel like Gladys tonight."

"Gladys?" O'Kanta looked questioningly at Mildred.

Mildred merely shook her head and quickly sat down, just in case O'Kanta decided to give her a hand.

"O'Kanta, will you do the honors?" Aunt Rose asked.

O'Kanta bowed his head and lifted his hands, palms up. "Oh Allah. We thank You for this food we're about to receive to nourish our bodies in Thy namesake of righteousness. Amen."

"Amen," Aunt Rose and Mildred repeated.

Aunt Rose and Mildred exchanged looks.

Mildred sat across the table and listened to the sounds that O'Kanta made. Aunt Rose often told her that the sounds that people made were important. Listen for grief in tears and hear the honesty in laughter, she said. Listen to the grunts and sounds that people make when they're eating. When you become a master at the sounds that people make, you'll never have to worry about trying to understand what they're saying to you. You'll know.

All of O'Kanta's sounds were delicious...

"What do you think, Mildred?" O'Kanta asked.

Mildred looked up in confusion. "Excuse me?"

"O'Kanta was just asking about our voter registration drive," Aunt Rose explained.

"Oh," Mildred looked down at her plate. "It's going okay, I guess," she whispered.

"Up and down, huh?" O'Kanta persisted.

Mildred nodded her head.

"Up and down is right," Aunt Rose put in. "Sometimes I feel like we movin' one step ahead for every two steps backward. Ain't that right, baby?" She looked meaningfully at Mildred.

Mildred nodded and reached for the butter dish.

O'Kanta picked up the dish and handed it to Mildred with an exaggerated flourish.

Mildred giggled and shook her head. She painstakingly buttered her slice of cornbread. "I was wondering how we can reach those people who are dead set against the very idea of a black mayor," she said.

"I was wondering the same, identical thing," Aunt Rose added.

"Well, first you have to realize that you're not going to reach everyone," O'Kanta said. "I've found that people can be broken into three main groups. You've got those of us who are afraid of having a black mayor; those who don't trust one of their own; and then there are those who couldn't care less about the mayoral election or any other election.

He took a forkful of okra and tomatoes. "Of course, there will be exceptions to this. Maybe you two have noticed different types.

"You know, it's funny," he continued. " But I've got three people in my building who seem to represent all of the people that I've come across."

O'Kanta leaned back in his chair with a thoughtful look.

"Chapman Jackson lives on the first floor. He's anywhere between 60 and 70 and is definitely against Raymond Williams."

"Why doesn't he like him?" Aunt Rose asked.

"'Oh, I ain't got nothing against your Raymond Williams personally,'" O'Kanta mimicked Jackson's voice. "'But I got to throw my weight behind young Tom Carroll. Now Tom is gonna run this city like his uncle did. Streets swept and garbage picked up on time.'"

"Yeah, but *whose* streets and *whose* garbage?" Aunt Rose wanted to know.

"What else does he say?" Mildred asked.

"'Son,'" O'Kanta continued, "'this city just ain't ready for no black mayor. Now don't get me wrong, we gon' be ready one day. But we sure ain't ready now.'"

"When I hear that from people, I always wonder if it means that they aren't ready," Mildred said.

"Could be," O'Kanta said. "I don't know for sure, but I always get the feeling that Chapman is afraid of having a black mayor."

"Why?" Mildred asked.

"Who knows?" O'Kanta threw up his hands. "Could be something in his past or something." He reached for another piece of chicken.

"But how do you reach people like Chapman Jackson?" Aunt Rose questioned.

"You don't," O'Kanta answered. "We won't be able to get everyone to come out and vote for Raymond Williams. We just have to keep talking to people one on one. Tell them about Raymond Williams, listen to their responses, and leave the literature. We're going to elect him one household at a time. But above all, don't get discouraged." He squeezed Aunt Rose's hand. "You're one of our best workers."

"Oh, I've been in the game far too long to back out now," Aunt Rose assured him.

O'Kanta pulled his chair away from the table. He smiled at Aunt Rose and Mildred. "I haven't had a home-cooked meal like that in a long time. It was delicious."

49

Aunt Rose grinned as she reached for her diet soda. "Yes, it was good, wasn't it? I'd really be worried now if I wasn't drinking this diet soda."

Mildred rolled her eyes.

O'Kanta turned to Mildred. "Wasn't that homemade fried corn?"

Mildred nodded and got up to clear the table.

"Baby, you don't have to do that." Aunt Rose looked meaningfully at Mildred. She turned to O'Kanta. "Are you ready for some pie?"

O'Kanta took a deep breath and winked at Mildred. "Yes, I believe I am."

Mildred started to get up.

"No, no," Aunt Rose waved at her to sit down. "I can get it." She smiled at Mildred. "You just relax and visit with our guest."

Mildred turned to the laughing eyes of O'Kanta.

"Alone at last," he whispered.

Mildred smiled and stirred her coffee.

O'Kanta placed his hand over hers. "Mildred."

Mildred looked up nervously.

"Mildred, I am not the enemy," O'Kanta said quietly.

"I know that," she whispered. "I'm sorry if I'm not what you're used to."

"And what am I used to?" O'Kanta questioned.

Mildred shrugged her shoulders.

O'Kanta took Mildred's hand and placed it between his own. "Listen to me; I've been waiting for someone like you for a long time. I don't mind waiting. I'm a patient man. All I'm asking for is your friendship. I want you to relax around me and smile sometimes." He squeezed her hand. "I mean—if you want to. You do want to, don't you?"

Mildred smiled. "You mean you're unsure about something?"

O'Kanta threw his arms up in frustration. "Who can be sure about anything with women?"

They both laughed.

"Where is Aunt Rose with the pie?" O'Kanta asked.

"Standing in the doorway, watching us," Mildred answered, looking at Aunt Rose.

"Well, are we ready for pie?" Aunt Rose hurried into the dining room, beaming at the two of them.

O'Kanta stared at the browncapped peaks of meringue. "That looks like a work of art."

"It *is* a work of art," Aunt Rose said as she set the pie down.

"You know, I couldn't believe it when you asked me if I liked lemon meringue pie," O'Kanta said as he looked at the pie. "It's one of my favorites."

"Well, I'll let you do the honors." Aunt Rose handed the knife to him.

O'Kanta stood up and made a big presentation over cutting the pie.

When the slices were all passed around, Aunt Rose got to her feet. "I'm going to propose a toast."

"With pie?" Mildred teased.

"Yes, with pie," Aunt Rose stated. She looked around the table. "I want to toast to Raymond Williams."

"Hear, hear," O'Kanta put in.

"Mr. Williams has put a lot of trust in us plain folk to get the word out about him. I'm toasting in his belief in us."

O'Kanta, Mildred, and Aunt Rose each took a bite of pie.

"MMmmmmmh," O'Kanta turned to Mildred. "Mildred, this is the best lemon meringue pie I've ever tasted."

Mildred brightened and nodded, "Thanks."

"The meringue is so light," O'Kanta continued, "and the lemon is tart, yet so sweet."

"Yes, that's lemon meringue pie," Mildred said dryly.

O'Kanta winked at her.

"You know," O'Kanta took a sip of coffee, "it's funny that you toasted Raymond Williams. There's a rally going on tonight at DuSable City College. Would you two like to come with me?"

51

"Oh, that really sounds like fun," Aunt Rose said. "But you know the next hour or two is my bedtime."

"Since when?" Mildred wanted to know.

"But I think you and Millie should go," Aunt Rose continued.

"I wouldn't feel right about going without you," Mildred put in hastily. "You're the one who's been behind Raymond Williams from the start. I'll stay here with you." She turned to O'Kanta. "But thank you for asking us."

"Nonsense," Aunt Rose said. "Will you bring her back here?" she asked O'Kanta.

"Of course," O'Kanta said, smiling at Mildred.

"Then it's all settled." Aunt Rose got up. "Mildred, you better put on a sweater under your coat; you know how easy you take cold."

Mildred stood up. "I think my sweater is in your room, Aunt Rose. Why don't you help me look for it?" She took her aunt's arm and led her into the bedroom.

She shut her aunt's bedroom door. "What are you trying to do?" she hissed.

Aunt Rose put her hands on her hips. "I'm trying to give you some time alone with him," she whispered. "I want you to go out with him."

"What about what *I* want?" Mildred began to pace her aunt's bedroom. "Do my feelings count for anything in this house?"

Aunt Rose snorted. "This is what you want. I know you better than you know yourself. You know you want to go out with him."

Mildred turned to her aunt. "Maybe I do. But *I* want to choose the time and place. I don't need you to shove it down my throat!"

Aunt Rose raised her arms in confusion. "If I left it up to you, you'd never do it. What am I supposed to do? Just sit back and watch a fine-looking black man like that slip through your fingers?"

"The meeting starts in an hour," O'Kanta spoke to the door.

"We're coming," Aunt Rose called. "Here," she grabbed an old blue sweater. "Put this on."

Mildred snatched the sweater and slipped it on. "Aunt Rose, what am I supposed to do?"

"Nothing." She looked at her niece meaningfully.

Mildred rolled her eyes and stopped her aunt from opening the bedroom door. "What am I supposed to talk about?"

"Not sex," Aunt Rose stated. "Here," she sprayed Mildred with her bottle of *Chanel N° 5*. "Go on and be the good girl that I raised. I'm gonna be waiting right here for you when you get back."

Mildred bent down and received her aunt's kiss and was pushed out of the bedroom.

O'Kanta was standing by the front door. "Is everything all right?" He smiled at Mildred gently.

"Here, baby." Aunt Rose handed Mildred her coat and purse. She held out her arms. "Come give me some sugar." As she hugged Mildred she whispered, "I put five dollars in your purse just in case you need to get a cab."

Mildred hugged her aunt.

"Well, are we ready?" O'Kanta held out his hand and looked at Mildred.

She took it.

* * *

Aunt Rose watched Mildred and O'Kanta leave from her living room window.

She walked back into the dining room and began to clear the table. She smiled with satisfaction as she picked up O'Kanta's plate. He had asked for seconds of everything. She lifted the white-lace tablecloth that he had admired and folded it carefully.

Rocking slowly with the tablecloth in her lap, she went over the dinner in her mind. She smiled at the sight of Millie slowly buttering her bread. Millie had her mother's hands. Big hands with long, thin fingers. Movie star hands, Millie's mother had called them. She'd noticed O'Kanta studying Millie's hands while she buttered her bread.

Movie star hands and *Tango Tangerine* lipstick. Rose began to rock and sing softly.

Seven

MILDRED WALKED BRISKLY AHEAD of O'Kanta down Jackson Boulevard. She thrust her hands in her pockets and looked straight ahead as she walked.

She started when she felt a tap on her shoulder.

O'Kanta stood behind her with an amused expression. "Mildred," he said carefully, "how about you and I going to this rally *together*?" He held out his hand tentatively.

Mildred offered O'Kanta a weak smile and gave him her hand. She looked up hesitantly.

O'Kanta winked at her.

"That's better," he said as he squeezed it.

"Uh, Mildred." O'Kanta looked at her sheepishly. "I'm sort of in between cars right now. Would you mind terribly if we took the El?"

Mildred smiled at O'Kanta. "Not at all," she whispered in an attempt to ease his embarrassment. "I like riding the El."

"Really?" O'Kanta looked relieved.

Mildred and O'Kanta climbed the El steps at Lake Street. As they approached the ticket booth, Mildred opened her purse.

"Excuse me," O'Kanta said in a loud voice.

Mildred turned around.

O'Kanta held up two dollars to the ticket agent. "I think I can manage this," he said.

"A true gentleman always pays," Aunt Rose reminded her.

Mildred leaned against the El railing and wondered if the people standing near her realized that she was on a date. She held her head down and smiled.

O'Kanta walked over to her. "I got us a couple of transfers," he said, "but it's kind of nice out. Would you like to walk to the rally from the El?"

Mildred nodded.

O'Kanta leaned against the railing and stared at Mildred. "I can't believe you agreed to go out with me," he said. "Tell me." He casually put his arm along the railing. "Did you really want to come, or did your aunt force you?" He draped his arm around her shoulder.

Mildred carefully eased herself free and leaned over the railing, looking down at the people below. "I guess it was a little of both," she said. She looked up at him and managed a smile. "Is that okay?"

O'Kanta returned her smile. "Hey, I'll take whatever I can get."

The approaching El slowed to a stop. O'Kanta took Mildred's arm and stepped aboard.

"Welcome aboard the friendship train! Everybody pick a card and make a friend!"

A young man grinned at Mildred and O'Kanta and motioned them to a seat. He was wearing an oversized jacket and a red bandanna tied around his head. A lone white feather stuck out at the back of the bandanna.

He had a brown briefcase on his lap with three cards spread out. He flipped and shuffled the cards with precision as he sized up his audience.

"Cherokee is my name and Three Card Molly is my game. Pick a card and don't be afraid to lose, 'cause I've got all kinds of money in my socks and shoes."

"Let's go to another car," Mildred suggested to O'Kanta.

"Why?" O'Kanta pulled Mildred to a seat across from Cherokee. "I've always wanted to watch this up close. Maybe I can win enough money to take you out to dinner."

Mildred looked at O'Kanta with disbelief. "What?"

"Just kiddin', just kiddin'." O'Kanta patted her hand. "But I've always wanted to watch this up close. Now that the El is half empty, I can figure this out."

"What do you want to figure it out for?" Mildred asked.

Cherokee continued. "You see, my great granddaddy was an Indian, and he had the power in his hands..."

"That explains the feather," O'Kanta whispered to Mildred.

Mildred turned to the window and smothered a laugh.

"I got the red lady in the middle," Cherokee said as he slid the ace of hearts between the ace of spades and the ace of clubs.

"How about a trial run?" Cherokee looked at O'Kanta and Mildred.

O'Kanta looked at Mildred questioningly.

Mildred shook her head.

"I want a trial run," an older man stated. He had on an old fedora with a rust-colored blazer over a tee shirt. "If the lady don't want to go." He tipped his hat to Mildred.

"Fellas, fellas," Cherokee shook his head. "The price is two dollars. Now I know y'all got two dollars in your pocket. If you don't you need to find another j-o-b."

O'Kanta laughed and turned to Mildred. "This guy is with him," he whispered. "That's how they work a crowd. Watch this."

"If you know what's going on, why do you want to get involved?" Mildred asked.

"Because I want to see the magic that he does with his hands," O'Kanta whispered back. "The magic that his great grandfather taught him."

Mildred groaned and shook her head. "Go on and play then," she suggested.

"He said he'd give you a free turn," O'Kanta pointed out.

"I'm not in this," Mildred said firmly.

She looked around the El car. A few passengers watched Cherokee with halfhearted interest. A young man and woman seemed totally absorbed in each other.

"I got the two dollars," the man in the fedora said. He held up two crumpled dollar bills.

"Put it down my man, put it down." Cherokee continued to switch the cards back and forth. He stopped abruptly and reached into his pocket and pulled out a thick wad of bills. He slowly peeled off two dollars and put the wad back in his pocket.

Cherokee smiled up at the man in the fedora. He picked up the ace of hearts and displayed it to the man, O'Kanta, Mildred, and the other passengers on the car. He shuffled the cards back and forth with speed.

Mildred watched Cherokee for a while and then turned to the window. She glanced at O'Kanta and smiled at his total absorption in the game.

O'Kanta had told her that he wanted her friendship. What did that mean in the 1980s? Was he saying that he just wanted them to be friends? Or did being "friends" today mean something else? Shannon, who worked at the bank with Mildred, called her boyfriend her "friend." Did O'Kanta mean that he wanted to be her boyfriend? She sighed heavily at the complexity of it all.

"Something wrong?" O'Kanta turned a concerned face to Mildred.

"Not at all," Mildred assured him. "Who won the card game?"

O'Kanta dismissed Cherokee with his hand. "They went off to find fresh bait."

He stared at Mildred intently. "What was the sigh for?"

Mildred looked down at her hands folded together in her lap. "I was just thinking about all of the labels that we put on each other," she said.

"Is someone trying to put a label on you?" O'Kanta's voice was very close to Mildred's ear.

"Uh-Uh," Mildred shook her head passionately.

She looked up at him and began to laugh.

"I think I missed something there," O'Kanta said as he gently placed a stray curl behind Mildred's ear.

"Tell me how you got involved with Raymond Williams," she said. "Do you know him?"

"I wish I did," O'Kanta said. "I know *of* him. I've followed his political career for the past five years, and I have an idea of what he's about."

"So how did you get this deeply involved in his campaign?"

The El slowed to a stop. O'Kanta stood up and held out his hand to Mildred. As they walked down the El steps and onto the street, Mildred marveled at how new and different the city seemed, now that she was walking with O'Kanta.

Holding hands with O'Kanta, Mildred walked the downtown streets of Chicago as if for the first time. Streetlights glowed. Store windows came alive. The warm air caressed her skin as curbside flowers gave off a sweet, heady perfume. Walking beside O'Kanta was like slow dancing. The warmth from his hand encircled the two of them.

"There I go, there I go, there I go, there I go..."

"Have you been to DuSable City College before?" O'Kanta suddenly asked.

Mildred quickly gathered her thoughts. "No. Is that where you went to school?" she questioned.

"No, I went to Malcolm X Junior College," O'Kanta replied.

"What are your undergraduate and graduate degrees in?" Mildred asked.

"I've never gone beyond junior college," O'Kanta answered.

"Really?" Mildred stopped walking to look at O'Kanta.

"Are you disappointed?" O'Kanta asked.

"No," Mildred shook her head slowly. "I just thought... I mean, you're so smart."

O'Kanta squeezed her hand. "But you don't have to have a degree to be.

How about you? Are you in school?"

"No," Mildred shrugged her shoulders. "I started at the University of Illinois after high school, but I stopped going."

"Why? What happened?"

Mildred looked down at the pointed toes of her brown pumps and shrugged her shoulders.

O'Kanta dropped Mildred's hand and placed both hands on her shoulders. "I think that's enough shoulder shrugging for tonight," he said. "Now, I want you to answer my question without moving your shoulders or looking down at your feet. Can you do that?"

Mildred looked into O'Kanta's face. "Do we have to stop right in the middle of the sidewalk to do this?"

O'Kanta nodded.

Mildred looked at the people who passed by her and O'Kanta. They seemed to smile their approval.

She looked down at her feet. "Well," she started.

O'Kanta squeezed her shoulders. "Look me dead in the face."

The warmth of his hands on her shoulders slowly pervaded her body.

She looked up into his smile. "It's nothing, really. It seemed that all of the classes that I wanted to take required you to get up before the class and either read a paper or make a presentation. So I decided to stop going."

"Aha," O'Kanta dropped his hands from her shoulders and started walking. "So you've got that 'I can't get up in front of people and talk' disease." He nodded his head. "I'm gonna change all that."

"Aunt Rose has been trying for years. Believe me, I'm hopeless."

"We'll see," O'Kanta replied. "Do you get to the library often?"

"Yes. Aunt Rose and I usually go about once a month. But," Mildred looked sideways at O'Kanta, "our taste usually leans toward the lighter side of fiction."

"Not Ebony Romances?" O'Kanta asked in mock horror.

"I plead guilty," Mildred confessed and started laughing.

"You know, I have to admit, I've casually flipped through a few of them in my day," O'Kanta winked at Mildred. "But I am shocked that you and your aunt—"

"Hey brother!" A voice rang out.

A man half sitting on the sidewalk looked up into O'Kanta's and Mildred's faces with his hand outstretched. His hair was dirty and matted. His once-white shirt was spotted and sweat stained.

Mildred tried to walk around the man but was held fast by O'Kanta.

"Brother, can you lay some change on me?" the man asked O'Kanta.

"Of course," O'Kanta replied as he reached into his pocket. He dropped a few coins into the man's dirty hand.

"Listen," he said. "My name is O'Kanta, and this is Mildred."

The man nodded.

"I work at the Center for Black Awareness on the West Side. We don't have much, but you can come in there anytime for a cup of coffee." O'Kanta pulled a leaflet out of his pocket and handed it to the man.

"We've got an election coming up, brother, and I need you to be involved."

The man nodded dubiously.

O'Kanta and Mildred continued walking.

"Do you do that often?" Mildred asked.

O'Kanta squeezed her hand. "Do what, love?"

"Stop and talk to people on the street like that."

"Yeah. Talk is usually about all that I can give, though." O'Kanta checked his pocket.

"What do you mean?"

"Well, usually I start out with about two dollars in change in my right pocket. Although," O'Kanta grinned at Mildred, "some days it's only a dollar. I try to make sure that before I go home at night that I've given it away. Once it's gone, all that I have left to offer is conversation."

"But why waste words on someone like that?" Mildred asked as she looked back at the man. "I could smell the alcohol on him before I saw him. Do you really think that he'll suddenly appear at the center one day and volunteer his time?"

O'Kanta turned to her. "What would you say if I told you that about five years ago I was out here on the street just like him?"

"I wouldn't believe you," Mildred said simply.

"You're lucky to have your aunt there for you. I mean, I can tell by the way she looks at you and talks to you that she loves you. And that's aside from what I heard through the bedroom door," he whispered.

Mildred ignored the last statement.

"But a lot of people don't have anyone there for them, and they make it," she pointed out.

"You're absolutely right," O'Kanta agreed. "I'm ashamed to say that I wasn't one of them. I wasn't an alcoholic or a junkie but I was just as bad. I came to a decision in my life that the white man was the cause of all of my suffering and pain. So I decided that I would let him support me."

"What do you mean 'support you?'" Mildred asked.

"I went down to the welfare office and told them that I was 'unable' to contribute to society. Then I claimed a corner on Jackson and Pulaski and set up house."

"Oh," Mildred said.

"But a funny thing happened on my corner," O'Kanta continued. "I rarely, if ever, got any money from the white man. The people who ended up supporting me were the brothers and sisters who lived in the neighborhood. The ones who seemed the least able to do so."

"What happened?" Mildred asked.

O'Kanta smiled. "I had a few regulars, you know. And I guess this one guy just got tired of giving me his change. Every time he stopped by he would lecture me and tell me that I was too young to be giving up. It got so bad that I told him that he could keep his change because I was so tired of his preaching.

"I was on my corner one afternoon and he came by with two young guys. He pointed to me and said 'that's him.' These guys picked me up and dumped me in the back of a station wagon."

"What!" Mildred exclaimed.

O'Kanta started laughing. "I'm serious. The old man told them to get in the back with me. But I was so filthy and smelly that they kept gagging."

61

"You mean you were kidnapped?" Mildred asked.

"Yes," O'Kanta said simply. "Literally."

"What about the people who were around? Didn't they try to help you?"

"Are you kidding? A few of them started clapping when they took me."

Mildred started to laugh. "Then what happened?"

"They took me to the 'Y' on Western. They stripped me and threw me in the shower. They would not even give me the courtesy of washing myself alone. They began to scrub me from head to toe. They washed my hair and would have brushed my teeth if I didn't snatch the toothbrush away from them."

"What were you thinking during all of this? How were you feeling? Were you angry? Did you try to fight them? Were you scared?"

"Are you kidding?" O'Kanta raised his eyebrows. "Those guys looked like they were raised on buffalo and beans. You could strike a match on either one of them. I really don't know what I was thinking. I was so shocked and surprised that I didn't know what to think. Then I thought that this old man must be crazy or something. He used to tell me that he'd lost a son in 'Nam, and I thought that maybe he had flipped." O'Kanta stopped in his tracks.

"Look," he pointed. "There's the college."

Mildred followed his gaze and saw the tall, gray structure of DuSable College. "Please finish the story before we go in," she urged.

"Okay. After I was clean, they gave me a pair of jeans, a tee shirt, and a pair of those—what do you call them? Flip-flops?"

Mildred nodded.

"Then we got back into the car. Nobody said anything during the ride. Out of the corner of my eye, I caught the old man looking back at me, but he didn't say anything. I remember wondering if he was some sort of religious fanatic or something. That maybe he was taking me to a church or something.

"But we pulled up to this apartment building and they ushered me in. The old man pushed me in front of a long hall mirror. You know the full-length kind?" He looked at Mildred.

She nodded.

"And he said to me,—" O'Kanta stopped and cleared his throat—"he said, 'look at yourself, goddammit! You're a man!' He kept saying it over and over. I think he must have said it a hundred times. Every time I tried to turn away he would force me back and repeat those words: 'You're a man.' I looked in that mirror, and it seemed like I saw a person who I hadn't seen in a long time. I broke down. I never cried so hard or for so long before."

Mildred squeezed his hand.

"I turned toward him and asked him what was I going to do?" O'Kanta shook his head. "He said that he didn't know, but that I was sure as hell going to do *something*." O'Kanta laughed.

"So I moved in with him. I started working a couple of odd jobs. I worked at Hamburger Heaven; I pumped gas; I mowed lawns..." O'Kanta winked at Mildred. "I can make burgers with the best of them.

"He made me pay back the money that I had collected from welfare. I started going to night school to get my GED and read everything that I could get my hands on. And, to make a long story short, a few friends and me eventually started the center."

"What about the old man? What happened to him?" Mildred wanted to know. "I'd like to meet him, and I know Aunt Rose would, too."

"I told you two about him tonight. He's Chapman Jackson, and he lives on the first floor." O'Kanta pulled Mildred's arm. "We'd better go in now and maybe we can get a good seat."

The two of them hurried into the lobby of DuSable City College.

Eight

THE DUSABLE CITY COLLEGE AUDITORIUM was filled to capacity. People milled about, talking to each other and trying to find seats. O'Kanta expertly navigated Mildred toward two empty ones near the front of the stage.

A group of people stood on the podium looking anxiously about as a young man adjusted the microphone.

"Who are all of those people up there?" Mildred whispered.

"Well, there's Alderman Hayes over there in the brown suit," O'Kanta answered.

Mildred stared at the podium. "He looks different in person. What about the others?"

"I'm not sure. Probably organizers, fund-raisers, and ministers."

The young man tapped the microphone a few times. No sound was heard.

Two huge color portraits of Raymond Williams occupied opposite ends of the stage. Underneath each was a large wicker basket. Poster

64

buttons and stickers were displayed on tables by the exit doors of the auditorium. All bore his smiling face.

"Is Raymond Williams going to be here?" Mildred asked.

"I doubt it. He doesn't usually come to the local rallies. A representative generally comes at the end and collects the money," O'Kanta answered.

"I hope they get the mike fixed. I'd sure hate to leave without hearing anybody," Mildred said.

"Are you kidding?" O'Kanta looked at Mildred. "These guys are so hungry for exposure they'll walk up and down the aisles shouting their message if push comes to shove."

A loud humming sounded through the auditorium.

The people on the stage seemed to heave a sigh of relief.

"Here we go," whispered O'Kanta.

A tall, shapely woman in a bright-yellow dress approached the microphone. "Good evening ladies and gentlemen," she crooned. "I want to thank each of you personally for coming out tonight and showing your support in our drive to elect the city's first black mayor!"

The crowd clapped and shouted their approval.

"My name is Beverly Winston and I will be your moderator for tonight." She flashed a red, glossy smile to the audience.

"Since we've already lost precious time in 'adjusting' our microphone," she looked meaningfully at the young man standing near the curtain, "let me introduce our first speaker to you. I don't know if we'll be able to get to all of our speakers tonight—"

An older woman got up from one of the chairs on the stage and motioned hurriedly to the speaker.

"We have many sponsors for tonight's rally," Beverly continued. "I'm proud to say that one of our sponsors is Edna Murray of Edna's Fashion Boutique, located at 5235 W. Madison Street. I happen to be wearing one of Edna's personal creations tonight."

Beverly stepped back from the microphone and slowly pirouetted on stage.

The audience clapped politely.

65

"Go on, Miss Beverly!" one man shouted.

"Oh, for heaven's sake," O'Kanta muttered.

Edna Murray stood up briefly and gratefully acknowledged the applause.

"Our first speaker," Beverly continued, "is a familiar face to those of you in the third ward. Alderman Hayes has taken time out of his busy schedule to speak with us about the importance of this election." Beverly gracefully extended a well-manicured hand. "Come on up here, Edward," she invited.

Edward Hayes rose, somewhat sheepishly, and approached the microphone.

A few titters were heard in the back.

Beverly handed Alderman Hayes the microphone and slowly moved to the end of the podium.

"How are y'all doing tonight?" Alderman Hayes asked. "I can't stay too long tonight with y'all, but I wanted to let you know that Raymond Williams has my total support. I want y'all to remember who was here. I know that our people have a way of forgetting around election time who said what and who did what. So I want y'all to take a good look at me." Alderman Hayes stepped away from the microphone and imitated the slow pirouette that Beverly Winston had done.

The crowd roared with laughter.

"I want y'all to remember that Alderman Hayes was here and that certain other individuals who are running for alderman of the third ward are not." He started to leave the microphone but stopped and came back.

"Raymond Williams has my full support in this mayoral election," he added as an afterthought. "I've known Raymond from his days as a lawyer, when he took the cases that nobody wanted. I mean, cases where folks didn't have no money and no nothing. Y'all hear me? I know his record in Congress, where he supported bills that y'all never knew about. All y'all knew was that they finally became a law."

"What bills?" Mildred asked O'Kanta.

O'Kanta put his arm along the back of Mildred's chair. "This is the world of politics," he whispered.

"... So I want y'all to vote for Raymond Williams for mayor and Edward Hayes for alderman of the third ward." Alderman Hayes waved to the crowd and bowed to Beverly before leaving.

"Someone told me that imitation is the truest form of flattery," Beverly told the crowd. "Our next guest is a personal friend of Raymond Williams and a friend of ours. Reverend Bishop would like to share a few words of inspiration with us."

Reverend Carl Bishop slowly approached the microphone. He nodded briefly to Beverly and looked out into the audience.

"I'd like to thank each and every one of you for taking the time to come out in support of Raymond Williams' candidacy," he said. "We, as a people, have been apart for far too long. We've broken apart from each other, turned on each other, and betrayed each other."

The crowd murmured words of assent.

"There are those who are in power who help to orchestrate this division, and they reap the many rewards that this division produces. But I'm here to tell you today, that we're together now!"

"Yes we are!" a few echoed.

"We're together as black, white, and Hispanic," Reverend Bishop continued. "This is not a black movement. It's a movement of the people. This is the campaign that Raymond Williams is running on. A movement of the people, by the people, and by God, for the people!"

Several people jumped to their feet and clapped and screamed their agreement.

"We're not trying to shove someone down your throat who is unqualified, inept, and incompetent."

"Well?" a woman asked.

"Do you know that this man was elected student body president in college? Did you know that he was only one of fifteen blacks in the entire student population at John Marshall Law School? Does that tell you something about this man?"

"Yes!" the audience screamed.

"Do you know his record in Congress?" Reverend Bishop glared

67

down at the crowd. "Don't let me recite it to you. Go down to the library and read about it!" He pointed to the crowd. "And take your *children* with you!

"We just don't need to hear you screaming at a rally or wearing a Raymond Williams button. We need volunteers in our district offices. We need you to go door to door and tell people about him. We need you to provide our senior citizens with transportation so they can get to the polls. We got enough chiefs, we need more Indians! Can I count on you?" Reverend Bishop shouted.

The crowd jumped to its feet and screamed their approval.

"When you talk to a brother or sister about Raymond Williams and you find that they're not receptive, don't get angry," Reverend Bishop continued. "Just say 'God Bless You' and go on to the next brother. Because we all know that everybody ain't saved." Reverend Bishop smiled at the crowd. "God seemed to have blessed some of us with the knowledge a little sooner than others!"

Mildred and O'Kanta laughed along with the crowd.

"I wish Aunt Rose was here," Mildred said. "She'd love this."

O'Kanta found Mildred's hand and squeezed it. "We'll bring her along next time," he promised.

Mildred settled back into the comforting cradle of O'Kanta's arm.

"I want you to be informed," Reverend Bishop continued. "Don't take my word or anyone else's about Raymond Williams. I want you to read, read, read! I want you to watch the debates. I want you to attend rallies like this. And I'm running out of time, y'all, but I want you to do one more thing for me."

The crowd leaned forward expectantly.

Reverend Bishop pointed to the two large wicker baskets at the end of the podium. "I want you to fill these baskets with everything that you possibly can. Raymond Williams doesn't have a large corporation supporting him. His people don't have money for television commercials and radio spots. All he has is us. Can you help him?"

"Watch out," O'Kanta cautioned Mildred.

Mildred turned to him questioningly.

O'Kanta picked up Mildred's legs and put them on his lap. He lifted his legs from the floor and angled them toward Mildred.

Mildred watched in amazement as the crowd surged forward to the baskets. People filled the aisles vertically and horizontally.

"This is incredible," she exclaimed.

"It's great to see, isn't it?" O'Kanta agreed. "This is the reaction that Raymond Williams inspires. The people truly believe in him."

"Do you think he'll win?" Mildred asked.

"Look around you at the people here tonight," O'Kanta looked at Mildred. "How can he not?"

* * *

It was a little after midnight when Mildred and O'Kanta returned to Jackson Boulevard.

Mildred walked slowly with her hand clasped in O'Kanta's thinking about the evening. She tried to remember every statement, every nuance, and every feeling. She had so much to tell Aunt Rose.

She wondered what O'Kanta was thinking. He whistled and walked down Jackson, seemingly oblivious to his surroundings.

"Well, Mildred, one more block and you're home," he said suddenly.

"Yeah," Mildred agreed.

"Do you think your aunt will still be up?" he asked.

"Are you kidding?" she smiled. "She's in the window right now, waiting for me."

"I see," O'Kanta tugged on his beard. "Well, in that case, let's step in here for a moment."

O'Kanta pulled Mildred into a gangway between two buildings.

She looked up at him with a frightened expression.

O'Kanta gently lifted her chin. "You don't have to ever be afraid of me, love," he said. "I just want to spend a few minutes alone with you before I step into your aunt's range of fire."

Mildred smiled.

"Did you enjoy yourself tonight?" O'Kanta asked.

"Oh, yes," Mildred nodded emphatically. "I loved everything. The El ride and Cherokee, the rally and all of the speakers—"

"How about the *company?*" O'Kanta broke in.

"Especially the company," Mildred addressed the ground.

"How about aiming that last sentence in my direction?" O'Kanta asked.

Mildred looked up into his eyes. "I especially liked the—"

O'Kanta leaned toward Mildred and touched her lips with his.

A window screeched open. Esther Patillo leaned out of her kitchen window. Her head was tied up with one of those "grease wraps," as Aunt Rose described them.

"Who's that down there?"

She clicked on a light and illuminated the gangway.

"Mildred? Is that you, Mildred Johnson?"

"Yes, Mrs. Patillo, it's me," Mildred answered.

"I thought that looked like you walking down the street and then I saw you turn into the gangway and didn't know what to think." She paused and looked from Mildred to O'Kanta.

O'Kanta put his hand in front of his face to shield his eyes. "Hello— Mrs. Patillo?" He looked at Mildred for confirmation. "My name is O'Kanta. How are you this evening?"

Mrs. Patillo nodded. "Been to the movies, have you?" she asked.

"No," O'Kanta replied. "I took Mildred to a rally for Raymond Williams at DuSable City College."

"Oh," Mrs. Patillo said.

"Are you familiar with the Raymond Williams campaign?" O'Kanta asked.

"No!" she said and slammed her window shut.

O'Kanta turned to Mildred, "I don't understand..."

"We should have never stopped here," Mildred said.

"Why?" O'Kanta asked. "I thought she was funny."

"Did you?" Mildred said. "Mrs. Patillo is one of the biggest gossips on Jackson. She's on the phone right now telling Aunt Rose that she

70

caught the two of us kissing in her gangway. Tomorrow she'll tell the rest of the block."

O'Kanta put his arm around Mildred's shoulder as they walked. "I guess there's only one thing left for us to do," he said.

"What's that?" Mildred asked.

"Kill her," O'Kanta said in a Clint Eastwood voice.

Mildred and O'Kanta were still laughing as they climbed the steps of Mildred's brownstone.

"Well..." Mildred began awkwardly, "I had a very nice time..."

"Did Mrs. Patillo spoil our first kiss?" O'Kanta asked.

"Uh, no," Mildred stammered.

"I could always kiss you again," he offered. "But then I wouldn't want to embarrass you." He grinned at Mildred. "What do you think?"

"I think that you like to embarrass me," Mildred replied.

"*I* should be the one embarrassed," O'Kanta said.

"Why?"

"Your aunt is staring at me."

Mildred looked up.

Aunt Rose hurriedly backed away from the window.

"I'd better go on up," Mildred said, laughing.

"Hold on a minute," O'Kanta took Mildred's hand. "I want you to know that this has been one of the best evenings that I've had in a long time," he said. "I'm glad that I spent it with you." O'Kanta moved closer to Mildred.

Mildred couldn't believe it. Was he going to kiss her twice in one evening? This time she was determined to do it right. She closed her eyes and parted her lips.

She felt a resounding smack on her forehead.

She opened her eyes to O'Kanta's broad grin.

"That should win me points with your aunt," he whispered. He winked broadly at Mildred and waved good-bye.

"That's what you think," Mildred muttered as she went inside. "You don't know my aunt."

* * *

Aunt Rose was rocking when Mildred opened the door. She had a skein of yarn in her hand and was examining it closely.

"Is that you, Millie?" she called.

"You can put the yarn down," Mildred locked the door behind her. "I saw you at the window."

Aunt Rose put the yarn aside and got up. "I only went to the window when I heard voices," she said defensively. "When I saw that it was you and O'Kanta, I drew back right away."

Mildred looked at her in amusement.

Aunt Rose followed Mildred to her bedroom.

Mildred slowly took off her earrings, watch, and sweater. She turned to Aunt Rose's beseeching expression. "I sure could use a cup of hot chocolate. How about you?" she asked.

"I'll get it right away," Aunt Rose hurried to the kitchen.

Mildred watched her aunt's departure with a smile. Aunt Rose deserved a medal for containing her curiosity this long.

Mildred put on her pajamas and housecoat and joined her in the kitchen.

Aunt Rose placed two steaming cups of hot chocolate on the kitchen table.

Mildred opened the refrigerator door and got out the whipped cream. She sprayed out generous toppings for them both.

She sat down at the table and gave her aunt a blow-by-blow report of her evening with O'Kanta. She told her about the El ride and Cherokee.

"I told you that fools ride the El," Aunt Rose commented. "O'Kanta didn't bet on the cards, did he?"

"No, no he didn't bet," Mildred assured her.

She told her aunt how Chappie had rescued O'Kanta from the street.

"My goodness," Aunt Rose wiped her eyes. "That poor child. What about his parents, Millie?"

"I don't know," Mildred answered. "He didn't say, and I didn't want to ask."

"Right, right," Aunt Rose agreed. She made a sympathetic sound. "Now that Mr. Chapman is somebody that we should meet. I don't understand how he could rescue O'Kanta and then not want to vote for Raymond Williams."

"He sounds like a fascinating man," Mildred agreed. "I told O'Kanta that I would like the two of you to meet." She looked innocently at her aunt as she took a sip of hot chocolate.

"What happened next?" Aunt Rose asked crisply.

She and Mildred laughed about the presentation of the speakers at the rally.

"Edward Hayes ought to be ashamed of himself carrying on like that." Aunt Rose cut a big slice of leftover lemon meringue pie. "I'd have liked to have heard Reverend Bishop, though. That man knows how to deliver the Word. Then what happened?" she asked.

"Well, nothing much. After the rally O'Kanta brought me home." Mildred cut a slice of pie and waited.

"Well, I'd sure like to know how you ended up in Esther Patillo's gangway!" Aunt Rose snapped. "I just sat here and waited to see if you'd tell me—"

"I knew you were waiting," Mildred interrupted. "I was waiting to see how long it would take for you to bring it up." She carefully sectioned off a bite of pie. "What did Mrs. Patillo tell you?" she asked casually.

"Never mind what she said," Aunt Rose waved her hand in the air. "I want you to tell me what you and O'Kanta were doing in her gangway at this time of night!"

"He said that he wanted to spend a few minutes with me alone before I got home," Mildred answered.

"He's been alone with you all evening," Aunt Rose pointed out. "What did he have to say to you there that he couldn't have said all night?"

"I don't know!" Mildred said defensively. "He, uh..." she stammered. "He just told me that he had a nice time and stuff."

"What's 'and stuff' mean?" Aunt Rose persisted.

"He didn't try anything, if that's what you mean," Mildred snapped. "I didn't know we were going into the gangway. Before I knew anything we were there."

Aunt Rose grunted. "Well, I knew that he wouldn't try anything. He's too much of a gentleman, my O'Kanta is. Take that kiss he gave you for instance. A true gentleman." She started to laugh.

Mildred got up and put her cup and saucer in the sink. "I knew you were watching. I hope you're satisfied."

Aunt Rose chuckled. "Oh *I* was satisfied, but you sure didn't look satisfied to me. You should have seen the expression on your face!" She began to laugh.

"Are you finished?" Mildred began to clear the table. "I'm going to bed. You coming?"

Aunt Rose wiped her eyes and chuckled. "Did he ask you out again?" she asked.

"No," Mildred shook her head.

"Well, don't worry," Aunt Rose got up from the kitchen table. "He will."

Mildred turned out the light and put her hand in her aunt's. "What makes you think so, Aunt Rose? He didn't say anything."

Aunt Rose kissed Mildred good night. "Trust me, baby. He will." She went into her bedroom slowly.

Mildred walked to her room. She looked at the dining room table that O'Kanta had sat at just a few hours before.

She sat at her desk and wondered if she could capture any of the feelings that she had experienced that night.

She tried to concentrate on what it was about O'Kanta that drew her to him the most. She picked up a sheaf of notebook paper and began to write.

Two hours later, she knelt down, said her prayers, and got into bed.

Folded carefully away in her personal box of trinkets, sachets, and memorabilia was a 12-line poem entitled "O'Kanta's Smile."

Nine

ELLEN, CURTIS, AND JOSEPH MATTHEWS sat across the dining room table, facing Aunt Rose and Mildred.

"Now is not the time," Joseph Matthews shook his head. At age 70, he was the undisputed head of the Matthews household.

"These things have to be planned years in advance. You can't just jump up and say you gonna be mayor and win."

"I don't know, Daddy," Ellen Matthews stood up. "If we wait for the right time, we gonna be waiting forever. We have to decide the time. I'm with Miss Johnson."

"Daughter, you ain't been in this world long enough to know what you saying. I can remember men being killed for just trying to vote. I'm too old to have to start worrying about my peoples!" Joseph ran his gnarled hand over his gray head. "Too old..." he muttered.

An uncomfortable silence descended upon the dining room table.

Aunt Rose cleared her throat. "Joseph, it's true that these children don't know what we had to go through in the forties, fifties, and sixties.

75

The lynchings that never made the news. The rapes that went unchallenged, the murders, the disappearances. But *you* and I know.

"We had it drummed into our heads by everything we read and everything that we saw on television that we were not good enough; we were not smart enough; our lives were not worth as much. It was up to us to pound into the heads of our children that they were good enough and that things were gonna change someday. Someday is *today*, Joseph. Now is the time for us to show our children that a black man can do more than sing and dance. We are gonna show them that a black man can run a whole city!"

Joseph jumped up. "And what are they gonna see when he tries to go into Bridgeport or Cicero?" He slammed his fist on the table. "Will they see him get killed? What will they see if my Baby Ellen goes to work with one of those buttons on her coat? Is some fool gonna try to hurt her? What if he gets elected and someone kills him? Will our city go up in flames again? What will we have won then?"

"Well, Joseph—" Aunt Rose started.

"I want your niece to answer me!" He pointed a bony finger at Mildred. "You're young. You tell me why I should let my family risk everything on this man!"

Four pairs of eyes focused on Mildred.

Aunt Rose looked at Mildred's tortured face and started to speak.

Mildred gently touched her aunt's arm and stood up. She wrapped both arms around her body as if shielding herself. "When I was younger..." she started. She cleared her throat and moved to stand behind her aunt's chair. Placing her hands on the back of the chair, she began again.

"When I was younger, I used to watch all of the film clips of the people who were involved in the Civil Rights Movement. Those people always seemed so much removed from me. They seemed larger than life. I couldn't understand how they could put their lives on the line like that. They were stoned, hosed down, and attacked by dogs. But they still pressed on."

"Yes, they did," Aunt Rose murmured.

"I thought they must be made of something different than me because I've always been so afraid of everything and everybody. Then one night I watched a clip of a reporter talking to Dr. Martin Luther King, Jr. The reporter asked Dr. King why he marched." Mildred shook her head at the memory of it. "Dr. King said that he didn't like to march. He said that he was tired and he was afraid. But he said that he marched on because he was a man and a child of God.

"When I heard him say that, it made him seem so much more human to me. I felt right then that I understood. I'm still afraid, Mr. Matthews. I'm afraid that someone will try to attack Raymond Williams. I'm afraid that someone will try to hurt my aunt because she doesn't care where she is—she just starts telling people about Raymond Williams. I'm afraid that when I go to work wearing this button that somebody will try to start something. But then I look at Raymond Williams and I feel so proud that he's trying to reach out to all of the people.

"I've seen him going into all-white neighborhoods and getting booed and jeered — but he just keeps smiling. Then I think about what Dr. King said to that reporter, and I just keep on trying and pray that everything will work out." Mildred sat down.

The dining room was quiet as everyone digested Mildred's speech.

"If I don't do nothing else in this world, I can go to my Maker knowing that I raised this child right," Aunt Rose sniffed, addressing no one in particular.

Joseph Matthews stared at Mildred thoughtfully. "What do you say, son?" he said, addressing his son-in-law Curtis.

"I don't know, Dad," Curtis shook his head. "I really don't think he can win. Half of these folks around here ain't even registered." He looked at Aunt Rose. "The man talks a good game, but how do we know that once he gets in office that he's not going to turn his back on us like everybody else?"

"He's been in Congress for ten years," Aunt Rose offered. "He didn't turn his back on us then. Look at his record and see for yourself." She pulled a few pamphlets out of her purse and laid them on the table.

Curtis picked them up. "Well, like I said, I don't think he'll win, but if the family agrees, I'll throw my vote behind him."

"Daughter?" Joseph Matthews looked at Ellen fondly. "What do you say?"

Ellen looked at Aunt Rose and Mildred. "We vote as a family," she explained. "We all sit down and talk about each candidate and we vote together. But we've never really got involved in anybody's campaign."

She turned to her father, "Daddy, I think that we ought to go out and help Raymond Williams." She reached over and covered her father's hand with her own. "Daddy, I know that you're scared. But I think that even though we're afraid, we should try like Mildred said. I think that you deserve to see a man like Raymond Williams in the mayor's seat in your lifetime, and I want to tell my children that you, me, and our family helped make it happen."

Joseph smiled at his daughter, and his eyes began to cloud over. "All right, daughter," he whispered. "All right."

Mildred watched the lined and weary face of Joseph Matthews glow with pride as he smiled at his daughter, and she turned and looked at her aunt, who was watching and dabbing her eyes with her handkerchief.

Curtis turned to Aunt Rose, "Can we cut that caramel cake now?"

"Goodness, yes!" Aunt Rose got up and picked up the cake from the buffet and set it in the middle of the dining room table. With a flourish, she lifted the cover of the cake pan.

"Now *that's* a cake," Curtis said, looking at Ellen Matthews meaningfully.

Mildred's six-layer caramel cake covered with pecans held the Matthews' attention.

"Who baked it?" Joseph Matthews asked as he pinched off a bit of caramel.

"My baby is the baker in our family," Aunt Rose said proudly.

"It looks delicious," Joseph stated. "I'm gonna get the kids."

Ellen disappeared into the kitchen to get forks and saucers.

"Well," Curtis looked at Aunt Rose, "what do we do now?"

"You need to go to the Center for Black Awareness on Sacramento." Aunt Rose advised. "Ask for O'Kanta and he'll tell you what to do."

Curtis picked a pecan off the cake. "O'Kanta," he repeated. "Got it."

Joseph Matthews came into the dining room with his three grand-children.

"Ooh, look at that cake," Curtis Jr. said.

"Cake," his younger brother echoed.

Joseph Matthews held the baby, Shawn, in his arms.

Ellen brought in the plates and silverware and passed them around.

"Who's gonna cut it?" Curtis Jr. asked. "Whose birthday is it?"

Mildred picked up the knife and handed it to Joseph. She held out her arms and took Shawn.

Joseph sliced the cake and placed it on each of the saucers. He passed the saucers around and picked his up.

"Mmmmmh," Aunt Rose bit into her slice of cake and dabbed her eyes. "I could really listen to some blues now.

* * *

"Ooooh. Thank you, Jesus," Aunt Rose plopped down heavily on her four-poster bed. "This body has had too much excitement for one night."

Mildred stood in the doorway of her aunt's bedroom and shook her head. "If you're exhausted, it's your own fault. Nobody told you to try to out dance and out sing everybody there."

Aunt Rose leaned back on her faded patchwork quilt and smiled up at her niece. "I had a lot to celebrate tonight. The Matthews are going to help us get Raymond Williams elected, and my baby came into her own tonight!"

Mildred walked over to her aunt's bed and flopped down. "I hope you aren't going to start that again." She turned over on her stomach and began to trace the patterns from some of her favorite discarded outfits that made up the multi-colored quilt.

Aunt Rose reached over and touched a faded blue patch. "Do you remember this one?"

Mildred glanced over at the square. "That's the blue dress that I wore to get my award in spelling in Mr. Fischer's class."

"What grade was that?" Aunt Rose looked at Mildred intently.

"You know it was the fifth," Mildred answered quietly. "That auditorium was surely packed that day." Aunt Rose leaned back and closed her eyes. "All of the children were dressed up in their Sunday best and the parents were all there just proud to bustin'. I bought you that blue dress with the big flounce on the bottom and you had two blue ribbons in your hair to match." Aunt Rose tugged on one of her niece's cornrows. "You were the prettiest girl there."

Mildred grunted.

"Mr. Fischer called each child's name and they came across the stage to get their award for the year. Oooh, the cameras were flashing so much I thought I was at the Academy Awards."

Mildred raised her arm to get up but was held fast by her aunt.

"Then Mr. Fischer said the next award goes to Mildred Johnson for spelling, and everybody waited for Mildred Johnson to walk across the stage. Do you remember?"

"How can I forget?" Mildred said. "Judy Dillon was sitting next to me and she kept saying, 'Go 'head Mildred. Go get your award.' The entire class turned around and stared at me like I was some sort of freak."

"Of course, I knew that there was no way that you were going up on that stage in front of all of those people," Aunt Rose said matter-of-factly.

"Of course," Mildred imitated.

"Mr. Fischer stood in front of all of those people and said that since Miss Johnson obviously doesn't want her award that she would..."

"... forfeit it." Mildred finished. "Why are you dredging all of this up?"

"I thought my heart would break in two as I watched you cry day in and day out over that award. I was so angry at your teacher that I went down to see him to give him a piece of my mind."

Mildred looked up in surprise. "You never told me that."

"I asked him how could he humiliate a child like that in front of all of those people and deny her something that she had worked hard for all year."

Mildred looked at her aunt curiously. "What did he say?"

Aunt Rose smiled lovingly at her. "He said that he wasn't trying to humiliate you. Said that winning that award took almost no effort on your part. You've always had a natural gift for spelling."

Mildred smiled and continued to trace patterns on the quilt.

"But he said that walking across that stage would take courage and effort on your part. He wanted to see if he could shame you into walking across the stage to get your award. He said that he felt that you would appreciate your award all the more if you really had to earn it."

"Well, that didn't stop him from giving it to someone else," Mildred said.

Aunt Rose got up from her bed and walked over to her chest of drawers. "Baby, I kind of agreed with Mr. Fischer. I knew that it would take something more powerful than an award to get you to walk across that stage that day. When Joseph Matthews called on you to give him a reason to support Raymond Williams, I saw that same look in your eyes that was there sevnteen years ago. Seventeen years ago you were too afraid to walk across the stage to accept your award for spelling." Aunt Rose pointed her finger at Mildred. "Tonight it took you two seconds to get out of your chair and stand up and preach!"

Mildred grinned. "Did I smoke?" She stretched out on Aunt Rose's bed. "Too bad Mr. Fischer wasn't there to see me."

Aunt Rose grinned and opened her drawer. She pulled out a brown picture frame. She looked at it proudly and rubbed it on her dress.

"Millie?" She turned to Mildred.

Mildred lay on the bed with her eyes closed. "Hmmm?"

Aunt Rose walked over to the bed and laid the picture frame on Mildred's stomach.

Mildred opened her eyes and picked up the picture. "What's this?"

Aunt Rose folded her arms across her chest and rocked back and forth on her heels. "You tell me."

Mildred sat up and stared at her spelling award carefully preserved in the brown picture frame. The white, rectangular sheet of paper was cut slightly off center so that it slid to one side inside of the frame. The stick lettering was smudged in places, making the "L" and "D" in Mildred look like one letter. Mildred touched the picture frame gently. It was beautiful. "It's my award," she whispered. "My award for spelling." She turned to her aunt. "Where did you get this?"

Aunt Rose grinned. "I told you that I went up to your school to give Mr. Fischer a piece of my mind."

"And he just gave you this?"

Aunt Rose sat on the bed and put her arms around her niece. "I told you that Mr. Fischer never wanted to take this away from you. He just wanted you to earn it."

"Why didn't he tell me any of that?" Mildred demanded.

"He said that he tried to talk to you several times in the hall but *somebody*," she looked at Mildred pointedly, "refused to speak to him."

"He didn't try too hard," Mildred said defensively.

Aunt Rose shrugged. "Well he knew that I had it."

Mildred turned to her aunt accusingly. "You mean you've had this for all these years and never gave it to me? How could you do that to me?"

Aunt Rose took the award from Mildred. "It was hard, baby. I watched you cry for it over and over for weeks. Then I watched you walk around here and act as if it didn't mean anything to you. Finally, I watched you go even deeper into yourself, and then I thought about what Mr. Fischer said and I understood." She lifted her niece's chin. "I kept it because I knew that when you came into your own that you would need it."

Mildred stared at her aunt for a long while. She slowly picked up the plaque and began to read:

"Delano Grammar School wishes to recognize Mildred Johnson for all around excellence such as self respect, respect for others, initiative, creativity, imagination, responsibility, growth in personhood, grasp of course material, and courage to question in the discipline of Spelling."

Mildred wiped her eyes and giggled. "Well, thank you very much, Aunt Rose," she said softly. "You know I couldn't have done it without you." She hugged her aunt fiercely.

"Whew, this had been some night." She held out her award and grinned. "Where should I put it?"

"On your dresser? The mantel?" Aunt Rose suggested.

"I don't know," Mildred stared at the award. "It's got to be a special place."

"Well, let me know tomorrow," Aunt Rose yawned. "I'm laying this body to rest."

"Good night," Mildred called over her shoulder as she carried the award to her room.

* * *

Aunt Rose lay awake long after Mildred left with her award. Right about now, Mildred would be writing a poem or a story about it. She chided herself again for letting Mildred know that she regularly went through the wastepaper basket in her bedroom. She had not found one poem since.

She sighed heavily. It looked like she'd just have to go back to reading the journal that Mildred kept in the shoebox in her chest.

When did Millie get so secretive? That's what she'd like to know. Seemed as if it was just yesterday when all she wanted to do was pour out all of her secrets to her Aunt Rose.

Rose yawned and looked at the clock again. Time truly flies, she thought as she closed her eyes.

Ten

CRAYTON, TENNESSEE, 1957

"ROSE JOHNSON! WHAT DO YOU MEAN you ain't goin' down to the courthouse with us?" Mildred Walker put her hands on her hips. "Don't you want the right to vote?"

Rose picked up a bowl of snap beans and carried it to the kitchen table.

"What I want, Miss Walker, is to marry Caleb Hawkins and have a nice house to raise our children in. Hitching Caleb takes up all my energy. I ain't got time for nothin' else."

Mildred dug into the bowl and took a handful of beans. "Well, at least come to the meetin' tonight." She popped a bean in her mouth. "I hear tell Caleb's gon' be there."

Rose looked up. "Who say he gon' be there?"

Mildred sauntered over to the mantel and pretended that she didn't hear Rose.

Rose stood up. "I say, who say Caleb's gon' be there, Mildred?"

Mildred began to pat her hair. Rose caught her looking at her out of the corner of her eye.

Rose carefully set the bowl on the kitchen table and wiped her hands on her apron.

Mildred inched toward the back door.

Rose flew after Mildred and chased her out of the brown frame house and into the backyard. She caught hold of Mildred's dress and Mildred tumbled to the ground.

Rose sat on her. "I said, who say Caleb's gon' be there?" Rose began to rock back and forth.

Mildred started laughing. "You gon' snap your purse at him, Rose?"

Rose reached down and began to tickle her.

"Okay, okay," Mildred gasped. "He tol' L.C. that he was comin'. Now get offa me!"

Rose got up and turned to help her best friend to her feet. "What time is the meetin'?"

Mildred began to brush the dirt off of her dress. "If this dirt don't come out, I'm gonna kick yo' butt!" She turned around. "Is the back dirty?"

"Yeah," Rose answered.

Mildred giggled. "I'm gonna tell L.C. that I was rollin' around in the dirt tryin' to fend off a hungry man."

Rose laughed. "You better tell him that the man just escaped from the chain gang and he was starving!"

Mildred laughed. "At least I got L.C. where I want him." She put her hands on her hips. "You comin'?"

Rose turned to go back into the house. "You ain't tol' me what time the meetin' is."

Mildred began to walk down the road. "Me and L.C.'ll come and get you at six o'clock."

Rose opened the back door. "Caleb better be there!" she hollered.

* * *

Rose sat on the hard, wooden bench of Sweet Water Baptist Church and tried to catch Caleb's eye.

Mildred jabbed her in the side. "Listen, here comes L.C."

Rose rolled her eyes.

L.C. Walker walked up and stood behind the pulpit. He looked uncomfortable as he stood in his faded overalls and faced the people. "We just plain folk y'all," he said.

"Yes, we are," a woman in the back agreed.

"Y'all know that I sharecrop for Mr. Pendleton, and my wife Mildred here takes in washin'." He paused and looked up. "But I ain't dirt! And I'm gettin' tired of people treatin' me like I'm dirt! It's time for us to take a stand y'all. How long we gon' let them scare us?"

"Not long," Caleb answered.

Rose puffed herself up.

"We got to answer this," L.C. held his right fist up, "with this;" he held up his left fist. "We can't be scared no more. If some of us get killed fightin', the ones who left standin' got to fight on!"

A few men clapped in the back.

"Why we gotta fight?" Rose turned to Mildred. "I don't want Caleb gettin' hurt."

"Hush up and listen," Mildred said.

"Now a few of us men are goin' down to the courthouse and register to vote just like they doin' next Sat'day. How many of y'all are comin' with us?"

Caleb stood up. "I'm comin'," he said.

"Git your purse ready," Mildred whispered.

"I got it ready, but he won't look this way," Rose whispered back.

"Well cough, sneeze, fart or somethin'," Mildred whispered.

Rose started laughing.

"Do you think this here is funny?" Caleb looked at Rose. "We are talkin' about our lives here and you're laughing? You see," he turned to the crowd, "it's silly women like this that gon' keep us back."

Rose turned a tearful face to Mildred, who stood up.

"Just you hold on a minute, Caleb Hawkins. This is my friend you talkin' about. For yo' information, I was sayin' that the women should go down to the courthouse with the men, and Rose started laughing."

"Well, she should have laughed," L.C. put in. "The women is stayin' right here. This here's a man's thang."

"I wanna vote," Mildred hollered.

Rose pulled her into her seat.

Mildred turned to Rose. "Ain't this some shit? I think we should walk out right now."

"Are you crazy?" Rose turned to look at Caleb. "Do you think I should snap my purse?"

"Is that all you can think of?" Mildred jabbed Rose in her side. "I'm gonna go up to that courthouse and march with my L.C.! I'm gonna help him vote." Mildred declared.

"What if they try to kill him?"

Rose saw Caleb frowning at them. She opened her purse carefully.

Caleb gave her a disgusted look.

"I'm gonna fight with my husband," Mildred vowed. "Come on, the meetin's over."

"L.C. said he don't want you there," Rose reminded her as they got up and filed out.

"What he don't know can't hurt him," Mildred retorted.

"Do you think Caleb's still mad at me?" Rose asked as they piled in the back of L.C.'s pickup truck.

Mildred turned and saw Caleb talking to a few men congregating in front of the church. "That Caleb is a bit stuck on hisself if you ask me."

"He is not!" Rose denied vehemently. "He just needs a wife to soften him up a bit."

Mildred grunted.

"What am I gon' do, Mildred?" Rose turned to her friend. "Remember it was me what introduced you to L.C."

"I ain't forgot; I ain't forgot," Mildred muttered. "Hold on a minute and let me think." She turned to L.C.

"Honey, why don't you ask Caleb if he needs a lift home?" Mildred asked L.C. in a sweet voice.

L.C. gave Mildred a dry look.

"Is that what y'all back there whispering on?" He turned to Rose. "Why don't you stop that purse-snapping foolishness and go over there and talk to him?"

"Ain't nobody asked you for your opinions, L.C.," Mildred retorted. "You just ask Caleb if he needs a ride home."

L.C. started up the truck and muttered under his breath. "Hey Caleb," he hollered.

Caleb Hawkins turned around and tipped his hat to L.C.

"Need a lift?" L.C. asked.

Caleb looked into the hopeful eyes of Rose and the suspicious eyes of Mildred and shook his head. "I got a heap of thinkin' to do tonight, L.C. I reckon it's best that I do it alone." He tipped his hat to Rose and Mildred and continued walking down the road.

Rose sighed and turned to watch Caleb as the pickup pulled off.

Eleven

ROSE JOHNSON SAT ON THE BACK PORCH STEPS in the Crayton noonday sun and contemplated her future. She let her chin rest in her hands and made circles in the red clay dirt with her toes. She was thirty-two years old and she was not married. She worked as a day cook at Baker's Hot Foods and she was not married. She lived alone in a house that she rented from the owners of the restaurant and she was not married. She looked up and shielded her eyes as the slim figure of Mildred Walker came into view. Mildred plopped down on the porch beside Rose.

"What's the matter with you? Your face is 'bout to touch the ground."

Rose shrugged her shoulders. "Where's Rosemary?" she asked.

"I got L.C. to watch her for me for a minute. I came down here 'specially to tell you somethin,' but you look like you don't want to hear no news." She looked sideways at Rose.

Rose looked at Mildred and frowned. "The last news you brought me got me into hot water with my Caleb."

Mildred stood up and stretched. "This here news might be the news that can fix your troubles."

Rose looked up with suspicion. "Like what?"

"Well," Mildred began to smooth her dress. She turned around in front of Rose. "Do you like this dress?"

Rose grinned. "I think I'd like it better with some dirt stains on it."

"Okay, okay," Mildred sat down beside Rose. "You know we all gonna march up to the courthouse next Saturday?"

"I'm not," Mildred stated. "And L.C. says you're not, either."

Mildred flipped her hand in the air, dismissing her husband's objections. "Well, I was thinkin'...this here is going to be a mighty big thing here in Crayton. So I said to myself, 'Mildred why not have a big party the night before the march to celebrate?'" She pinched Rose. "You can come and wear your red and white dress and just walk in front of Caleb." Mildred stood up and demonstrated the type of strut that Rose should do. "Then we'll have a Sadie Hawkins dance and you can go up to him and ask him to dance."

Rose stood up. "What if someone beats me to him?"

Mildred flipped her hand in the air. "I'll take care of all that. Don't you worry none."

Rose began to get excited. "Who all you gon' invite, Millie?" she asked.

"Just the ones who gonna march and they women." Mildred jumped up. "I got to go. I told L.C. that I'd be right back. He's gonna have a fit." She began to hurry down the road and turned back suddenly. "You gonna help me cook?"

Rose made a face. "What you gon' have?"

"Catfish and spaghetti. L.C. said he's gonna get some beer."

"Mildred!" L.C.'s voice carried across the yard.

"Lord, I gotta haul ass before that man hurts my child!"

Rose laughed and hugged herself, wondering how things could be so bad one minute and so wonderful the next. She hurried into the house to press her red and white dress.

* * *

Mildred and L.C.'s house was truly festive. Rose and Mildred decorated the tiny front room with red and white streamers. When they ran out of streamers, they used old Christmas decorations. A bright orange pumpkin hung from the ceiling.

Mildred had on an emerald-green straight dress with padded shoulders. The dress had a deep V in the back that L.C. said she'd better keep covered. Mildred laughed and told L.C. that she was wearing it just for him. L.C. snorted in his way and kept his eyes on Mildred's back.

Rose's red and white checked dress was straight and tight with a slit on the side.

She and Mildred spent an hour in the bathroom before they decided on Ruby Red lipstick for Rose and Tango Tangerine for Mildred.

L.C. shook his head.

The music was screaming and every square inch of space in the front room was taken up by a hip, elbow, or bust. The kitchen was also packed with people waiting for the catfish to come out of the skillet.

Rose tried to catch Caleb's eye several times but he was always surrounded by someone, specifically, Lucille Jenkins. She quietly slipped into Mildred and L.C.'s bedroom to think about what her next move should be.

Rose bent over the makeshift crib in the bedroom and picked up five-month-old Rosemary. "Hey, sugar," she crooned. "Whose fat baby are you?" She buried her nose in the creases of Rosemary's neck.

The bedroom door opened a crack and Mildred peeked inside. "What are you doing in here?" she whispered. "The party is going on outside."

Rose put Rosemary back in her crib. "Not for me it ain't," she whispered.

Mildred came inside and closed the door.

"What do you mean, but for you it ain't? I saw Caleb standing out there."

"Did you see him dancing record after record with Lucille Jenkins? Her husband ain't been buried six months yet, and she's out there waggin' her tail at Caleb!"

Mildred walked over to Rose. "And what are you doing? How come you ain't waggin' yours at him?"

Rose put her hand over her mouth to smother a giggle.

Mildred put her hands on her hips. "At the first sign of trouble, you go runnin.' You got to show him that you interested."

"I'm trying," Rose moaned. "I slept on ten wave clamps to get Marcel waves, didn't I? I put on red lipstick and sprayed myself with that Interlude perfume you gave me, didn't I?" She shook her hand. "Face it, Mildred, I have. He just ain't interested in me. And I'm going to die an old maid!"

Mildred put her arm around Rose. "Don't you talk like that, Honey. You just got to be more sure of yourself. Every man don't like a big butt like Lucille got. You got to let Caleb know that you interested in him. Go up and talk to him tonight."

Rose shook her head. "I just can't, Millie," she sniffed. "Every time I get close to him I forget how to talk. I just stand there staring at him—deaf and dumb."

Mildred shook her head. "Snap out of it. I don't want to hear this crazy kind of talk. Look! How would you like your namesake to hear you talkin' like this?" She reached into her bodice and pulled out a tissue. "Here. Wipe your face and come out to the party."

Mildred peeked at her daughter and blew her a kiss. "I'm gonna wink at you before I announce the Sadie Hawkins dance. You git yo' butt next to Caleb and grab him." Mildred hurried out.

Rose walked over to the crib and smiled at Rosemary. "What do you think about all this, Miss Rosemary?" She pinched Rosemary's cheek and turned to leave.

The bedroom door opened abruptly.

"Mildred, I'll be out in a minute." Rose gave the baby a final kiss and turned around to the serious face of Caleb Hawkins.

"What are you doing in here?" she whispered.

Caleb folded his arms across his chest. "I was told that someone in here wanted to talk to me." He looked at Rose critically. "Is this more of you and Mildred's foolishness?"

Rose began to trace patterns on the edge of Rosemary's crib.

Caleb snorted and turned to leave.

"Wait a minute," Rose whispered.

Caleb turned around but kept his hand on the doorknob.

Rose looked at Rosemary and took a deep breath. "I was wondering if you wanted to dance with me," she whispered.

"What?" Caleb frowned.

Rose faced him. "Mildred's going to play a Sadie Hawkins record. That's when the women ask the men to dance. I was wondering if I picked you, if you would dance with me."

"Is that why Mildred asked me to come in here?" Caleb demanded. "Don't you know that I got too much on my mind to worry with this foolishness? I'm going to give that Mildred a piece of my mind." He said as he opened the door.

"Hold on one minute!" Rose hollered. She walked over and closed the door. "Before you march out there and give my best friend a piece of your mind, let me give you a piece of mine! I know that you don't think much of me. You think that I'm just a silly good for nuthin' woman. Well, this silly woman cares more about you than any woman out there!" She jerked her thumb towards the door.

"I'm the one that worries if you're eatin' right up there in your house all by yourself. I'm the one who worries when I hear L.C. say that you're laid up with a cold! I'm the one who wants to do your washin', mendin', and cookin', I'm the one who wants to have your children," she whispered. "But I ain't never had the nerve to tell you all this. I told my best friend instead. So before you go to tell her off with your hard words, I want you to know that she was doing it for me. She knew that I'd just die if I asked you to dance and you turned me down in front of all of my friends." Rose threw her hands up in the air. "So don't bother giving her a piece of your mind. She and I won't be bothering you no more." She brushed past Caleb and walked out of the bedroom and into the crooning sounds of Billie Holiday.

"...I wanna pigfoot and a bottle of beer
Send me daddy, cos I don't care
I feel just like I wanna clown

Give the piano player a drink. Cause he brought me down.
He's got rhythm when he stomps his feet
He moves me right off to sleep
Check all your razors and your guns
I'm gonna be arrested when the wagon comes..."

Rose took a sip of beer and made a face. "Millie, What kind of beer is this?"

"The kind that gets you drunk," Mildred stated. "Now what else happened?"

Rose took another sip. "Nothing else happened. I told you after I said that to him, I walked out."

Mildred grunted. "Since you went that far, you mighta went ahead and planted one on him."

Rose giggled. "After that speech, if I'd tried to kiss him he probably would have hit me."

Mildred put down her cup. "Well, I'm going to play my Sadie Hawkins anyway. It won't hurt to show old L.C. that I still pick him over anybody else."

"What's all that shoutin' about in the kitchen?" Rose asked.

"Just colored folks with too much liquor." Mildred flipped her hand in the air. "A bunch of the men wanna go down to the courthouse tonight and bust a few windows."

Rose shook her head. "What for? Ain't they going tomorrow?"

"Yeah," Mildred retorted. "But they drunk with courage tonight. I'm going to put the record on. You gonna ask Caleb?"

"Not the time of day." Rose rolled her eyes.

Mildred disappeared into the crowd.

Rose went into the kitchen to get rid of her beer.

94

L.C. and Caleb were surrounded by about eight men.

"L.C., I'm a man," Lew Jones was saying. "I say let's go down there tonight and let them know that we are men!"

"Yes!" the men agreed.

"Hold on now, Lew," L.C. patted him on the back. "I know you're a man. But what's breaking a few windows gonna prove? Now we all decided to go down tomorrow and try to register."

"I ain't gonna try nothin'!" a man that Rose didn't recognize screamed. "Why the colored man always got to be the one tryin'? I don't see none of them crackers tryin' to do shit but kick our ass. Well, I'm gonna kick some ass tonight!"

He folded his arms across his chest. "I hear tell that Sharon Wood was paid a visit last Saturday night by two or three insurance men."

"What?" L.C. looked confused.

The man ignored L.C. and turned to Lew. "A few of yo'"— he pointed at L.C.— upright citizens paid her a visit at twelve o'clock at night!"

"What happened?" Caleb asked quietly.

Rose tried to picture Sharon. She remembered her as a tiny dark-skinned woman who always sang in church.

"They did things to her that a self-respectin' man wouldn't do to a dog," the man said.

"Where is she now?" L.C. asked.

"She went to stay with an aunt in St. Louis," the man answered. "She didn't have no husband or brother to look out for her. Well, I'm gonna kick some ass for her tonight!"

A few of the men murmured their consent.

Rose hurried out. She spotted Mildred talking to Silas, who was spinning records. She motioned to Mildred.

Mildred danced her way over to Rose with her eyes sparkling.

Rose grabbed her hand. "Millie, you better put that record on now. Them men are talking crazy in the kitchen. They wanna go down to the courthouse and start trouble!"

Mildred shrugged her shoulders. "L.C.'ll talk them out of it. Come

95

on, girl!" She squeezed Rose's arm. "Time for some sho nuff grindin' music," she whispered.

"Hey!" Mildred hollered. "Everybody! I want y'all's attention for one minute!" She looked toward the kitchen. "L.C.! Y'all come on out here for a minute!"

L.C. came into the front room still trying to appease a few of the men. Caleb was the last to enter. Rose began to busy herself with rearranging the red and white streamers.

"What's going on?" L.C. asked Mildred.

"I have an announcement to make," Mildred giggled. "This here record is a Sadie Hawkins dance. This dance is for the women to pick their partners." She pointed to Silas.

The soft strains of "I Only Have Eyes for You" began to fill the front room. "I just want everybody here to know that after these five years of marriage that I still choose you, baby." She blew L.C. a kiss.

"There you go, L.C.!" Silas hollered.

L.C. laughed and opened his arms. Mildred hugged him and whispered something in his ear.

Rose felt her eyes begin to well up as she watched Mildred and L.C. Slow dancing couples began to fill up the front room. Rose decided to hide out in Mildred's bedroom until the record was over.

She turned and walked into Caleb.

"Excuse me," she said and moved to walk around him.

Caleb reached out and caught her elbow. "I thought you wanted to dance," he said.

Rose stared at him intently. "So did I," she answered. "Excuse me, please," she tried to shake off his arm.

"Now hold on a minute," Caleb said gruffly.

Rose looked up.

"I ain't got no fancy speech for you," Caleb said matter-of-factly. "I guess I ain't used to nobody caring about whether I eat or not and such." Caleb looked uncomfortable. "I didn't mean to holler at you back there," he muttered.

Rose shrugged indifferently. "Forget it, Caleb," she whispered.

"Oh, and one other thing," Caleb stammered. He cleared his throat and looked past her. "I meant to tell you that that's a real pretty dress you got on."

Rose looked up in amazement. "Do you really like my dress, Caleb?"

"I just told you, didn't I?" Caleb answered gruffly.

Recognition dawned on Rose.

"Caleb?" Rose reached up and turned Caleb's face toward her. "Will you dance with me?" She put her arms around his neck without waiting for an answer.

Rose felt Caleb's solid arms clumsily surround her. As they stumbled through the song, she felt her love for Caleb deepen. She looked up at him and wondered if he could see it on her face.

"Don't be gettin' no fancy ideas," Caleb whispered in her ear. "We'll take this here thing one step at a time. Do you hear me?"

Rose buried her face in Caleb's neck and sighed happily.

"Uh, sorry to break this up folks," L.C. said.

Rose opened her eyes.

Caleb removed Rose's grip from his neck. "What is it?" he asked L.C.

"I need to speak to you in the kitchen." L.C. looked at the pout on Rose's face. "I'm real sorry, Rose." He smiled and winked at her. "I'll bring him right back."

With her hands on her hips, Rose watched L.C. and Caleb leave.

"Well, for somebody who said she wasn't going to ask a certain person to dance, *somebody* was sho nuff holding on to him!"

Rose turned to the teasing eyes of Mildred. "What's going on Millie?"

"I don't know," Mildred shrugged. "L.C. saw something or heard something and stopped dancing right in the middle of my song."

"Saw what?"

"I don't know, but I'm going to find out." Mildred headed for the kitchen.

Rose followed her hesitantly.

L.C. and Caleb were speaking in low tones as Mildred and Rose entered the kitchen.

"What's going on?" Mildred demanded.

L.C. looked up guiltily. "Nothing, baby. Go on back to the party. I'll be out in a minute."

Mildred put her hands on her hips. "I ain't going nowhere until you tell my why you stopped dancing with your wife in the middle of my song that I 'specially dedicated to you."

L.C. walked over to his wife. "Caleb and me have got to run over to the courthouse for a minute, sugar. Some of the guys are headed over there asking for trouble."

Mildred put her arms around L.C. "Why do you have to go down there? You tried to talk them out of it, didn't you?" She rested her head on L.C.'s shoulder. "I don't want you to be in the middle of all this, baby."

"I'm just going to bring the boys back before any trouble starts," L.C. promised. He kissed her on the forehead." I'll be back before you know it. You stay here with Rose and keep the party going until I get back. Okay?" L.C. searched Mildred's face.

"Okay, sugar," Mildred agreed sweetly.

"I mean it, Mildred. I want you to stay inside this house until I get back."

Mildred looked up innocently. "I said okay, honey. I'll stay right here."

L.C. glared at her threateningly. "If I catch sight of you down there Mildred, I'm gonna wear your tail out!"

"I'm stayin' here with Rose!" Mildred hollered.

"Okay." L.C. gave Mildred a kiss and motioned to Caleb.

"I'll meet you outside," Caleb said, looking at Rose.

Caleb turned to Mildred. "Will you give us a minute?"

Mildred grunted and left the room.

"Everything's gonna be all right, ain't it, Caleb?" Rose asked fearfully.

Caleb walked over to her and placed his hands on her shoulders. "This here ain't nothin' to worry about. We just gonna grab Lew and his friends before they get theyself hurt." He tweaked Rose's nose playfully. "Don't you be out there shaking your tail with everybody while I'm gone."

Rose shook her head fiercely.

Caleb laughed and awkwardly bent down.

"Caleb!" L.C. yelled.

"I'll be back," Caleb whispered and hurried out.

"I heard the back door slam. Is he gone?" Mildred peeked around the doorway.

"Yeah," Rose answered breathlessly.

"We'll give them a few minutes before I throw these folks out of my house," Mildred stated.

"You mean you're going to end the party?" Rose asked. "What for?"

"Snap out of it, girl!" Mildred shook Rose hard. I'm going down to that courthouse."

"Mildred Walker!" Rose whispered. "L.C. said—"

"I don't care what L.C. said," Mildred broke in. "Do you think I'm just gonna sit back and dance while my man is in trouble?"

"But L.C. said that there wasn't gonna be no trouble." Rose began to wring her hands.

"It's what he didn't say that I'm actin' on," Mildred said in a quiet voice. "Do you really think that Lew and that bunch are gonna be led back by the hand like children? These men have been shoved, kicked, and spit on one time too many. They ain't going down there to discuss the weather. They drunk and they want to hurt somebody!"

"But Mildred—" Rose began.

"I got to get these folks out of my house." Mildred hurried into the front room.

Rose could hear her calling for everyone's attention. She heard the groans and protests that followed Mildred's announcement. She leaned against the sink and began to dream about the life that awaited her as Mrs. Caleb Hawkins. She smiled and shook her head as she thought of the wrinkles in his shirt tonight. Once they got married, that would be one of the first things that she would take care of.

She wondered what his house looked like on the inside. One night when L.C. and Caleb were midnight fishin', she made Mildred walk up there with her. She had tried to peek through the windows, but everything was too dark. Maybe now Caleb would invite her over and show her the inside. Or maybe they could...

"You ready?"

Rose jumped at the sound of Mildred's voice.

"Ready for what?" she asked.

"What is the matter with you?" Mildred demanded. "What do you think I'm talkin' about? Dancin'? Are you ready to go down to the courthouse?"

"Mildred, L.C. said—" Rose began.

"I don't care what L.C. said," Mildred interrupted. "I said are you ready?"

"What about Caleb?" Rose whispered. "Do you think he'll get mad at me?"

"Do you want to see him mad or alive?" Mildred asked.

Rose's eyes opened wide. "What do you mean?" she demanded.

"I mean that if somethin' were to happen to L.C., I would want to be right there in the middle of it. I don't want to be at home waitin' to hear the news. I mean that I love him." She looked at Rose questioningly.

"I love Caleb," Rose said quietly. "But what can we do if something happens?"

Mildred raised her dress to show Rose the 38 that was strapped to her thigh.

"Mildred Walker!" Rose exclaimed.

"L.C. says that I'm a better shot than he is," Mildred said proudly. She looked at Rose. "Now what can we get for you?"

Rose backed away. "I can't shoot no gun, Mildred!"

"Don't we know it," Mildred said dryly as she walked around the kitchen.

"Here!" She picked up a butcher knife from the kitchen sink. "You put this in your purse."

"What am I supposed to do with this?" Rose struggled to fit the knife inside her purse.

"Hopefully, nothing," Mildred muttered. "Come on, we've got to get moving." She opened the back door and motioned to Rose.

"What about Rosemary? Who's going to watch her?" Rose asked.

"I left Lucille Jenkins watching her," Mildred said.

"Lucille Jenkins!" Rose exclaimed. "How can you trust that woman with Rosemary?"

"I told her that Caleb told me to tell her to wait for him." Mildred grinned and slapped Rose on the back and opened the kitchen door. "Honey, she planted herself in that bedroom and she ain't moving!"

Rose giggled and hurried to catch up with Mildred's long strides.

Twelve

"COULDN'T YOU HAVE FOUND a better shortcut than this?" Rose looked down at her mud-stained white pumps. "I don't think I'll ever get the dirt off of these shoes."

Mildred wiped her forehead with the back of her hand. "That's why it's called a shortcut." She peered into the darkness on her right. "I think we'll be right behind the library in the next mile or so."

"I'm not going to walk a mile in these shoes," Rose groaned. "They'll be ruined for sure. Hold on a minute." She reached down and took off her shoes.

"Good idea," Mildred agreed. "I'm gonna take these stockings off, too."

Rose laughed and kicked the dirt as she walked. "I'd sure hate for my Caleb to see me looking like this."

"That Caleb sure is a sly one," Mildred remarked. "Just imagine, a big rusty man like that—shy!" She shook her head.

"Isn't it wonderful?" Rose said dreamily. "Do you think he's gonna ask me to marry him, Mildred?" Rose looked at her friend anxiously.

"Of course he is," Mildred said with confidence. "What else can he do?"

"He's gonna be real mad though, seeing me here tonight." Rose shook her head sadly. "We are doing the right thing, ain't we Mildred?"

"I've tol' you over and over Rose. When you see your man headin' in the wrong direction, you got to make a move to put 'em on the right track."

"Right," Rose agreed somewhat absently as she smoothed her dress. "Mildred, how long do you think we should wait before we get married?"

"That depends." Mildred reached up and plucked a leaf off of a sycamore tree and twirled it.

"Depends on what?"

"On how long you can wait." Mildred grinned sideways at Rose. "I say the sooner the better!"

Rose began to laugh. "Who all should I invite, Mildred?" She jumped nimbly over a branch. "I don't have any kin down here. I got one aunt in Chicago, what lives on Adams, but by the time I find her address, Rosemary'll be grown."

"Why don't you just have me and L.C. to stand up for y'all, and then have a big party afterwards?" Mildred suggested.

Rose nodded her head in agreement. "I think I can get Mrs. Brooks to help me make a dress and," she looked sideways at Mildred, "some underthings."

"Don't waste too much time on them *underthings*," Mildred advised. "They won't be with you for long!"

Rose and Mildred stopped walking to laugh.

"Stop!" Mildred gasped as she put her hand to her side. "I've got a stitch in my side!"

Rose wiped her eyes and shook her head.

"Hold on a minute," Mildred pointed to her left. "There's the library up yonder."

Rose strained her eyes to make out the building. "I don't see anything," she whispered.

"What are you whispering for?" Mildred nudged her from behind. "Let's go up to the courthouse."

The two of them slowly entered the main street. The library, the general store, and post office appeared grotesque in the twilight. The street was deserted. Mildred and Rose crept against the edges of the buildings toward the courthouse.

Rose felt the heaviness of the butcher knife shift inside her pocketbook. She felt the need to explain to somebody, anybody, that bringing the knife was not her idea.

"We gonna have to cross the street to get to the courthouse," Mildred informed her.

"I can see it from here," Rose said.

"Don't be such a scaredy cat," Mildred grabbed Rose's hand. "We got to see if L.C. and Caleb is here."

Mildred headed purposely across the empty street, looking neither to the left nor right. Rose was jerked along beside her. When they reached the courthouse, they both stopped and stared. Crayton, Tennessee's courthouse, built in 1922, was devastated. Every window appeared to be broken. The jagged panes of glass that were left made monstrous shapes that seemed to mock Rose. The U.S. flag fluttered feebly atop the building's roof.

"Lord, have mercy," whispered Rose.

"Lew and his gang been here all right," Mildred said matter-of-factly. "I wonder if L.C. and Caleb caught up to them."

Rose, unable to pull her eyes away from the courthouse, shook her head.

"I hope to God they didn't do nothing else." Mildred stepped over a piece of glass on the ground and knelt down to put on her shoes. She looked up at Rose. "Do you wanna go inside and see if they did anything else?"

Rose clutched her pocketbook in one hand and her shoes in the other. She shook her head dumbly.

"I wonder where L.C. is," Mildred muttered.

A siren pierced the silence, its pitch sharpening as it drew closer.

"We better hide in here," Mildred whispered. She ran up the courthouse steps and tried the door. Opening it, she disappeared inside.

Rose, frozen in fear, continued to stand in front of the court-house with her shoes in one hand and her pocketbook in the other.

Mildred flung open the courthouse door and jumped down the steps. She grabbed Rose and dragged her up the steps and into the building.

The lobby floor of the courthouse was covered with broken glass and wood. Benches, chairs, and bookcases were overturned, some lying in broken pieces. Books were strewn about with their covers torn. Plants were upside down, ashtrays and trashcans were overturned, and debris covered the floor.

Mildred and Rose stood in the shadows inside the darkened building and peeked through one of the broken windows.

The familiar black and red car of the county sheriff pulled into view. Rose looked at the black and red stripes on the side of the car that immediately demanded respect or terror—depending on what color you were.

Sheriff Bob Tucker and his nephew Deputy Bill Tucker stepped out and leaned against the car.

Sheriff Tucker was known in the colored community as Stick Face.

Sheriff Tucker's nephew was a thin young man with a chalky white complexion who suffered miserably from eczema.

Rose crouched in front of the broken windows in the lobby of the courthouse. She couldn't stop shaking. It was surely only a matter of time before Sheriff Tucker came in to get her.

"You better put your shoes on, Rose," Mildred whispered. "With all this glass you're liable to cut yourself for sure." Mildred kicked away glass and wreckage to make a path toward the window.

"Mildred, I'm scared," Rose began to rock from side to side. "I'm scared; I'm scared—"

"Will you be quiet!" Mildred hissed. "I'm trying to hear what they're sayin'."

"I want to go home," Rose moaned.

"Just listen to you," Mildred pointed her finger at Rose. "A few minutes ago you loved Caleb and wanted to protect him. Now at the first sign of trouble you ready to go home. What would Caleb say if he heard you talkin' like that?"

Rose sniffed.

"He'd say she's got a hell of a lot more sense than you," L.C.'s baritone voice rose up out of nowhere.

Mildred jerked around. "L.C.?" Her eyes and body strained toward the area that the voice came from.

Rose dropped her purse. "It's a haint," she whispered.

L.C.'s dark frame seemed to come to life from the overturned trashcans, bookcase, books, and chairs.

Rose dropped her shoes.

"Ssh," L.C. put his finger to his lips. "Git away from the window."

Rose backed away. She ignored the wreckage that lay in her path. She kept moving until her back hit the wall. Her eyes stayed fixed on L.C.

Mildred put her hands over her mouth, squealed and leaped over the overturned chair, throwing herself into her husband's arms.

"Why can't you ever listen to what I say?" L.C. demanded. "Didn't I tell you to stay at home?"

Mildred began to cover his face with kisses.

"Do you want to git yo'self killed?" L.C. started to shake Mildred and then held her close.

"Caleb?" Rose whispered.

L.C. and Mildred continued to hug.

"Caleb?" she repeated.

"I'm here." Caleb emerged from behind a partially opened door that had been kicked in.

"Caleb, you're in the wrong washroom," Rose said simply.

The "'Whites Only'" sign above the men's restroom hung loosely by a single nail.

Silently Caleb made his way towards Rose.

Rose looked at the expression on Caleb's face and tried to back further away into the wall.

Caleb placed both hands on her shoulders. "Don't ever do anything like this again."

Rose shook her head. "Never," she whispered as tears fell.
"All right, all right." Caleb put his arms around her and tenderly patted her shoulder. "Don't cry."

"What happened?" Mildred broke in. "Did Lew and them do all this?"

L.C. nodded. "He got a few, others to join him. When we got here they had just about finished."

"Where are they now?" Rose asked.

"We convinced them to go back to Sweet Water," Caleb answered. "We gonna have a special meetin' tonight."

"Tonight?" Mildred asked.

"Yeah," L.C. answered. "Lew got a lot of people to help him do this." He waved his hand around the lobby. "Seems like it's more folks that follow his way of thinkin' than mine. We need to get together and talk. See if we can come up with one plan that everybody can agree on that's gonna help us git the vote."

"But why tonight?" Rose asked.

"Cause we figured that everybody would still be at the party." L.C. looked at Mildred. "I suppose you tol' them all to go home."

Mildred nodded.

"Well, knowin' Lew, he'll round up a bunch of folks on his own," L.C. said.

"Can you tell what they sayin'," Caleb asked.

L.C. slowly approached the window.

"Naw, but it looks like they're gettin' ready to leave."

"What if they come in here?" Rose put her arms around Caleb.

"They've already been in here." L.C. pulled Mildred away from the window.

"While you and Caleb were here?" Mildred asked.

L.C. nodded.

"They didn't see you?" Mildred grabbed L.C.'s arm. "What would y'all have done if they found you?"

"All they did was look around," L.C. said. "They wasn't gonna get they hands dirty liftin' and movin' stuff."

"They're leaving now," Caleb said.

"Let's get a move on," L.C. said.

Rose reached down to put on her shoes.

Caleb picked up her purse. "Why is this so heavy?" he asked.

Rose took her purse from him and hurried past.

L.C. and Caleb waited until the echoes of the siren were no longer audible before leading Mildred and Rose out into the night.

Walking a few feet behind Mildred and L.C., Rose and Caleb were silent. Rose could hear Mildred's voice and L.C.'s laughter in the darkness. She wondered if Caleb was still angry with her. Maybe he'd changed his mind about the two of them.

"Not many women would leave a party to come trackin' clear across town to make sure they men is okay," Caleb suddenly commented.

Rose didn't dare answer.

"It was a dumb thing to do," he continued, "but I guess your heart was in the right place."

Rose could feel herself glow.

Caleb cleared his throat. "When I was in that washroom, I heard Mildred say that you said that you loved me. I knew right then that what I cared about more than anything was gettin' out of there and bein' with you."

Caleb stopped walking and took both of Rose's hands. "I wanted to be with someone who cared enough to come after me with a butcher knife in her purse."

Rose concentrated on the toes of her shoes.

"Rosemary."

Rose looked up at this rare, full pronunciation of her name.

"I want to be part of a family," Caleb said softly. "Do you... I mean, would you..." he stammered.

"I love you, Caleb Hawkins," Rose said softly.

Caleb opened his arms.

Rose entered.

"Would y'all hurry up!" Mildred hollered.

"We'll talk later," Caleb whispered.

Rose nodded and hugged him tighter.

* * *

Sweet Water Baptist Church appeared as a welcoming haven to Rose. She and Caleb entered the church still holding hands.

Mildred, L.C., Lew Jones, and several others were already inside.

"Where is everybody?" Lew demanded.

"They left the party," L.C. answered.

"That's all right," Lew boasted. "I told enough folks on the way." He walked up to the pulpit.

"Just what did you tell everybody?" Caleb asked. "Did you tell them to meet us here for the meetin'?"

"Hell, no!" Lew shouted. He stood behind the pulpit and looked out at those gathered. "I tol' em that we tore up that courthouse. The same courthouse that we can't get a fair trial in and that we can't vote in!"

Several of his friends clapped.

"And I tol' them that we was meetin' here tonight to decide on what we was gonna tear down next!" He pounded the pulpit with his fist.

"You tol' them what!" L.C. shouted.

"Are you crazy?" Caleb asked.

Lew smiled. "You see, L.C., that's the big difference between you and me. I'm a man of action—" he began.

"You're a fool!" L.C. shouted. "Don't you know that one of them folks you tol' is gonna want to make points with Sheriff Tucker and tell 'em what you said?"

Lew looked confused.

L.C. went up to the pulpit and shoved Lew aside. "You tol' 'em what you did, and that we're meetin' here tonight. It's only a matter of time before they come here!" L.C. began to shake Lew. "You drunk fool!" he shouted.

Caleb grabbed Rose. "I want you to git out of here," he said.

"What?" Rose tore her eyes away from L.C. and Lew. "What?" she asked.

"I want you to get out of here now." Caleb began to push her toward the door.

"Wait a minute!" Rose screamed. "Do you think Sheriff Tucker is comin'?"

"I don't know, but I want you out." Caleb walked Rose out of the church.

"Let me get Mildred," Rose said.

"*I'll* get Mildred," Caleb answered. "Start running now. I'll get Mildred, and me and L.C. will catch up with you later."

"Promise?" Rose looked up at Caleb and smiled.

"Promise. Now go!" Caleb pointed his arm in the direction that she should take.

Rose began running the mile or so it took to get to her house. She was more than halfway there when she heard the explosion. She looked back and saw black plumes of smoke spiraling in the sky. She turned and began to head back to Sweet Water, screaming as she ran. Each step carried her closer to a curtain of thick, black smoke that filled her eyes, nose, and throat.

Rose put her hand over her mouth and strained to make out the church through the smoke, but she couldn't see the church at all. All she could see was a red blaze of fire that jumped and danced crazily.

"Mildred and them must have come out through the back door," she thought wildly. She ran crazily around to the back of the church. Small circles of people were beginning to gather there.

Rose scanned the crowd for Mildred's, Caleb's, and L.C.'s faces. "Has anybody seen Mildred and L.C.?" she shouted.

A few shook their heads.

She spotted Silas in the crowd and ran to him. "Silas, have you seen L.C. and Caleb?" She grabbed his arm.

"Wasn't Caleb and L.C. in the church?" Silas asked.

Rose nodded.

Silas put his arm around Rose. "Baby, nobody that was in that church came out," he said softly.

"No!" Rose screamed. "Caleb was comin' out right after me. And L.C. and Mildred were comin' out." She began to lash out at Silas with her fists. "You must have seen them!"

She began to run through the crowd. "Have you seen Mildred?" she asked. "Have you seen Caleb and L.C.?"

The sympathetic looks cast at her struck terror in her heart.

She ran toward the church, screaming Mildred's name. Dropping to her knees, she began to moan Caleb's name over and over. She hugged her stomach and tried to keep back the bile that rose in her throat. Smoke was in her eyes, nose, and mouth.

"Please, Father," she moaned. "Please, God. Please! Please!" she began to scream and pound the ground with her fists.

"Rose, Rose..." Silas held her fast. "Listen to me. Everybody that was in that church is gone, child."

"We need to help them! We need water! Lots of water!" Rose tried to free herself from Silas.

"It's too late for that now," Silas said. He pulled her down to the ground and began to rock her.

"Caleb promised me," she cried. "He promised me; he promised me. Oh my God. What happened? What happened, Silas?"

"I don't rightly know. I just heard a loud noise. John was one of the first ones out here. He said he heard glass breaking and then the noise."

"Glass breaking?" Rose exclaimed. "Somebody threw somethin' in the window! We've got to call the sheriff." She started to get up.

Silas pulled her back down. "Look over there," he whispered.

111

Rose looked to her right and saw Sheriff Tucker and nephew Billy leaning against their car, watching the fire.

"How long have they been here?"

"John said that they were here when he got here."

"Well, did they see anybody? Did they do anything?"

Silas looked at Rose. "John said that they were *here* when he got here," he repeated.

Rose stared at Silas.

"Do you know what they was meetin' about tonight?" Silas asked.

Rose dropped her eyes.

Silas shook her. "If you know anything about what was goin' on in that church or what happened at the courthouse tonight, you better be mighty careful."

"What do you mean?" she whispered.

"I'm sayin' that people here are talkin' about a group of folks that went down and tore up the courthouse tonight. They sayin' that the same group was inside Sweet Water tonight when it caught fire. Tucker ain't gonna leave it just like that. They gonna want more than that."

Rose turned a frightened face to Silas. "What should I do?" she whispered.

"You got some kin somewhere that you can stay with for a while until this blows over?"

"I don't know," Rose stammered. "I can't think," she shook her head.

"Leave," Silas said simply. He slowly pulled her to her feet.

More people began to crowd around the fire.

"Do you have any money?" Silas asked.

"I've got a little bit saved up."

Silas hugged Rose. "Go now," he whispered. "Don't stop for good-byes, child. Run now."

Rose ran. She fell twice but clambered to her knees, refusing to stop.

The outline of Mildred and L.C.'s house finally came into view. Mildred's weekly wash blew in the breeze.

Rose leaned against the porch and tried to catch her breath. She sat on the bottom steps of the porch and began to take long, deep breaths. When she began to breathe normally she reached down and slipped off her shoes and tiptoed onto the porch. She eased in the back door and headed for Mildred and L.C.'s bedroom.

Lucille Jenkins lay sprawled across Mildred and L.C.'s bed, snoring loudly. Rose tiptoed past her and went over to Rosemary's crib. Rosemary looked up at Rose and grinned.

Rose picked up her namesake and left the bedroom noiselessly. She opened the back door and put on her shoes. She ran the few yards to her house with Rosemary in her arms.

Laying Rosemary on her bed, she began to throw a few clothes into a shopping bag. She looked under her bed and pulled a mason jar that held all of her life savings. She opened the jar and counted out seventeen dollars and thirty-five cents.

She pulled her Sunday coat over her cocktail dress and grabbed the paper bag. She picked up Rosemary and swore softly. "How could I forget to bring you any clothes?" she muttered. She looked around her house nervously as the early morning rays began to break outside. She finally pulled her dining room tablecloth off of the table and wrapped it around the baby.

She hurried outside and refused to look back.

* * *

The 2:50 A.M. Greyhound bus en route to Chicago was nearly full when it stopped in Crayton to pick up a solitary passenger. A young woman boarded with a heavy coat that parted to reveal a muddy, bloodstained red and white dress. She held a brown shopping bag in one hand and cradled a baby wrapped in a white-lace tablecloth in the other arm.

The bus was quiet as she boarded and looked around nervously for a seat. She finally saw an empty one next to a heavyset older woman. The woman looked at Rose intently. She held out her arms for Rosemary. Rose instinctively clutched the baby to her chest and looked at the woman with frightened eyes.

The older woman smiled gently. Rose handed Rosemary over and burst into tears.

"There, there now," she patted Rose's shoulders. "It's gon' be all right."

A few other passengers nearby murmured their sympathies and clicked their tongues. Someone passed back a warm facecloth.

Rose wiped her face and her bloody knees.

"Where's your baby's clothes?" the woman wanted to know.

Rose shook her head.

Diapers and two tee shirts were passed back.

Rose started crying.

"Probably had to leave the man with just the clothes on her back," someone commented.

"Lucky she got away with what she did," another woman put in.

Two chicken drumsticks and a bottle were passed back.

"What's your baby's name?" the older woman asked as she fed Rosemary.

Rose dried her eyes and took a bite of chicken.

"Mildred," she said in a clear voice.

Thirteen

CHICAGO, ILLINOIS, 1957

ROSE SHIFTED MILDRED to her other arm and knocked softly on the door. She could hear the sounds of music playing and loud voices coming from inside the building.

Mildred started to cry.

Rose shifted the child to her other hip and checked the address again. "3925 W. Adams," she read aloud. She looked at the door.

"Ssh, baby, ssh," she murmured to Mildred.

She tried the front door, which opened into a hallway. A single light bulb burned dimly and revealed walls that were a faded, orange color. Candy wrappers and a few cigarette butts were scattered about the floor. A row of boxes and buttons were attached to one side of the wall.

"Now what's this?" she asked. She walked over to the boxes. Underneath each box were a name and a black button. She saw a faded note in childish script taped under the boxes that read, "Mailman, please ring bell twice for checks."

115

"Boxes for mail?" Rose questioned. "And bells?" She found the name of Delores Johnson under the third box. "Now what am I supposed to do?" she asked aloud.

Mildred's whimper turned into a loud wail.

Rose punched the bell twice in desperation.

She heard the creak of a door being opened.

"Come on up!" a woman yelled down.

Rose started at the sound. She walked a few feet and stopped.

"Hey!" the woman yelled. "Who's down there? You comin' on up or what?"

"Aunt Dee?" Rose called.

"Huh?" the voice answered.

Rose cleared her throat. "Is Delores Johnson here?" she called.

"Of course she's here, baby," the woman said. "Who do you think is throwin' the party?"

"Oh," Rose didn't know what to make of that.

"Who you talkin' to, Pearl?" Rose heard a woman ask.

"Somebody down there what called you Aunt Dee," Pearl answered.

"What? You talkin' to some kin of mine and ain't told them to come on up?"

Rose heard the clacketyclack of high-heeled shoes hammering down the stairs. She chewed her lip nervously and hugged Mildred tighter.

A middle-aged woman in a white dress covered with bright red flowers suddenly appeared before her. Her hair was straightened and flipped up at the ends. Redstreaked bangs fell into her eyes. Her dress was fitted around the bodice and cinched in at the waist. The skirt fell in pleats around her hips. Her fingers, wrists, and ears sparkled with jewelry.

Rose had never seen a more beautiful colored woman before in her life.

The woman looked at Rose intently.

"Hi, Aunt Dee," Rose stuttered. "It's me. I mean, it's Rose Johnson. I'm Rose Johnson," she said finally.

116

"Do you think you have to tell me who you is?" Delores said. "Don't you think I'd know Mary's girl when I see her? Come here, baby!" Delores opened her arms wide, embracing Rose and Mildred at once.

"Lord, Lord, Lord," Delores said.

Rose began to cry.

"Don't start none of that now," Delores admonished and hugged Rose tighter.

"Well, wait a second," she exclaimed. "Who have we here?" She stared at Mildred and pulled back the blanket covering her face. "Is this your child?"

"Yes. I mean no..." Rose stammered.

"Well, y'all just come on up," Delores said. She turned to the staircase, leading the way.

Rose shifted Mildred and began to follow her upstairs.

Delores suddenly turned around. "I'm throwin' a rent party," she said, winking at Rose.

Delores ushered Rose and Mildred past Pearl, who was still hanging over the banister absorbing the entire scene. Pearl looked at Rose curiously.

Rose looked down at her mud-stained dress and bloody knees. She shifted Mildred and pulled her coat closer together.

"I'm not really dressed for a party, Aunt Dee," she whispered. "I've been riding the bus all night and today. Could I just—"

Delores waved away Rose's protests. "Honey, you look better and smell sweeter than most of the folks here. Don't worry none about that."

Delores walked into the living room ahead of Rose and Mildred. "Everybody! Hey, everybody!" She grabbed Rose's hand and pulled her into the room. "This here is my niece from down South and her baby!"

Rose pulled her coat closer together and tried to smile. About twenty people occupied the living room. A few couples were dancing in one corner. Others were sitting on a couch or standing around. There was a table of people playing cards in another corner.

Some looked up when Delores made her announcement and smiled. Others glanced up from their activities briefly and then continued with what they were doing. Rose was impressed with how sophisticated the women seemed with their fancy dresses and straightened hair.

"Hey!" A man at the card table motioned to Rose. "Do you play Bid?"

Rose shook her head. She had no idea what "Bid" was and decided not to ask.

"Sam, ain't you got a partner sittin' right there?" Delores asked.

"Yeah," Sam replied. "That's why I'm askin'."

Delores laughed and grabbed Rose's hand. "Come on, baby. Let me fix you a plate and catch up on what's going on in Crayton." She reached over and took Mildred from Rose's grip.

Mildred began to howl.

"Is she a fussy baby?" Delores asked as she turned into the kitchen.

"Not really," Rose answered and fell into a chair. "Aunt Dee, we've been on the bus for almost two days. We haven't had much to eat and we need a bath. We're both just hungry and bone tired. I apologize for springing on you unannounced like this... I promise I'll tell you all about it tomorrow. But right now me and Mildred need to eat, bathe, and find someplace to sleep."

Delores sat down at the kitchen table and rocked Mildred. "It's me that should be doing the apologizing. Here I am ready to show you off and throw you into my party without thinking once about you." She got up with a start. "I'm gonna get rid of these folks right now," she announced.

"No, no, Aunt Dee," Rose protested. "Don't do that. Don't you have a back room or someplace where we can sleep?"

"Uh-uh, I sure don't." Delores sat down and continued to rock Mildred. "Hold on a minute and let me think." I got it!" she jumped up and thrust Mildred at Rose. She went over to the cabinet and took out two plates. Taking them to the stove, she began to fill them with barbecued ribs, greens, potato salad, and corn bread, all the while humming to the music playing in the front room.

She turned abruptly to Rose. "How old is the baby?"

"Five months," Rose answered.

"Miss Roberta won't mind putting y'all up for the night," Delores answered.

"I didn't mean to intrude, Aunt Dee. God knows I didn't," Rose answered.

"Don't worry, baby," Delores turned to Rose. "Miss Roberta is my best friend in the building. She got two bedrooms and a heart of gold. She made this potato salad for my rent party. So make sure you say how good it is when you're down there." She turned back to the stove.

"Now this here bowl of cornbread and pot liquor is for the baby. I'm sending milk down, too. Roberta's a real angel but ain't no sense pressing our luck."

She turned to Rose. "What else do you need? You got something to sleep in?"

Rose nodded. Tears began to collect in the corners of her eyes. "Thank you, Aunt Dee," she whispered.

Delores came around to the table and kissed her. "Come on, sweetie," she said. "I don't know what brought y'all up here, but it sure feels good to have my kin around me. I'll be down in the morning and we'll talk about everything." She turned to Mildred, who was starting to whimper. "Just wait until that baby tastes my pot liquor." She put the plates and milk in a shopping bag and looked critically around the kitchen. Picking up a sweet potato pie, she slid it into the bag. "I don't know how this tastes. It ain't one of mine, but Pearl swears by it."

She turned to Rose, "Let's go."

Rose followed Delores into the living room and out of the front door.

"Pearl," Delores motioned to her friend. "Keep an eye out for me. I'll be right back."

Rose followed Delores down to the first floor of the building.

Delores tapped on Miss Roberta's door.

There was no answer.

"It's all right, Miss Roberta, it's me—Dee!" she hollered.

Rose first heard the shuffle of feet and then a series of clicks before the door eased open.

A woman wearing a flowered housedress stood in the doorway. "What you out there hollerin' about Delores?" she asked.

"Miss Roberta, I got a big favor to ask of you," Delores began.

"Uhh," Miss Roberta grunted as she stood in the doorway and stared at Rose and Mildred. "Who this with you?" she asked.

"This is my niece Rose and her baby." Delores answered. "They just got in from Crayton, Tennessee."

"How do you do, Ma'am?" Rose whispered.

"Bring that baby out of the night air and come on inside," Miss Roberta said.

Rose followed Delores inside.

Delores put the shopping bag down. "You see, here it is—" she began.

"Have a seat," Miss Roberta told Rose. "What's wrong with the baby?"

"She hungry, wet, and tired," Delores broke in. "They just got off the bus from Crayton. Been ridin' for two days and caught me by surprise."

"Don't say?" Miss Roberta answered.

"Here I am in the middle of a rent party and my niece and great niece come knockin' on my door—"

"She throws a rent party every month. Sometimes twice a month," Miss Roberta informed Rose. "And the fools just keep right on comin'. Payin' and comin.'"

Rose smiled.

"I started to clear them folks outta my house, but Rose says no," Delores continued. "All they need is a bath and a place to spend the night. You ain't got to feed 'em. I brought food down here myself. I fixed you a plate, too."

"I already ate," Miss Roberta broke in. "You say your name's Rose?" she asked.

"Rose Johnson," Rose answered. "And this here's Mildred."

"Well, Rose and Mildred, like I said, I already ate. Because it is," she looked meaningfully at Delores, "eleven o'clock."

Rose wearily began to turn towards the door.

"But I got plenty of hot water and I could sure use some company. You and the baby can stay here with me tonight."

Rose tried to form the words of thanks, but her throat was too full. She nodded.

"Well, thank you, Miss Roberta," Delores said. She jumped to her feet. "That sure takes a load off of my mind. Now I hafta get back upstairs." She blew Rose and Mildred a kiss. "I'm gonna come and get you first thing in the morning," she promised. She turned to Miss Roberta. "Thank you again, Miss Roberta. I'll see you in the morning."

"Uhh," Miss Roberta grunted and got up to let Delores out. When the door closed she turned to Rose. "If she gets up before noon, she's doin' something."

Rose didn't reply.

"Well," Miss Roberta turned to Rose, "I'll take the baby and bathe her in the sink while you soak in the tub." She held out her hands for Mildred.

"Oh, no," Rose clutched Mildred tighter. "I can bathe her and then take care of myself later."

"Nonsense." Miss Roberta reached down for Mildred. "I'll bathe and feed her while you take a load off."

"With all due respect, Miss Roberta!" Rose's voice climbed. "Mildred is my responsibility, and I'll take care of her."

"Why of course she's your responsibility, child," Miss Roberta said. "She's your baby, ain't she?"

Rose began to rock Mildred.

Miss Roberta watched her.

"I said, she is yourn', ain't she?" she repeated.

Rose sprang to her feet. "I'm sorry that we bothered you, Miss Roberta," she said. "We'll be going now."

"And just where will you be going at eleven o'clock at night with a baby on your hip?" Miss Roberta questioned.

Rose shifted Mildred and studied the floor.

"Sit down, child," Miss Roberta said.

Rose perched on the end of the chair.

"I don't know what's all going on here," Miss Roberta said. "But what I do know is that here is a baby that looks worn out. You say she ain't had much to eat and needs a bath. I see a young woman who ain't far from a baby herself who looks like she been through hell and back. I ain't gonna ask what happened to you, but there is one thing that I have to know while you stayin' in my house."

She walked over to Rose and stood directly in front of her. "Are you a God fearin' child?" she asked.

Rose looked up into Miss Roberta's eyes. "Oh yes, Ma'am," she whispered. "Yes, Ma'am," she nodded. "Yes, Ma'am," she repeated as the tears fell.

"All right, then, all right," Miss Roberta held out her arms for Mildred.

Rose got up and put Mildred in her seat and ran to Miss Roberta.

"Please help me, Ma'am," she moaned as she laid her head on Miss Roberta's shoulder. "Please help me. I don't have anyone; I don't know nobody..."

Miss Roberta put her arms around Rose. "Ssh, child, ssh. It's going to be all right."

She waited until Rose's cries subsided. "Let's get this baby bathed and fed. We'll put her to bed, and then we'll work on you."

She walked over and picked up Mildred and headed toward the back of the house.

Rose wearily followed her.

She sat on the toilet seat and watched Miss Roberta skillfully bathe Mildred in the bathroom sink. When she finished, she got up and wrapped Mildred in a towel.

"Now, while you're taking your bath, I'm gonna feed this child and put her to bed."

Miss Roberta shook Mildred to wake her up. "This poor thing is tuckered out. But I want to get some food in her before she goes to sleep."

She turned to Rose. "When you come out of the tub, I'll have your plate ready for you."

Rose nodded. "Thank you," she said simply.

She closed the bathroom door behind Miss Roberta, turned on the bathroom faucet, and began to take off her clothes. She turned to the mirror above the sink. The reflection showed a woman whom she did not recognize. Her eyes were hardly visible through the puffy lids. There were lines around her mouth that she had never seen before. Her cheeks were covered with streaks of dirt whose paths were only broken by tearstains. Her hair stood up in some places and was matted down in others. She closed her eyes and got into the tub, welcoming the sting of the water as it hit her knees and arms.

Sweet Water Baptist Church. The woods. Mildred. Caleb. L.C. "Lord, please give me strength. I can't handle this!" she whispered through clenched teeth. "Strength!" she moaned. "Strength!"

She washed her aching body with trembling hands.

About a half an hour later, Miss Roberta knocked on the door.

"Come in," Rose said.

The door opened and Miss Roberta peeked around the corner. "You 'bout ready to come out?" she asked.

Rose nodded.

Miss Roberta brought in a white gown and a housecoat. "Here's a jar of Vaseline, too." She placed it on the sink. "Child, you should have seen that baby working with that spoon of cornbread and pot liquor." Miss Roberta laughed. "Bless her heart, she was sure tryin'."

She darted a look over at Rose. "Well, I'll be in the kitchen when you're done."

Rose smiled and nodded.

She leaned back in the tub when Miss Roberta had gone and took a deep breath.

Stepping out of the water, she smiled at the size of the gown that Miss Roberta had given her. She looked into the mirror again and promised herself that she'd wash her hair tomorrow.

Miss Roberta was sitting at the kitchen table when Rose entered. Her eyes were closed.

"I'm sorry to be keepin' you up, Ma'am," Rose said.

Miss Roberta's eyes flew open. "Oh, you're not keepin' me up, child," she said. "Here sit down and eat." She pulled up a chair for Rose.

Rose sat down. She looked down at the barbecued ribs, greens, and cornbread. "What happened to the potato salad?" she asked.

"Oh, I dumped that," Miss Roberta said.

"But I thought Aunt Dee said that it was your potato salad." Rose picked up a fork.

Miss Roberta got up. "That's the potato salad that I make for her so-called rent parties."

She took a bowl out of the refrigerator.

"This is the potato salad that *I* eat." She winked at Rose.

Rose lay down her fork and laughed with Miss Roberta, who spooned a generous helping onto her plate. "Now you can eat," she said.

Rose picked up her fork. "I guess you want to know why I'm here—" she began.

Miss Roberta put her hand up. "Child, you look just as worn out as that baby in there. You eat and get a good night's sleep. We'll talk in the morning."

"Thank you ever so much, Miss Roberta," Rose said. She murmured a few words of grace and started eating.

After she cleaned her plate, Miss Roberta showed her the room where she and Mildred would sleep.

Rose tiptoed in and looked at Mildred lying in the center of the bed.

Once alone, she knelt down and prayed.

Rose gently placed Mildred on one side of the bed, bolstered her with a pillow to keep her from rolling off, and slipped under the covers next to her. She sighed at the luxury of being in a bed again.

Before drifting off to sleep, she smiled to herself and thought how comforting it felt to *finally* meet someone in Chicago whose hair was as kinky as hers.

Fourteen

CHICAGO, ILLINOIS, 1984

"KNOCK," AUNT ROSE ORDERED.

Mildred knocked faintly on the door of the Giles residence.

"I don't know what you're so scared about," Aunt Rose shook her head. "Reverend Giles isn't going to bite you."

"I just don't like the way he stares at me," Mildred whispered. "He always wants to preach at me."

"He's a reverend ain't he? He's supposed to preach at you."

"Not with those big eyes."

"Stop being silly. You know what?" Aunt Rose looked at Mildred innocently. "I wonder if this is the weekend that Charles Gilbert is home from college. You could talk to him, you know, and give him the young person's view about the Williams' campaign while I work on persuading Reverend and Flossie to have Raymond Williams talk to the church." She winked at Mildred.

Mildred glared at her aunt, "If I find out that you knew Charles Gilbert was coming…"

Flossie Giles opened the door and beamed at Mildred and Aunt Rose. "Well, what a surprise! Charles Gilbert! Charles Gilbert! Come see who's here!"

Aunt Rose laughed nervously and pulled the basket from Mildred's stiff fingers. "We didn't come to breakfast empty-handed Flossie; my baby made some blueberry muffins that will knock your socks off!"

Flossie Giles embraced Mildred like a long-lost daughter. "You mean you can bake, too, child?" She smiled into Mildred's face and reached for the basket.

"Are we going to be able to visit with Sister Rose and Mildred?" Reverend Giles voice boomed from inside.

Flossie laughed. "Forgive me, you two. Come on inside."

Following Flossie Giles inside, Rose turned to Mildred imploringly. "I didn't know for sure that Charles Gilbert was visiting," she whispered.

Mildred followed her inside.

Mildred always thought of the Giles' kitchen as a warm and friendly place. The kitchen table was white and one of the largest that she had ever sat down at. Reverend Giles always said that the kitchen table was for those members in his congregation who didn't know how to go home. Red and white curtains covered the large bay windows and the wallpaper was red and white checked. The stove had six eyes and Flossie Giles would use all six as she stood with one hand on her hip while the other hand flipped pancakes for the nurse's board's pancake breakfasts.

"Well! Well! Well!" Reverend Giles grinned at Mildred and Aunt Rose. "Come sit down and break bread with us. Charles Gilbert was here a minute ago, but when he heard you were on the porch, he took off like 40 going north! I wonder what that means?" he asked Mildred in an exaggerated whisper.

"I've told my testimony many times that it took Sister Giles to help turn me the right way. She's several years," Reverend Giles cleared his throat and winked at his wife, "older than me and look at us now." Reverend Giles thumped his chest for emphasis. "Married almost 50 years. History just might repeat itself with my son. What do you think?" He smiled at Mildred.

"Reverend, stop embarrassing the girl," Flossie admonished.

Reverend Giles shook with laughter. "Then feed me, woman!" He winked at Mildred. "Are you one of these modern women who doesn't know how to cook?"

"Mildred made the muffins that we brought," Aunt Rose put in.

"Because, you know, the Good Book says..." Reverend Giles continued.

Flossie put a steaming plate of ham, grits, and eggs in front of her husband.

Reverend Giles stopped talking and stared at the plate as though mesmerized.

"What can I get for you, Rose?" Flossie picked up a plate and walked toward the stove.

"Ummmmh-ummmh, everything smells so good," Aunt Rose smiled at Flossie. "How about some of that country ham, a couple of big spoonfuls of grits, and two of my baby's muffins," she smiled at Mildred.

"Good choice, good choice," Reverend Giles reached for the basket. "I think I'll try a couple of these myself."

Flossie sat Aunt Rose's plate down in front of her and picked up another. "Baby, what will you have?" she asked, smiling at Mildred.

"Give her a little bit of everything," Reverend Giles decided. "These girls today are way too skinny." He looked up at his wife's ample hips approvingly.

Mildred sighed and glanced at her watch.

Charles Gilbert, Jr. nervously walked into the kitchen and awkwardly pulled out a chair and sat down.

"Well hello, Charles Gilbert," Aunt Rose smiled. "I declare, every time I see you, you look more handsome."

"Hello, Miss Johnson," he mumbled.

"Charles Gilbert, aren't you going to say hi to Mildred?" Flossie prompted.

He fixed Mildred with a desperate stare and stiffly nodded in her direction.

"Here you go, baby," Mrs. Giles sat a heaping plate directly in front of Mildred.

Mildred stared at her plate and watched the yolk from her scrambled eggs running into the grits. She saw her blueberry muffins begin to soak up the grease from the ham and felt slightly sick.

"Is something the matter, Mildred?" Mrs. Giles looked at Mildred's strange expression.

Mildred faintly shook her head.

"Don't be silly, Millie," Aunt Rose admonished.

She turned to Mrs. Giles. "My baby is a strange eater, Sister Giles. She doesn't like to have her food touch on her plate."

"Oh." Mrs. Giles looked at Mildred. "I see," she nodded as if trying to understand.

"What kind of foolishness is that?" Reverend Giles looked up from his plate. "It's all meeting up in the end." He pointed a chubby finger at Mildred. "Who's going to wash up all of these extra dishes?"

"I'm really not very hungry anyway," Mildred said.

"Nonsense, child. Don't pay the reverend no mind. He's just teasing you. Let me fix you another plate." Flossie got up from her chair, still staring at Mildred.

"I'll take her plate," Charles Gilbert offered.

"Now let's see, how about the ham and eggs in one plate and a saucer for the grits?" Flossie looked at Aunt Rose for confirmation.

"That's fine," Aunt Rose nodded. "And give her a separate saucer for the muffins."

Mildred looked up from her lap into the laughing eyes of Reverend Giles.

"Do you need separate forks, too?" he questioned Mildred.

"Quit teasing the child, Reverend," Flossie shook her head. She turned to Mildred as an afterthought. "Do you?"

Mildred shook her head no and looked pointedly at her aunt.

"Uh, Charles Gilbert," Aunt Rose cleared her throat. "How do you like college?"

Flossie sat Mildred's plate and saucers in front of her and turned to Reverend Giles. "Well, I guess we're ready now."

Reverend Giles bowed his head. "Lord, we want to thank You for the food we're about to receive. We want to thank You for gracing our home this morning with Sisters Rose and Mildred and Your presence. We pray for those of us who do not have anything to eat today, and we give thanks to You for allowing us to be here and share in the glory of Your name. Amen."

"Amen," the table echoed.

"Mmmmh, Flossie where did you get this ham? It's delicious." Aunt Rose winked at Mildred.

"Isn't it?" Flossie agreed. "The reverend's brother Lester lives in Memphis and he sends us a ham whenever somebody goes down to visit."

Mildred looked up from her plate into the eyes of Reverend Giles.

"Well, Mildred," he boomed. "What do you think of my son—the college man?"

Mildred nodded gravely.

"What are you studying, Charles Gilbert?" Aunt Rose beamed.

"I haven't really decided," Charles mumbled.

"Theology," the Reverend answered.

"Charles Gilbert is in a liberal arts program for now because he's not totally sure what his major will be," Flossie explained. "We're hoping that he'll decide on theology but he hasn't received the call yet."

"He will," Reverend Giles stated.

"I see," Aunt Rose commented. "What classes do you like the best, Charles Gilbert?"

"Art," Charles stated softly.

"So, you are an artist." Aunt Rose smiled at Charles. "I've always wanted to be able to draw. What do you do? Draw? Paint?"

"It's just a hobby," Reverend Giles put in. "Just something that he does to relieve stress. It's not going to be a career or anything like that."

"Oh," Aunt Rose looked at Charles thoughtfully.

Mildred looked at her aunt and wondered what that expression meant. She glanced at Charles Gilbert and felt a pang of sympathy.

"How's the registration drive going?" Flossie asked Aunt Rose.

"Good, good." Aunt Rose bit into a muffin. "We've been getting a good response from some of the people who want to be involved in the Williams campaign." She shook her head. "I never knew so many people were not registered. You know, it's funny — my baby and I have been to a lot of homes, telling people about Raymond Williams. Some people you can tell right off whether you've got a chance to convince them to join you or not. But you know, the people that say 'no' have the strangest reasons for not supporting him." Aunt Rose shook her head.

"What do they say?" Flossie asked.

"Well," Aunt Rose took a spoonful of grits. "I've had a few young people tell me and Millie that the city is not ready for a black mayor, and some of them are college people. That's an answer that I thought I'd hear from someone my age."

"It's hard to undo one hundred years of brainwashing," Reverend Giles commented and shook his head.

"What else?" Flossie prompted.

Aunt Rose turned to Mildred. "What was that Miss Sharon told you, baby?"

"She said that the Reynolds campaign had better-looking men in it and that she was supporting Parker Reynolds." Mildred grinned. "It was so crazy that I had to laugh."

"Sad," Reverend Giles shook his head. "You should have brought her to Wisdom Seat. Maybe hearing the Word would knock some sense into her head."

"But I still think that Mrs. Richards took the cake. Didn't she, baby?" Aunt Rose began to laugh.

"Mrs. Richards?" Reverend Giles said thoughtfully. "Isn't she a member of Wisdom Seat?" He stared at Aunt Rose.

"I wouldn't be so bold as to say," Aunt Rose retorted. "But I can say that I've never heard a stranger response."

"Mrs. Richards." Reverend Giles leaned back in his chair and focused on Mildred. "Does she sit in the front of the church on the Washington Boulevard side?"

Mildred took a big bite of ham and indicated that she couldn't talk with her mouth full.

Laughing, Flossie said, "You can forget it, Reverend. They are not going to tell you who she is."

"They don't have to *tell* me," Reverend Giles retorted as he picked up a spoonful of grits. "I think I know who it is."

Flossie turned to Aunt Rose. "What did she say?"

Aunt Rose leaned back in her chair and waited until she had everyone's attention. "I said, 'Sister Richards, can we count on your vote for Raymond Williams'? She looked at me and said, 'Sister Rose, I've been thinkin' on this a spell—yes, I have. Now you know that Tom Carroll has been saying some mean and nasty things about Mr. Williams.'" Aunt Rose turned to Flossie. "I nodded and said 'yes,' he sure has." Aunt Rose nodded.

"Now I *know* who Mrs. Richards is," Reverend Giles put in.

Flossie waved her hand at her husband to hush.

Aunt Rose continued. "Sister Richards said, 'As a matter of fact, Mr. Carroll has been giving Mr. Williams *pure dee hell.* So Sister Johnson, I think that I'm gonna vote for Mr. Carroll, and if he's elected—I'm gonna give him hell!'"

"What!" Flossie laughed. "What are you saying, Rose?"

Aunt Rose shook with laughter. "Y'all heard what I said. She's gonna vote for Tom Carroll and give him hell."

"An idiot," Reverend Giles decided as he bit into a blueberry muffin. "A mind that is totally null and void."

Charles Gilbert giggled and turned to Mildred. "These are very good muffins."

Mildred smiled her thanks.

"What's that?" Reverend Giles looked at Charles Gilbert.

Charles Gilbert shook his head.

Reverend Giles smiled a knowing smile at Mildred.

"You know, Sister Rose," he said as he reached for another blueberry muffin, "it could be that your approach is all wrong. Some people need the strong word of a man to persuade them."

Charles Gilbert rolled his eyes at Mildred.

"You know, you may be right," Aunt Rose agreed. "Some of the men that we've talked to don't even look like they're listenin' half the time when I'm talking."

She looked innocently at Reverend Giles. "What do you think I'm doin' wrong?"

Reverend Giles leaned back in his chair and wiped his mouth with a napkin. He took great pains to fold it into a small triangle. He finally looked up. "I don't know, Sister Johnson. It could be several things. Perhaps your presentation isn't forceful enough. Maybe you don't give eye contact — which is always very important. "He held up his hands and began to count off possible weaknesses in Aunt Rose's delivery, tone, and execution.

"I could come out with you sometime and give you a few pointers," he offered.

"Are you familiar with Raymond Williams' campaign?" Mildred asked.

Reverend Giles reached in the basket for another muffin. He took a big bite. "I don't have to be. An accomplished speaker can speak on any subject, warm up any crowd—"

"That's it!" Aunt Rose pounded her fist on the kitchen table.

"That's what?" Flossie asked excitedly.

"Yes, what?" Reverend Giles repeated.

"You have just provided the answer to our problem," Aunt Rose said.

Mildred watched her aunt with amusement.

"Who would know better than you how to warm up Wisdom Seat?" She smiled at Reverend Giles.

"Wisdom Seat? What has Wisdom Seat got to do with us?" Reverend Giles demanded.

"You'll set the stage, warm up the audience..." Aunt Rose continued.

"Set the stage for who? You?" Reverend Giles asked. "I hardly think Wisdom Seat is the place for you to practice your—"

"Not me," Aunt Rose interrupted. "Raymond Williams."

"Raymond Williams!" Flossie exclaimed. "Would Raymond Williams actually come to Wisdom Seat?"

"I don't see why not," Aunt Rose answered.

"Oh, I don't know about that," Reverend Giles began.

"Just think, Raymond Williams in *our* church." Flossie turned to Aunt Rose. "Why we'd be the envy of every church on the West Side of Chicago. The first black man to run for office—speaking at Wisdom Seat!"

"It might make the news," Aunt Rose said.

"If it's advertised well enough," Charles put in.

"That where *you* come in." Aunt Rose pointed her finger at Charles Gilbert. "You can make up posters and signs, and we'll let the kids put them up all over the neighborhood."

"Wait a minute, wait just a minute," Reverend Giles held up his hand. "Just what do we know about this Raymond Williams? You all seem to forget one important thing." The reverend paused and looked around the table.

"*I* am the pastor at Wisdom Seat Baptist Church. *I* decide who comes into my church and who will speak at my church. Just *who* is this Raymond Williams? I don't know anything about him and I will not," he slammed his fist down on the table, "let my church be used as someone's podium for politics!"

There was silence at the kitchen table.

Flossie turned to Aunt Rose. "So what will you wear?" she asked.

"My black dress?" Aunt Rose looked at Mildred for confirmation.

Mildred nodded.

Reverend Giles picked up two muffins and left the table.

"What do you think?" Aunt Rose asked Flossie.

"Give him some time," Flossie said. She leaned over to Aunt Rose. "If you had told me what was on your mind earlier, I could have had time to work on him."

Aunt Rose shook her head. "I just now thought of it myself."

"Do you have some information on Raymond Williams? I'll just spread a few pieces around the house."

Fifteen

"CAN I HAVE EVERYBODY'S attention please?" O'Kanta's voice boomed out over the noisy crowd. "We're gonna make sure that we get to each and every one of you, but we need some help here. Would you please line up at each table and have your identification ready so that—"

"Identification?" A young man in army fatigues interrupted. "What kind of identification? How come y'all didn't say nothin' 'bout identification before I came all the way down here from 15th Street?"

O'Kanta smiled patiently.

Mildred looked out at the mass of faces. "We're going to be here all day," she whispered to Aunt Rose.

"Isn't it wonderful?" Aunt Rose answered.

Mildred sighed.

Four rectangular tables were stuffed into the main room of the Center for Black Awareness. An assortment of folding chairs, stackable chairs, and milk crates surrounded them.

The center's first official voter registration drive was under way.

Mildred and Aunt Rose, O'Kanta, Nate, and Nikki each manned a table.

"Name?" Mildred asked.

"Martin Malcolm Marlow," a young man said loudly.

"What a beautiful name!" Aunt Rose exclaimed. "You must be very proud to carry a name with so much history behind it."

"Yes, Ma'am."

"Address," Mildred continued.

"4336 W. 19th Street."

"Aren't you near the Church of God and Christ?" Aunt Rose interrupted.

"Uhmmm, I'm not sure," Martin stammered.

"Well, it's a beautiful church, anyway, if you ever get the chance to go." Aunt Rose smiled.

Mildred looked at Martin's hands as he filled out the application. O'Kanta's hands were large and dark with long fingers and short clean nails. His hands had totally enveloped hers as they walked downtown.

"He's looking at you."

Startled out of her daydream, Mildred turned to her aunt. "Huh?"

"O'Kanta. I been watchin' him out of the corner of my eye and he's been looking at you."

"I'm really not interested," she commented.

"Name?" she addressed the next young lady in line.

"Jennifer Miles," the woman answered. "Hey, uh, girlfriend," she leaned toward Mildred conspiratorially. "Do you know if that man over there in the dreads is married?"

Mildred followed her gaze to O'Kanta, who was busy filling out an application.

"I wouldn't know," she answered crisply.

"Well, if you don't mind, I think I'll wait in line at *his* table." Jennifer sauntered over to O'Kanta's table.

"How is he looking at me?" Mildred asked.

"I *don't* know, kind of confused like."

"Well, what kind of a look is that?"

"Maybe he's wondering why you're acting so distant."

"I'm not being distant. I'm being sensible," Mildred snapped.

"Look, baby, I know he hasn't called since your date," Aunt Rose said soothingly.

"That hasn't, got a thing to do with it."

"Excuse me?" A young man interrupted.

Mildred and Aunt Rose looked up.

"Name?" Mildred asked quickly.

"I think you ought to go over and say something to him," Aunt Rose whispered.

"I don't," Mildred replied as she greeted the next would-be voter.

"What are you being sensible about?" Aunt Rose wanted to know.

"He hasn't called me since we went out, Aunt Rose. Now doesn't that tell you something?"

"What does it tell you? Other than that he's a busy man?"

"It tells me that maybe he's not interested. It tells me that maybe he's not looking for the same thing that I'm looking for. Maybe he's trying to let me down easy."

"Have you told him what you're looking for?"

"No."

"Well, what are you waiting for?"

Mildred turned to her aunt. "Now is not the time to discuss this," she whispered.

Aunt Rose leaned back in her chair and crossed her arms over her chest. "I bet you that young lady over there is telling him exactly what's *she's* looking for."

Mildred looked over and spotted Jennifer Miles talking and smiling at O'Kanta. She quickly turned her head away.

"Aunt Rose, will you take over for me for a minute? I need to go to the bathroom."

Aunt Rose looked at her niece intently. "Sure, baby. Hurry back."

Mildred eased away from the table and headed toward the back of the center.

She closed the door quietly behind her and leaned against it. There was really no need for her to be so upset. O'Kanta had not made her any promises. They were not boyfriend and girlfriend.

She walked over to the tiny mirror above the sink and stared at her reflection.

A bleak, dejected Mildred stared back at her. This would definitely not do.

She began to splash cold water on her face. Looking into the mirror again, she forced herself to smile.

A knock sounded at the door.

"Just a minute," she answered. She gave herself a final shake and opened the door.

O'Kanta stood outside.

"Are you all right?" he asked.

Mildred nodded and attempted a smile. "Just fine," she mumbled as she eased around him.

"Hold on," O'Kanta caught her hand. "I want to talk to you."

"I left Aunt Rose alone registering people and I should really get back to her," Mildred said quickly.

"Aunt Rose can handle it." O'Kanta ushered Mildred into a small, makeshift office.

The room was barely large enough for the two of them. The wall facing her was filled with books and magazines. A small card table and folding chair completed the office.

"I've missed you." O'Kanta said. His six-foot-plus frame seemed to take up the additional space in the office.

Mildred looked into his eyes.

"Have you missed me?" he asked.

"Yes," she whispered.

"I went to Indiana to speak at a rally and try to get money for the center."

"Oh," Mildred said.

"It came up so suddenly that I didn't get a chance to talk to you."

"How did you do?"

"Not too bad. The crowd was pretty receptive." O'Kanta leaned against the card table. "I talked to a few brothers there about opening up a center in their neighborhood."

"That's a great idea." Mildred stared at O'Kanta's mouth. He had nice full lips. She remembered them being soft.

"I brought you something."

"Yes," she said dreamily.

"Mildred!"

Mildred jumped.

"I'm sorry. What did you say?"

"I said I brought you something." O'Kanta reached under the card table and pulled out a folded newspaper. He handed it to Mildred and pulled her onto his lap.

Mildred slowly opened the newspaper.

Several stems of black-spotted, bright reddish-orange flowers were nestled inside.

"They're beautiful," she exclaimed. "What are they?"

"Tiger lilies." O'Kanta wrapped his arms around her. "They made me think of the Nile River, African kings, queens, and you."

Mildred turned around to face him.

"And one more thing…" he continued.

She raised her eyebrows.

"The next time a woman asks you if I'm spoken for — you'd better say…"

"Yes," Mildred answered as O'Kanta kissed her.

Mildred came back to her table hand-in-hand with O'Kanta. She put the newspaper-wrapped tiger lilies under the table and winked at Aunt Rose.

"Next!" she called out cheerfully.

* * *

Six hours later, she massaged the aching fingers of her left hand and yawned. "I can't believe that we processed all of those people."

"The Center for Black Awareness' first voter registration drive is officially over!" O'Kanta announced.

"I'm going to go home and lay this body down," Aunt Rose said.

"Don't forget the debate tonight!" Nikki called out as she left.

"What time does it start?" Aunt Rose asked.

"Eight o'clock," O'Kanta answered. "Channel 11."

"Who are you going to watch it with?" Aunt Rose wanted to know.

"I don't know," O'Kanta said as he looked at Mildred. "I guess I'll watch it in the back on my 12-inch black and white."

Mildred picked up the bundle of flowers and began to wrap them in the newspaper slowly.

"Mildred!" Aunt Rose admonished.

She looked up innocently.

O'Kanta leaned his head on her shoulder and looked up at her beseechingly.

She laughed. "Would you like to come over and watch the debate with us?"

O'Kanta nodded. "Thanks for the invite. I'll come by at about seven thirty?"

Aunt Rose nodded and stretched. "Let's get a move on, Millie."

O'Kanta held the door open for them. "Hey! Is it all right if I bring a friend with me?" He asked suddenly.

Mildred looked at him questioningly.

"Of course, son," Aunt Rose said. "Any friend of yours is a friend of ours."

Mildred and Aunt Rose walked out into the night air.

"Who do you think he's going to bring, Aunt Rose?" she asked. "Do you think he's going to bring another woman?"

"Don't be silly. Didn't he just tell you in there to tell any and all women that he's spoken for?"

"Well, who could it be then?"

"I don't know. What about Nate?"

"I don't think he'd bring Nate. Would he actually have the nerve to bring a woman to our house?"

"We'll find out soon enough."

Sixteen

MILDRED CAREFULLY MEASURED A CUP of coffee beans into the grinder.

"Make sure you make enough for everyone to have at least two cups," Aunt Rose said as she came into the kitchen. "What kind of coffee are you making?"

"Good old-fashioned Colombian," Mildred answered as she turned the grinder on.

"Why don't you make some different kind of coffee for tonight? Something fancy. I know we got some flavored coffee here." Aunt Rose went into the kitchen pantry.

"Regular Colombian coffee will bring out the vanilla flavor in my sweet potato pies," Mildred said.

"Oh right, right..."Aunt Rose agreed as she stepped back into the kitchen.

"Now let's see, we've got two pies on the table, the coffee's grinding, and the television is on." Aunt Rose walked into the living room and admired the vase of tiger lilies on the table.

142

"Lord have mercy. O'Kanta did it up this time didn't he?" She sniffed the flowers. "What was that he said when he gave them to you?" She turned toward Mildred.

"I told you," Mildred answered shyly. "I'd just like to know who he's bringing with him."

"Well." Aunt Rose sank into the multi-colored sofa. "We'll find out directly."

Mildred looked at the kitchen clock. "It's already five minutes to—"

A sharp knock sounded at the door.

"You get it," Mildred whispered.

"Don't be silly." Aunt Rose got up from the sofa. "You go and welcome our guests in. I'll be right behind you."

"But what if it's a woman?" Mildred whispered.

"Get the door," Aunt Rose said sharply.

Mildred wiped her hands on her apron and slowly untied it. Tentatively, she walked to the door and opened it.

O'Kanta smiled at her and stood with his arm around a gentleman who looked to be around sixty years old.

O'Kanta had on a dark-blue dashiki and a pair of blue jeans. The gentleman had on a dark gray three-piece suit and tie. In his hand was a matching gray fedora with a black band around it. He twirled the hat nervously between his fingers.

"Mildred, I'd like you to meet Mr. Chapman Jackson," O'Kanta said. "This is the man I was telling you about earlier—the one who saved my life."

Mildred smiled and extended her hand. "Mr. Jackson, I'm pleased to meet you, sir."

"Please, please, call me Chappie," he said as he pumped Mildred's hand energetically.

"Chap," O'Kanta continued, "Mildred Johnson. Mildred is the woman who is slowly becoming my life."

"Yes, yes," Chapman Jackson nodded as he stared at Mildred with a critical eye. "She sure is pretty... just like you said."

Aunt Rose cleared her throat.

"Oh, forgive me. Please come in," Mildred stammered as she ushered the two inside.

"Uh, Mr. Jackson, Chappie, I'd like you to meet my aunt, Miss Rose Johnson."

"How do you do, Mr. Jackson," Aunt Rose said formally as she held out her hand.

"Miss Johnson, it is indeed a pleasure." Chapman Jackson kissed Aunt Rose's hand with deference.

Mildred looked at her aunt's startled face. "Well, let's all sit down," she suggested.

As Mildred followed O'Kanta into the living room, she felt a slight tug at her skirt.

"Millie, let O'Kanta and Mr. Jackson sit on the good sofa. We can take the love seat."

"All right, Aunt Rose," Mildred said, puzzled.

The two men sat on the living room sofa while Aunt Rose and Mildred sat stiffly on the love seat facing them.

Mildred looked at O'Kanta.

He winked broadly back at her.

Chapman Jackson gazed intently at Aunt Rose.

Aunt Rose stared straight ahead.

"Well, can I interest anyone in coffee and sweet potato pie?" Mildred asked.

"I'd love some," O'Kanta answered.

"I thought you said that she was going to make that lemon—"

"Ssh," O'Kanta nudged Chapman Jackson.

"What was that?" Mildred asked.

"Nothing," O'Kanta answered. He jumped to his feet. "Let me help you with the pie and coffee."

"Oh, I can help Millie," Aunt Rose broke in as she started to get up.

"I wouldn't think of it," O'Kanta said. "I'll leave you and Chap to get better acquainted. You know, Aunt Rose, Chap was born in Tennessee. Who knows? Maybe you two have some friends in common." He followed Mildred into the kitchen.

"What was it Chappie said?" Mildred asked O'Kanta as she poured the coffee.

"How about a kiss?" O'Kanta put his arms around her waist.

"How about an answer?"

"Okay, okay. But after I tell you, will I get a kiss?"

Mildred looked into O'Kanta's smile and smiled back. "I'll think about it."

"Well, Chappie wasn't all that keen on coming over here tonight. It took some talking on my part to get him out the front door." O'Kanta scooped up a hunk of sweet potato pie with his finger.

"Why didn't he want to come?" Mildred asked as she tried to smooth over the top of the pie with a knife.

"I told you that he's not a Williams supporter and, I don't know... when I told him about you and your aunt, he seemed nervous or something."

O'Kanta looked hungrily at the second pie.

"Don't touch it," Mildred warned. "Well, he could have fooled me. What made him kiss her hand like that?"

"I don't know." O'Kanta's voice dropped to a whisper. "Maybe it was something in her eyes. Maybe it was her Chanel N° 5..." he speculated.

"Ssh," Mildred giggled. "So what made him finally decide to come?"

"I told him that you were making his favorite dessert..."

"Lemon meringue pie," Mildred finished.

"Right. Now come here..." O'Kanta reached for Mildred.

"Millie! Do you need some help in there?" Aunt Rose's voice rang out.

"Gotta go," Mildred whispered and grinned at O'Kanta as she handed him the tray of cups and saucers.

As Mildred came into the living room, Aunt Rose got up to help her set the dining room table.

Mildred watched her aunt fuss over the arrangement of cups, saucers, and silverware.

145

"I think it looks okay," she ventured.

"Well, I don't," Aunt Rose snapped.

"I was just telling Miss Johnson here that I believe I might know some of her kinfolk in Crayton," Chapman Jackson said. "Is that where your folks are from, too?" he asked Mildred.

"Of course that's where her people are from," Aunt Rose called out from the dining room. "Where else would they be from?"

Mildred took her aunt's hand and led her back into the living room.

"Isn't it time yet?" Aunt Rose asked Mildred.

"It's not quite eight," O'Kanta said. "Well," he looked from Chapman Jackson to Aunt Rose to Mildred. "What do you say, Chap? Did you and Aunt Rose have some friends in common in Tennessee?"

"I'm not quite—" Chapman Jackson started.

"No," Aunt Rose finished his sentence.

"Although I do recall a Johnson on my mother's side who I believe stayed near Crayton," he continued.

"No relation," Aunt Rose snapped. "There's a heap of Johnsons in Tennessee. Johnson is a very common name..."

"Yes sir," Chapman Jackson continued as he took a sip of coffee and nodded at no one in particular. "I believe I recollect that a Johnson—"

"Did you live in Tennessee a long time before you came up to Chicago?" Mildred asked.

"Yes, indeed," Chapman Jackson answered. "I lived in Memphis goin' on about 40 years before I came up North. Forty wonderful years."

He turned to Aunt Rose. "Did you ever make it over to Memphis from Crayton? It's only about sixty or seventy miles north of there."

"Not that I can recall," Aunt Rose answered.

"But Aunt Rose, didn't you say that you and..." Mildred started.

Aunt Rose silenced her with a stern look.

"There's no way that anybody could come to Memphis and not remember her." Chapman Jackson stated. "Memphis has a way of keeping herself on your mind."

Mildred laughed. "You make Memphis sound like a person. A woman or something."

Chapman Jackson looked at Mildred as one would look at a child. "Memphis *is* a woman, daughter. Didn't you know that?"

"What channel is the debate on?" Aunt Rose wanted to know.

"Memphis teases you with her scent, her ways, and her sounds. Oh, she'll put a hurtin' on you with her sounds all right." Chapman Jackson shook his head.

"What kind of sounds?" Mildred wanted to know.

"Watch out now," O'Kanta warned.

"There's only one sound that comes from Memphis," Chapman Jackson said. "The sound heard from the moment you're brought into the world 'til you're laid to rest. The one sound that'll carry you through the hills and valleys that living in this world will bring."

Aunt Rose leaned back in her seat and took off her glasses. She polished the lens carefully with a white-lace handkerchief and slowly put them back on.

"A sound that was born out of the Negro work songs," Chapman Jackson continued, "and carried up through the generation of a people. A sound that came long before jazz, rhythm and blues, and what's that new one?" He looked at O'Kanta.

"Rap," O'Kanta answered.

"Rap," Chapman Jackson repeated. "It's like Aretha said, "...*with-out a word of warning' the blues walked in this mornin'—and sat right down in my living room...*"

"Hold on now, Chap," O'Kanta interrupted. "You've got a couple of blues aficionados here. You better watch it."

"Is that right?" Chapman Jackson looked at Aunt Rose.

"But we've got a problem here," O'Kanta continued. "Aunt Rose is of the opinion that B.B. King is the king of the blues. I tried to tell her that there is no equal to Muddy Waters, but she wouldn't hear none of it."

"Then I'd say that Miss Johnson and I have quite a lot to talk about," Chapman Jackson said. "Isn't that right?" he turned to Aunt Rose.

Aunt Rose smoothed the sides of her dress. "Would you like a slice of sweet potato pie?" she asked him.

"I'd love some," Chapman Jackson beamed.

"It's on," O'Kanta announced. "Turn the sound up."

Sherry Smith, moderator for the League of Women Voters, introduced the three mayoral candidates.

Parker Reynolds, Tom Carroll, and Raymond Williams faced the cameras as the debate began.

"Do you believe it?" Mildred asked. "We're now down to the final three. We started out with seven and we're down to three candidates."

"Look at that Parker Reynolds," Aunt Rose pointed to the television. "Now tell me this. How can somebody with that much money and livin'..." She turned to Mildred, "Where is that area that's he's from?"

"Carriage Estates," Mildred answered.

"Right, Carriage Estates. How can he know what our problems are over here on the West Side?"

"I don't think he's ever been in this neighborhood," Mildred added. "He didn't go to school here and he doesn't practice law here, either, but he says he wants to be mayor for *all* of us."

"Well, I can't blame the guy for being rich," O'Kanta said. "But it seems to me that if he really wants to be mayor for the entire city, that he would spend some time getting to know the city and its people. I called his office a couple of years ago when Bernard Johnson was beaten up and his store torched when he testified against those police officers. Remember that case? I asked if his law firm would represent Johnson, or if he could at least recommend somebody."

"I remember that case," Aunt Rose said. "Lord, when it came out that the police were behind that..."

"They wouldn't even talk to me," O'Kanta continued. "I called his office again last year when the council came up with their version of the redistricting map. I couldn't get past his secretary."

"Yes, I'm wealthy," Parker Reynolds said with a smile. "Is that a crime? My grandparents came to America with a dream. A dream and a desire to work.

They didn't ask for any handouts. They didn't ask for any special treatment. Ladies and gentlemen, I come to you tonight with a dream. A dream and a desire to work for this great city that we call Chicago..."

"What do you think about Tom Carroll?" Chapman Jackson asked Aunt Rose. "Now that's a man who knows the city. His uncle spoon-fed him on politics. He knows what you have to do to get things done in this city."

"Have you ever been to his neighborhood?" Aunt Rose asked.

"She's got you there, Chap," O'Kanta laughed.

"I don't know," Mildred commented. "I just can't bring myself to vote for someone who lives in a neighborhood that is known for bigotry and racism." I mean," she continued, "two guys were attacked there just three months ago. Their only crime was being there after dark, and I never heard Tom Carroll say anything about that."

"*I'm sick and tired of these vicious and unworthy attacks on my community,*" Tom Carroll interrupted. "*There are many good people in my neighborhood and I'll defend them. And there are a few bad people in my neighborhood and I'll prosecute them. My uncle wasn't born with a silver spoon in his mouth. He was raised right here in the city and he showed me how to treat people fairly and decently...*"

"Now, that he did," Chapman Jackson agreed.

"We're going to convert you yet," Mildred said as she refilled Chapman Jackson's cup. "Aren't we, Aunt Rose?"

"Ssh, here he is," Aunt Rose motioned to Mildred.

Raymond Williams looked directly into the Johnson's living room.

"*There are some who believe that I should avoid the race issue,*" he began, "*but I will not avoid it because it permeates our entire city and it has devastating implications. My opponents can run, but they can't hide. Because I will challenge you in every neighborhood of this city to tell me what you will do to sustain the educational system of this city and what you will do to balance its budget. What will you do to provide jobs for the inner city and what will you say to each and every one who is listening to make them believe that you care about them and their lives? That you care as much for the families that are fighting for* survival on the West Side and the South Sides of Chicago, as well as the affluent neighborhoods of Lincoln Park and the Gold Coast."

"Well," Aunt Rose said. "As we say in Wisdom Seat, 'Well...'

* * *

"Okay, what do you think?" Mildred asked as she washed the dishes.

"About what?" Aunt Rose dried the plate carefully.

"Well, for one thing, you've dried that plate for the last five minutes."

Aunt Rose put the plate down.

"I want to know what you think about Chapman Jackson." Mildred stopped washing and turned to her aunt.

"What am I supposed to think about him?"

"You know what I'm talking about. He seemed to really take an interest in you."

Aunt Rose picked up the plate and continued to dry.

"Does he remind you of anyone—"

"No!"

"I mean, does seeing him remind you—"

"I said no."

"—of being in Memphis," Mildred continued.

Aunt Rose continued drying.

"He seems like a nice man," Mildred offered. "Would you mind if he came by again with O'Kanta?" Mildred gently removed the plate from her aunt's hands.

Aunt Rose shrugged her shoulders. "It's a free country."

"They both have a sweet tooth," Mildred commented. "Maybe we can invite them over again for pie and coffee."

"I think he likes lemon meringue," Aunt Rose commented.

Mildred smiled and continued to wash dishes.

Seventeen

CHICAGO, ILLINOIS, 1960

"MAMA," MILDRED SAID.

"Aunt Rose," Rose corrected her.

"Mama!"

"Aunt Rose!"

"Don' wanna say Aunt Wose," three-year-old Mildred said stubbornly. "Wanna, wanna," she labored, "wanna say Momma!" She smiled triumphantly and held up her arms to be picked up.

Rose took her hands out of the dishwater and sighed. She wiped them on her apron and sighed again.

She picked Mildred up and carried her into the living room, walking over to the window and looked down at the city below.

"Down, wanna get down!" Mildred's voice broke in.

Rose lowered Mildred and sat down on the radiator in front of the window. Looking out, she wondered if she would ever feel at home in Chicago. After three years, she still felt like an outsider.

The bright, orange lettering of Andy's Food & Liquors faced her. Following in quick succession were the laundromat, the currency exchange, Chicken Delight, and Mount Calvary Apostolic Church. She closed her eyes and remembered a kitchen window in Crayton that looked out on a backyard filled with jonquils and forget-me-nots. A stream with fat perch and tadpoles. A place where she had envisioned her and Caleb...

The shrill sound of the doorbell interrupted her thoughts. She looked out of the first -floor window into Miss Roberta's frowning face.

Miss Roberta had on a flowered-print housedress with a white shawl draped around her shoulders. She had a cloth-covered basket in one hand that Rose was sure contained a batch of fried catfish and hush puppies. A bulging shopping bag and her black leather pocketbook dangled from the other hand.

"I just wanted to see how long I would have to stand here before you'd see me!" Miss Roberta fussed good-naturedly.

"Well, well, look at Miss Roberta comin' to call with both arms full," Rose teased. "I thought I asked you to stop bringing dinner every time you visit. Don't you think we'd let you come in—even if you came by empty-handed?"

"Don't you be concerned with what's all in my basket," Miss Roberta retorted. "Ain't none of it for you anyhow. It's all for my baby. That is, if you plan on letting me come up and see her."

"I don't rightly know," Rose teased. "You mean ain't nothin' in them bags for me?"

"Rose Johnson!"

Rose laughed and ran from the window.

"Millie! Millie!" she called. "Come see who's here!" She ran down the stairs and opened the front door for Miss Roberta.

"How you feelin', Miss Roberta?" Rose asked sweetly as she removed the basket from her arm.

"I might have known you'd take the basket," Miss Roberta replied. "Lord, Lord," she exclaimed as she climbed the flight of stairs leading to Rose's apartment. "I thought I'd never get here. Where's my baby?"

"She'd better be waiting at the top of the stairs," Rose said loudly as she looked up. "Because she knows better than to come down by herself."

Millie stood at the top of the landing with one hand clutched tightly on the banister. The other hand reached out for Miss Roberta.

"Is that Grandma's baby?" Miss Roberta cooed as she climbed the stairs toward Millie. "Is that Grandma's baby?"

Millie nodded her head fervently as Miss Roberta picked her up and covered her face with kisses.

Rose picked up the bags that Miss Roberta dropped and followed the two inside. She laid the cloth-covered basket on the kitchen table after checking under the cover to confirm that it indeed held catfish.

"What's in the shopping bag?" she called out.

Miss Roberta slowly walked into the kitchen carrying Millie.

"Miss Roberta, will you put that big child down and have a seat?" Rose pulled out a chair. "You want some coffee?"

"Not in this heat," Miss Roberta sat down heavily with Millie on her lap. "I'll take a jar of ice water though." She leaned back into the chair. "I'm telling you, I thought that Pulaski bus would never come."

Rose handed her the water and sat down. "When are you going to start riding the El? You are the only person I know that takes three buses to get here when you could take one bus and the Douglas B train."

"I come the way I know how and the way I've been coming for years," Miss Roberta snapped. "Now if you don't want my company..." she stared at Rose.

Rose laughed and picked up the basket. "What are we eating tonight?"

Miss Roberta grunted. "You know exactly what's in that bag because I know that you looked. But before we eat, I was down at Goldblatt's the other day, and I bought Millie a few things."

Rose smiled and shook her head as Miss Roberta pulled out an assortment of dresses, short sets, and accessories for Millie. "Good gracious, Miss Roberta, did you leave anything in the store?" Ignoring Rose,

Miss Roberta reached into the bag and pulled out a red and white striped ball and handed it to Millie.

With a squeal of laughter, Millie took the ball and ran into the living room.

"Well, Miss Roberta, now that you're retired, I guess that child is really going to be spoiled." Rose shook her head and picked up the shopping bag.

"She's supposed to be spoiled," Miss Roberta retorted. "Don't throw that bag away. There's something else in there."

"You mean there's more?" Rose teased as she reached into the bag.

She lifted out a parcel that was wrapped in tissue paper. "What's this?"

"What does it look like?"

Rose unfolded a black-satin dress with a velvet bow on the side. It had short, velvet sleeves, which were also accented with tiny bows.

"Do you like it?" Miss Roberta asked hopefully. "It's an evening dress."

"Uh, it's very nice," Rose said. "Is it for me?"

"Who else would it be for?"

"Oh. Well, ah..." Rose studied the dress carefully and turned it over. She smiled at the sash at the back of the dress, which sported another velvet bow.

"It used to be one of my all-time favorite evening dresses," Miss Roberta continued. "I wanted you to have it."

"Thank you, Miss Roberta," Rose said, kissing her on the cheek. "I'll have to wait for a really special occasion to wear it."

"You can wear it Saturday night," Miss Roberta informed her.

"What?"

"Delores is giving a party."

"You know I don't go to Aunt Dee's rent parties."

"This is not a rent party. It's a kind of get-acquainted party," Miss Roberta said as she busied herself with smoothing out the dress.

"A what kind of party?"

"A get-acquainted party," Miss Roberta said slowly and with emphasis.

"What kind of party is that?"

"It's the kind of party that lets folks get acquainted with each other."

"I can't go."

"And why not?"

"Since when do you like Aunt Dee's parties?"

"It doesn't matter what *I* like, *I'm* not the one invited."

"Well, *I* don't like them either."

"How do you know if you like them or not? You've never been in three years."

"I've got to take care of Millie."

"*I'll* watch Millie."

"Well thanks, but no thanks. I have no intention of meeting and greeting Aunt Dee's friends."

"It won't exactly be Delores's friends that are coming," Miss Roberta said as she stood up and took the cloth off of the basket of catfish.

Rose looked intently at Miss Roberta's face. "Well, if Aunt Dee's friends aren't going to be there, then who is?"

"I've invited a few upstanding young men from my church..." Miss Roberta began.

"Forget it."

"I've already told them about you..."

"Forget it."

Miss Roberta sat back down and faced Rose. "How long is it going to be, child?"

"How long is what going to be?" Rose stood up and walked over to the sink.

"How long are you going to grieve for that young man?" Miss Roberta followed Rose and stood behind her.

"Please, Miss Roberta, don't start." Rose shook her head.

"Baby, you know I'm not one to meddle," Miss Roberta gently put her hand on Rose's back, "but don't you think it's time now for you to start thinking about your future? That child in there needs a father and, whether you believe it or not, you need a husband."

"Miss Roberta, we've gone over this before—," Rose began.

"Wait a minute, I'm not through. Now is the time."

"Now is definitely *not* the time."

"Now *is* the time. Who would know better than me? These eyes of mine don't miss much. I have watched you over the years go from a terrified child to a grown woman. And I've watched you make a life for you and Millie. But I haven't seen you make a life for yourself. You go to work, you pick up Millie from me, and you go home. You go to church on Sundays and you call me"—Miss Roberta thumped her chest emphatically "to go the movies with you. What's going to happen when that child grows up, meets a man, and wants to leave you?"

"I'll let her go!" Rose said loudly. "Because then I can rest and be satisfied that I did my duty. That I raised Mildred's child the best way that I knew how." Her voice began to tremble. "I'll let her go," she whispered.

"Then who will you have to hold on to?" Miss Roberta asked. "Child, a house feels mighty empty and lonely when you're rattling around in it all by yourself. That's all I'm trying to tell you. And you're much too young to start preparing for it now."

Rose shook her head as tears began to fall.

"I'll let her go," she repeated.

"Okay, okay," Miss Roberta said as she patted Rose's back. "We'll give it a little more time."

Eighteen

"SO, HAS OUR O'KANTA MENTIONED the 'M' word yet?" Aunt Rose asked as she deftly snapped the ends off of a green bean and passed it to Mildred.

"Hmmmm?" Mildred snapped the green bean in two and tossed it in the bowl that separated them at the kitchen table.

"The 'M' word. Has he asked you to marry him yet?"

"Marry him! What are you talking about? We've only been on a few dates together. No, he has not asked me to marry him!"

"Well don't act like it's something that's never crossed your mind." Aunt Rose picked up the bowl of beans and carried it over to the sink. "How much longer do you think it will take? One month, two months?" She began to rinse the beans.

"I have no idea," Mildred replied. "I haven't even thought about it, and neither should you."

"Why not? You don't need to date someone for a year before you

157

know he's the one. You know when you know."

"Well, I guess I just don't know right now. You wanna watch the six o'clock news?" Mildred got up and turned on the television set.

"Yeah, let's see how Mr. Williams is doing in the polls." Aunt Rose returned to the table with a few beans in her hand.

"Angry demonstrators disrupted a visit to a northwest side Catholic church service being attended by Raymond Williams and Vice President Shepherd," Harry Phillips reported.

Aunt Rose stopped chewing. Mildred turned and focused on the 12-inch black-and-white television set.

"Williams was invited to attend the Palm Sunday church service, along with Republican candidate, Sherman DeGault," Phillips continued. "Approximately 200 DeGault supporters surrounded the mayoral candidate, shouting and jeering at him. Williams and Vice President Shepherd decided not to attend the service and had to be escorted by police to their cars. Parishioners at St. Jude Catholic Church, located in a predominantly white community, said that they were opposed to Williams' pro-abortion stance, although Father Murillo, pastor of the church, stated that the stands taken by Williams and his opponent, Republican candidate DeGault, were identical."

Mildred and Aunt Rose watched the angry, taunting faces of the crowd as they surrounded Williams and Vice President Shepherd.

"Lord, Lord," Aunt Rose whispered. "Is this what it's all coming to?"

"He's all right, Aunt Rose," Mildred said. "The police came and walked with him back to his car."

"Look how far we've come," murmured Aunt Rose. "Just look at us."

"An apologetic Father Murillo said most of the demonstrators were members of his parish."

"I've been a priest for 37 years," Father Murillo said, shaking his head, "I guess I didn't get the message of love across."

"More on this late-breaking story at ten," Phillips continued.

"I don't understand." Mildred frowned at the television and turned to her aunt.

"What are they so angry about? Did you see the hate on their faces? I just don't understand it."

"That's a hate that's about two hundred years old, baby," Aunt Rose replied. "If you asked most of them, they probably couldn't tell you why they are so angry."

"If we could figure out why they are so angry, maybe we could reach them. O'Kanta said that we need at least 20 percent of the white vote to get Williams elected."

"Not *that* white vote," Aunt Rose said as she opened the refrigerator and took out four white potatoes.

"Well, what white vote then? It's not like we can pick and choose."

Aunt Rose sat down at the kitchen table and began peeling the potatoes.

"Did you see the looks on their faces? O'Kanta can't compete with that type of hate. And that was the hatred standing on the steps of the church. Can you imagine what the hatred would be like away from the church?"

Mildred got up from the table. "I wonder if O'Kanta saw the news?"

"If he didn't, it will be on every channel tonight," Aunt Rose answered.

"He was just talking about organizing a team to go into some of the white neighborhoods. I hope he wasn't thinking about going into that neighborhood."

"Well, if you talk to him, tell him that I said that we should concentrate on our home base here."

"The inner city will not be enough to elect Williams. He's running for mayor of *all* of the people. That's his platform."

"I don't see Tom Carroll coming on the West Side and asking for any votes," Aunt Rose pointed out.

"That's true," Mildred smiled. "I can't see him going into Esther Patillo's house, can you?"

Aunt Rose put the diced potatoes and string beans in a pot of water. She turned to Mildred. "Are we going to go for healthy or fat tonight?"

"Healthy," Mildred answered.

Aunt Rose sighed and took a smoked turkey wing out of the refrigerator. "What are we going to do, just let these ham hocks spoil?" She gazed longingly at the package of ham hocks on the refrigerator shelf before she closed the door.

"How are the preparations coming for Williams' speech at Wisdom Seat?"

"Great. You should see the poster that Charles Gilbert drew. Raymond Williams looks like he's going to jump off the page at you. Charles Gilbert has posters up all over town, and O'Kanta has got it advertised on WGDI. I think it's going to be a big turnout at the church. How is Reverend Giles taking it?"

"Flossie is working on him. That reminds me. I've got to call her and find out what's going on."

"I wonder how many—" Mildred's question was interrupted by the sound of the telephone. She leaned over and picked up the receiver from the kitchen wall unit.

"Hello? Hi, O'Kanta. Yeah, we saw it too. It was a shame."

"It surely was!" Aunt Rose added.

"I know. We were just talking about that."

"What did he say?" Aunt Rose asked loudly.

Mildred waved her off.

"Yeah, that's a good idea. What time?"

"Is there going to be a meeting?" Aunt Rose got up from the table and walked over to Mildred.

"I'll tell her," Mildred continued. "Okay, we'll see you there." Mildred hung up the telephone. "O'Kanta says that he wants to have an emergency meeting tonight. There are about four groups that were planning to go onto the Northwest Side, and he wants to tell them what to do in case they run into something like what happened today."

"That's a good idea." Aunt Rose sat back down at the table. "When is the meeting?"

"Tonight at eight o'clock. He's going to come by and pick us up on his way to the center."

"Well, you go and tell me what happened." Aunt Rose got up and went over to the stove.

"Aren't you coming?"

"No. I'm going to stay here and finish cooking dinner. I'll have it ready when you get back." Aunt Rose lifted the top off of the pot and added seasonings. "Make sure you ask O'Kanta to stop by and get some dinner before he goes home."

Aunt Rose looked at Mildred critically. "I hope you're going to change clothes before he gets here."

Mildred looked down at her faded tee shirt and blue jeans. "Oh, I don't know. This is probably all right."

"Mildred Johnson!" Aunt Rose exclaimed.

"All right, all right." Mildred walked toward her bedroom. She turned around suddenly.

"By the way, Aunt Rose, did you know that O'Kanta doesn't eat pork?"

Aunt Rose put her hands on her hips. "Why are you telling me that?"

"I'm letting you know, just in case those ham hocks happen to find their way into the pot of string beans and potatoes." Mildred gave her aunt her brightest smile and walked into her bedroom.

Aunt Rose sighed and sat back down at the kitchen table.

* * *

The discussion was loud and fierce in the center as Mildred and O'Kanta walked in.

"Hey, O'Kanta! It's about time you got here," a young man that Mildred didn't recognize shouted.

There were about fifty individuals milling around and about the center. Several discussions were being held simultaneously. Most were very loud. Mildred sat down quickly in one of the folding chairs.

"What are we going to do now?" the man who greeted O'Kanta asked.

"Yeah, O'Kanta." Terrance Williams, treasurer of the center, addressed him. "I know we ain't going to let this shit go unanswered."

"That's right," another said. "We got to let them know that this ain't Martin Luther King, Jr. they messing with. We got to send them a message—"

"Oh, this is just great," Dwayne Anderson said. He stood up with his daughter Jamila in his arms. "Then we'll have a nice race war on our hands. The city will be divided and some Bozo that nobody ever heard of will waltz in and become mayor. Do you want that?"

"The first thing we've got to do is calm down." O'Kanta walked up to the front of the assembly. "Nothing happened that we didn't expect to happen. This is Chicago we're dealing with. Did you think that Raymond Williams could go into some of these neighborhoods and be greeted with a handshake and a smile?

"Folks, this is a wake-up call. This is what may happen to any and all of us as we travel throughout this city."

"But what about those of us who won't have a police escort like Williams did?" A young woman asked. "I don't want to get hurt. They already told us to take off our Raymond Williams buttons down at the bookstore where I work. My supervisor said that some of the customers were complaining."

"What are we supposed to do? Turn the other cheek? I say we go over to Bridgeport packing. I know where we can get about five 38s real cheap," another said.

"And I know where we can get five caskets real cheap," Dwayne answered. "Do you really think that they are going to listen to what we have to say about Raymond Williams with a gun sticking out of our pocket?"

"Please," O'Kanta broke in. "The first order of business is for us to all calm down. This should have been expected by all of us. This is serious. We are attempting to change a way of life for some people who refuse to entertain the thought of Chicago having a black mayor. We are in the process of making history. These people feel the need to protect a way of life, an institution that they have based their very existence on. We are going to change that. I ask that each of you calm down and listen to me. Even if we don't agree with what happened tonight, we must respect each and every one of those people. We are planning to go into their neighborhoods, their homes, their places of business, and their places of worship. We will show them the utmost respect and tolerance. We must be an example to any hotheads that are out there just waiting for any form of retaliation."

"That's right, brother, that's right," someone interjected.

"I heard someone say that this ain't or we ain't no Martin Luther King. Well, I say that we should strive to be. Whoever said that, I have a book of King's called *The Law of Civil Disobedience* that I would love to share with him.

"In the Gospel of Matthew, Jesus teaches his disciples how to handle those people who were not responsive to their message. Jesus says, 'As you enter his home, bless it. If the home is deserving, your blessing will descend on it. If it is not, your blessing will return to you. If anyone does not receive you or listen to what you have to say, leave that house or town, and once outside it shake its dust from your feet.'"

"That's right, that's what the Bible says," a woman agreed.

Mildred's heart swelled with pride.

"If anyone needs a direction or focus, let this be it. We will travel in teams or groups. We will look out for each other and protect each other. Now, let's get down to business. This is how we will set up our groups."

As O'Kanta began to discuss planning strategies, Mildred looked around her and marveled at his ability to settle an unruly crowd. Even Terrance Williams was paying attention. She wondered if Aunt Rose had believed her when she told her that she never thought about her and O'Kanta getting married. She doubted it. Her aunt knew her far too well. Lately it seemed that that was all she was able to think about — her and Aunt Rose's future with O'Kanta. She wondered if O'Kanta ever thought about it. Maybe he'd already decided to remain a bachelor.

"Don't no man want to take care of a woman and her mama," her co-worker Shannon pointed out. "It's hard enough for a man and a woman to make it. You go bringing in mama, and you just askin' for trouble."

I guess we could just keep dating, Mildred supposed. Some people dated for years and years without ever getting married.

"How are you doing tonight?" Nikki Anderson's voice broke into Mildred's thoughts.

"Is 'Kanta still yo' boyfriend?" Jamila asked.

"Jamila!" Nikki exclaimed. She sat down next to Mildred.

"I'm glad to see you here tonight. How is your aunt?"

"Fine," Mildred answered.

"It looks like O'Kanta was able to calm some of the folks down. Dwayne and I couldn't believe what we were seeing on TV."

"Neither could we."

"Are you and your aunt planning on going to the North Side with any of the groups?"

"I'm not sure. We were thinking about it."

"Good. I want to be with the group that you're with. So let me know when and where."

Mildred nodded and pulled Jamila's fingers out of her mouth.

Jamila's grin revealed several missing teeth.

"Well, I've got to get this young lady home and put to bed," Nikki said. "Be sure to let me know which group you're with." She picked up Jamila and headed toward the front of the group where Dwayne stood talking with several people.

Mildred leaned back against a table and put her hands in her pockets. Aaron, the owner of the liquor store, turned the heat off when the store was closed. The three space heaters scattered around the center were no match for January's hawk in Chicago.

Mildred listened to the group discussions and watched the faces of the people. The incident at St. Jude's brought the election of Raymond Williams into a clear picture of black versus white. She and Aunt Rose had planned on going to the Northwest Side and pass out fliers and information the next weekend. Now, she wasn't so sure.

Aunt Rose would never put her safety ahead of her "mission," so it was up to Mildred. She couldn't insist upon O'Kanta coming along with them every time, but then again...

"Hey, Love, what are you sitting here frowning about?"

O'Kanta stood in front of Mildred and lightly touched her face. "I have a surprise for you."

"What is it?" Mildred asked as she pulled her wool cap closer to her head.

"It wouldn't be a surprise if I told you now, would it?" O'Kanta opened the exit door to Ray's Liquors and gave Mildred his arm.

"It is freezing out here!" Mildred exclaimed.

"Yep, it is," O'Kanta answered. "Every year I try to decide which month is colder, January or February, and every year I decide that it's got to be a tie."

"Where are you going?" he asked as Mildred turned down Jackson Boulevard.

"To the El."

"Why are you going to the El?" he asked.

Mildred looked at him as one would look at a child. "To ride it," she answered.

"But why would you ride the El when a brother got a car?" O'Kanta answered.

"O'Kanta, you got a car?" Mildred smiled in amazement. "Where is it? What kind of car is it? Why didn't you pick me up? What year is it? What color?"

"Hold on, hold on!" O'Kanta laughed and grabbed both of her hands. "Let's not get too excited. It's not a Towncar or a Seville. "I didn't pick you up because Herbert hadn't finished detailing it. He told me that he'd be finished tonight and would drop it off at the center for me."

"I don't care what it is," Mildred answered. "A car is a car. Where is it?"

O'Kanta took her hand and pulled her back in front of the liquor store.

Parked in front of Ray's Liquors was a very large, very shiny, dark blue automobile.

"Is this it?" Mildred asked.

"Uh huh."

"What kind is it?"

"It is a 1976 Oldsmobile 88 sedan. This is a classic American car. This baby's got a V8 engine, bench seats, and only 42,000 miles," O'Kanta recited proudly.

"Wow," Mildred whispered as she walked around the car.

"Allow me." O'Kanta walked around to the passenger's side and opened the door.

Mildred sunk back against the seat and closed her eyes.

"Wait until Aunt Rose sees this."

O'Kanta slid behind the wheel. "Next stop, 3216 West Jackson!"

Nineteen

"ARE YOU READY YET?" Mildred stuck her head inside Aunt Rose's bedroom door.

"No, I'm not!" Aunt Rose snapped. "I'm just too nervous. I can't decide what to wear, and my hat don't look right." She readjusted her black pillbox and frowned at her reflection in the mirror.

"I thought we decided on the blue dress. What happened?" Mildred picked up the dress from the floor, shook it, and lay it on the bed.

Aunt Rose stared at the blue dress and fingered the sequins on the front. "I can't wear this old thing. This is the first time that I'm going to see Mr. Raymond Williams. My dress has got to be special."

"Did I tell you that Lucinda went out and bought herself a new dress, after telling me that she wouldn't? She looked me right in the eye and said she was goin' to wear her brown dress with her beige hat. I should have known better."

Mildred sat on the bed and smiled.

"Don't just sit there," Aunt Rose said, "help me find something. I refuse to wear my blue dress and let Lucinda think that she won. She'll be expecting that. I'm goin' to let her know that I've got more than *one* good dress."

Mildred opened her aunt's closet and looked inside.

"What about this?" She pulled out a dark-green dress with a gold braid on the shoulder. "You could wear this with your gold hat."

Aunt Rose looked over her shoulder. "Uh-uh. I wore that for the Christmas service. She's already seen it."

"What about the red dress that I bought you last year? I haven't seen you in that yet..."

"I'm saving it, baby; I'm saving it. You know perfectly well that I can't walk up in Wisdom Seat in red. Boy, am I going to fix that Lucinda. Trying to be slick is what she's doing..."

"If you keep combing your hair, you're going to comb out every curl that I put in," Mildred said.

Aunt Rose put the comb down and walked over to the edge of the bed.

"You think I'm being silly don't you?" She folded her hands together and sat down on the bed. "You'd think I was going to be the one up there speaking, the way I'm acting."

Mildred went over and put her arms around her aunt. "You should be a little nervous and excited. You initiated the entire event. Raymond Williams wouldn't be coming to Wisdom Seat if it wasn't for you. You suggested—no—I think you *told* Reverend Giles that Raymond Williams was going to speak. We have been handing out fliers, knocking on doors, and collecting money from every restaurant from Jimmy's Chicken Shack to Brothers' Tacos. Charles Gilbert has been making posters and has got his entire art class involved. Everybody who's anybody is goin' to be there. You've been announcing it in church for the past three months, and I think that Ms. Lucinda is jealous of all of the attention that you've been getting. That's why she lied to you about the dress."

"Don't say 'lie,' baby. That's not ladylike," Aunt Rose interrupted.

Mildred began to rub her aunt's shoulders.

"Okay, she didn't tell you the entire truth. That's why you've got to step in there looking glamorous and confident. You need to go right up to her and say, 'Lucinda', Mildred mimicked her aunt's voice, 'how nice to see you.'"

"Yes, yes," Aunt Rose agreed. "Rub just a little more... right there, but what dress, baby? What dress?"

Mildred whispered, "The red!"

"I can't..." Aunt Rose started.

"The red dress with your new black hat and black pumps," Mildred continued. "Now you know you can wear that dress. This is not a church service, it is a fundraiser for Raymond Williams."

"But—"

"What other dress is going to show Ms. Lucinda up and let everybody else know how special this event is to you? You put it on and be sure to wear some of my red lipstick."

"I just don't think—"

"O'Kanta will be here any minute, and it's already pressed."

"Well."

Aunt Rose got up, walked to the closet, and pulled out the dress. She held it in front of her and turned back to her niece. "Are you sure, baby?"

"I'm sure," Mildred got up and headed for the door.

"And you know what else?" She turned back to face her aunt. "As many red ties as Mr. Raymond Williams wears, I think red is one of his favorite colors."

"Go and get me the scissors to cut these tags off," Aunt Rose answered.

* * *

"My." O'Kanta looked from Mildred to Aunt Rose. "My," he repeated.

"Don't we look grand?" Aunt Rose asked. She turned around slowly in front of O'Kanta.

"My baby picked this out for me," she continued. "Millie says that red is one of Raymond Williams' favorite colors."

169

"As many red ties as he wears, I think she may be right," O'Kanta agreed.

"Look at Millie," Aunt Rose gestured. "Turn around, baby."

"I don't think so," Mildred replied. She tugged on her skirt and wondered if she'd been too hasty in agreeing to the gold suit that Aunt Rose and the sales lady assured her was "definitely her."

The gold suit shimmered in the afternoon sun. It was a silk, double-breasted, tailored suit with a tiny split in the back.

The saleslady assured Mildred that she did not need to wear a blouse under it, just a frilly camisole.

Mildred and her aunt exchanged looks when she made the statement.

"Mildred," O'Kanta said, "you look beautiful."

Aunt Rose beamed.

"I don't know if I can handle escorting two gorgeous women to this event. I am, after all, merely a humble servant."

Mildred looked appreciatively at O'Kanta's two-piece white dashiki outfit. "You look very nice yourself."

"He doesn't look nice," Aunt Rose interrupted. "He looks handsome."

"Yes," Mildred agreed.

"You think so?" O'Kanta grinned and slowly imitated Aunt Rose's pirouette. "I had to get a new suit for this special occasion."

A knock sounded at the door.

"Are you expecting someone?" Aunt Rose asked Mildred.

Mildred shook her head.

"Oh, that's probably Chappie." O'Kanta walked toward the door. "I invited him to join us." He turned around suddenly. "You don't mind do you?" He smiled at Aunt Rose. "I think Old Chappie is kind of sweet on you."

Aunt Rose stared straight ahead.

"No," Mildred answered for her. "We don't mind. It will be nice to have him here. Maybe he'll change his mind after hearing Raymond Williams speak."

As O'Kanta ushered Chappie in, Mildred leaned over to her aunt and whispered, "Does this mean we're on a double date?"

* * *

Mildred entered Wisdom Seat Baptist Church on the arm of O'Kanta and tried not to look at the eyes that focused on their entrance. Aunt Rose walked on the other side of her, leaving Chapman Jackson to bring up the rear.

"I see Miss Lucinda checking you out," Mildred whispered to her aunt.

Aunt Rose smiled as she looked from aisle to aisle. "How you doing, Miss Evans?"

"Nice to see you, Patricia. My, that child has grown."

"Glad you could make it, Mrs. Jeffrey."

She stopped at Miss Lucinda's pew.

"Lucinda," she exclaimed, "don't you look nice. Is that a new dress?" Miss Lucinda turned to Aunt Rose.

"Why, hello, Rose. I wasn't sure who it was speaking to me. All I could see was red. I knew that couldn't be *you* coming to church in a red dress."

"Lucinda, Lucinda," Rose smiled. "You've got to get in step with the times. This is the 80's, after all. My baby bought me this dress for a special occasion, and I can't think of an occasion more special than this one. After all, red is one of Mr. Williams' favorite colors."

"And one of mine."

Aunt Rose turned around to face the smile of Chapman Jackson.

"My name is Chapman Jackson." He extended his hand to Miss Lucinda.

"Oh, hello. Are you a friend of Rose's?" she inquired. She nudged Mrs. Patillo, who had also turned around.

"Of course," Chappie answered.

"Oh, I don't recall Sister Rose ever mentioning your name... Rose?" Miss Lucinda looked at Rose.

171

"Where did you say you were from?" Mrs. Patillo asked.

"Rose and I are both from Tennessee," Chappie answered.

He took Rose's arm and ushered her into the pew in front of Miss Lucinda and Mrs. Patillo.

"Good evening, Miss Lucinda, Mrs. Patillo." Mildred smiled and entered the pew next to Aunt Rose.

"Ladies," O'Kanta nodded as he sat down next to Mildred.

"Well," Mildred heard Miss Lucinda mutter.

"Uh-huh," Mrs. Patillo answered.

Mildred squeezed her aunt's hand. "How we doing?"

Aunt Rose squeezed back.

"This is a large church," O'Kanta whispered. "How many people does it hold?"

"About a thousand. When was the last time you were in church?"

"At my mom's funeral."

"O'Kanta! You never told me..."

"Ssssh. Looks like we're ready to start."

Reverend Giles strode up to the pulpit. "Good evening ladies and gentlemen," he began. "I would like to welcome all of you to Wisdom Seat Missionary Baptist Church. I greet you in the only way that I know, with the love of Jesus in my heart. Our motto here at Wisdom Seat is, '*You're never a stranger in the house of the Lord.*' For those of you who are visiting us for the first time, all we can say is that we hope to see you again. To Wisdom Seat members, thank you for coming back out this way. We had a powerful sermon here this morning. And I'm not saying it was powerful because I brought the message." He paused and laughed.

A few titters broke out.

"Let's everybody look to your right and say, 'Welcome,' 'how you doin',' 'glad to see you.' Y'all don't have to stay in your seat. Get up and say hello to somebody!"

The organist started to play.

"Mildred!" Catherine Jones slowly walked up the aisle and greeted Mildred like a long-lost friend. "Who is this young man that you brought this evening?" Catherine smiled provocatively and extended her hand to O'Kanta.

"Excuse me, excuse me," Mother Evelyn Washington squeezed past Catherine.

"Rose Johnson, is this gentleman with you?" Mother Washington beamed at Chapman Jackson.

"Uh, Mr. Jackson, may I—" Rose began.

"I'm Mother Evelyn Washington. Just call me Ev. Ever since my husband passed in 1976, God rest his soul—"

"Evelyn Washington, the rest of us would like to welcome Rose's guest too!"

Mildred looked up and saw several members of the Mothers' Board lined up to meet Chapman Jackson.

"Show our visitors some of that Wisdom Seat love," Reverend Giles continued.

"Sister Rose! Sister Rose!" Mother Hattie Clark called as her granddaughter Jessica wheeled her up the aisle.

Mother Clark tried to speed up Jessica's efforts by pushing the wheelchair's wheels faster with her hands.

"My goodness," Mildred whispered. "I can't believe this. We've never been so popular."

"Well, it's obvious that you have never been escorted by two handsome gents such as Chappie and myself," O'Kanta replied. "Right Chap?" O' Kanta looked over at Chapman Jackson, who was trying to say hello to three members of Wisdom Seat's Mothers' Board.

Mildred was also aware that several women were trying to catch O'Kanta's eye.

"Good evening, ladies," Mother Flossie Giles broke in. "You ladies will have to excuse me for interrupting." She firmly pulled Mother Hattie's wheelchair out of the aisle.

"Since Sister Rose first brought the idea of inviting Raymond Williams to Wisdom Seat, she, Mildred, and their guests will sit up front with me and the Pastor."

"Oh, what an honor!" Rose exclaimed. "Mr. Jackson, I would like you to meet the First Lady of Wisdom Seat M.B. Church, Mother Flossie Giles."

"Millie, introduce O'Kanta to Mother Giles."

O'Kanta extended his hand. "I'm glad to be here. You have a beautiful church."

"Why, thank you," Flossie replied. "Where is your church home?"

"Well, I'm kind of in-between churches right now," O'Kanta stammered. "I haven't found a church home yet, but I'm still looking."

"Well, don't look too long. You need to join with a body of believers to pray with, laugh with, and grieve with."

"Yes, Ma'am."

Flossie led them to a pew festooned with a large red bow.

"Thank you," Rose whispered as she slid in.

"Do we have a lot to talk about," Flossie whispered back. She nodded to Mildred. "Mildred, did you forget that Charles Gilbert was coming?"

* * *

Raymond Williams looked out at the sea of faces.

Mildred glanced around too. Although the crowd was mostly made up of African Americans, there was a sizeable number of Hispanics. Several white college students from Charles Gilbert's art class were also in attendance. Never had Wisdom Seat been packed so tightly before. The Brotherhood kept bringing folding chairs from the fellowship hall. The chairs were filled as soon as they were set out.

Everyone was waiting.

"I'm nervous," Mildred whispered to O'Kanta.

O'Kanta squeezed her hand. "Everything'll be fine."

"How do you think the people will receive him?"

"Good evening," Raymond Williams addressed the crowd.

"Good evening," the throng responded.

"I want to thank you all for coming out tonight. I'd like to thank Reverend Giles for inviting me. Wisdom Seat Baptist Church. I like the name of your church. As I look out among you, I see faces of every color. Chicago is reflected in you. I bring you the same message that I take to the West Side, the South Side, the North Side, and the suburbs. It's no different. I don't speak any different here than I do anywhere else because I love *all* of Chicago. I want to be mayor of all of Chicago.

"I have a problem when I go to a police headquarters in a city where the black population in Chicago is 36 percent, and the Hispanic population is 25 percent, and I don't see it reflected in the ranks of the police department!

"I have a problem when I go to the Chicago School Board and see the board made up of 99.9 percent whites and we have an attendance of 89 percent black children."

The crowd applauded.

"My fellow candidates don't like to talk about race. How can we solve the problem if we don't talk about it? We're not living in an all-white or all-black society. We're living in a city that boasts the rich cultural heritage of Hispanics, Greeks, African Americans, Irish, Polish, and Vietnamese. America is no longer a melting pot. It is now a tossed salad. How can we ignore the gifts that each of these cultures bring to the table?

"We are all brothers and sisters in a quest for greatness. Our creativity and energy are unmatched by any city anywhere in the world.

"But there is a fine, new spirit that seems to be taking root. I call it the spirit of renewal. It's like the spring coming here after a long winter. It is the spirit of change. The dictionary defines change as: 'To cause to be different, to alter, to transform. To lay aside, abandon. To go from one phase to another...' I submit to you that when a people are ready to 'transform' or to 'move from one phase to another' that they got to have faith. The Bible says "Faith is the substance of things hoped for and the evidence of things not seen...'"

"That's what it says!" Reverend Giles shouted.

"I believe that we black folk know a little something about that kind of faith. It was faith that sustained African Americans who were enslaved in these United States. They held onto the faith that one day their children would be free. This is the same faith that carried Jews trapped in the prisons of Auschwitz. It is faith that makes scores of Vietnamese risk their lives coming to America in leaky boats—home of the free.

"It is..." He put his hand to his ear and focused on the crowd.

"Faith!" the crowd repeated.

"...that brings scores of Mexican Americans across the borders each year to the promise of a better life," he exhorted the crowd.

"It is..."

"Faith," the crowd repeated.

"...that brings you here to lay claim to the change that Chicago will undergo this election year! Jesus says if you have the faith the size of a mustard seed, you can say to a mountain, 'move!' And it will be done. You don't have to have a lot of faith, just a little."

"That's right!" Aunt Rose shouted.

"I take that to mean that you don't have to have a lot of people with faith—just a few. We're not going to convince all of Chicago to unite with us to move this city forward. All we need is a few!"

"Preach, brother!" Dwayne Anderson shouted.

"We don't need the prayers of everybody in Chicago—just a few. The prayers of a righteous man prevaileth much..."

"Pray, servant!"

"Hear me good. Change is going to come. Change will come whether I'm ready for it"—he touched his chest— "or whether you"—he pointed to the congregation—"are ready for it. Change is going to come... "Mordecai told Esther that if she remained silent at this time, deliverance would come from another place, but who knows whether you have come for such a time as this?"

"Yes," Mildred whispered. "For such a time as this," she repeated.

"I want to help bring about a change in this government, but I can't do it without you. I want you to help me bring about a change in this city that'll have the rest of the country asking, 'How did they do it'?

"Elect me your mayor and give me your support. Don't quit after I'm elected. Give me your ideas. Let us govern this city together. Chicago can be an example of how government should be run. Let the cities of New York and Washington, D.C. ask, 'How did they do it?' Become more involved in your community. Invest your time and talent in *your* neighborhood. I don't care if it's in public housing or on the Gold Coast. It's your neighborhood! Do you know who your alderman is? Do you know where your city councilman lives? Who's representing you in Washington?"

Wisdom Seat rose to its feet.

"Start a letter-writing campaign. Hold those people who represent you accountable to your community. Hold me accountable as mayor. Make the people in Congress and the House of Representatives ask, 'How did they do it'?

"And do you know what we'll say?" He paused. "We had the faith!"

He stared out at the congregation.

"Are you one of the faithful few?"

"Yes!" Wisdom screamed.

"My brothers and sisters, I cannot be successful without you. But with you, I can't fail."

He stretched out his hands, "Will you work with me?"

Wisdom Seat stood on its feet and clapped and screamed, "Yes!"

Reverend Giles rushed to the pulpit and grabbed Raymond Williams' hand. "Yes. Work with us!" he shouted.

"Work with us!" he repeated.

Mildred looked over at Aunt Rose, who was wiping her eyes while Chapman Jackson softly patted her shoulder.

She turned to O'Kanta. "This is it!"

"No, love." O'Kanta threw his arm around her. "*This* has just only begun."

Twenty

CHICAGO, ILLINOIS, 1975

AUNT ROSE'S FIFTIETH BIRTHDAY fell on a Sunday. It was Women's Day at Wisdom Seat. Mildred pretended that she didn't feel well, and begged off going to church. Aunt Rose was on the Women's Day committee. Reverend Estelle Hereford, Pastor of Greater Love Missionary Baptist Church, was the guest speaker, and she was bringing the renowned Greater Love Choir with her. The Women's Day program immediately followed morning worship service.

"You go on to church and stay for the second program," Mildred suggested. Then come home, and I'll take you to dinner. I'm going to take some aspirin and rest here. I'll be ready when you get back."

"Are you sure you don't want me to stay here with you?" Aunt Rose felt Mildred's forehead. "I don't have to go to church, or I could come back after morning service."

"No," Mildred said firmly. "You're on the Women's Day committee. You need to stay to make sure that everything goes smoothly. I'll be right here when you come back."

"All right."

Aunt Rose adjusted her hat more firmly on her head. "I sure don't like to leave my baby here alone. I'll go and get the thermometer and you can—"

"I don't *need* the thermometer. I don't have a temperature. I just need to lie down. I'm eighteen now, remember?" Mildred reminded her. "I'll be fine."

Aunt Rose left the house, giving Mildred instructions to take her temperature and drink hot tea.

Mildred watched her aunt wait at the bus stop from the window. After she had boarded the bus, Mildred hurriedly threw her clothes on and left for the store. She had been planning her aunt's fiftieth birthday dinner for weeks. The Women's Day program would give her just enough time to have everything ready when she came home from church.

* * *

She was putting the finishing touches on the dining room table when she heard her aunt coming up the stairs. She opened the door and greeted her aunt.

"How are you feeling, baby?"

Aunt Rose carefully checked her niece's face. "I wanted to call you after the first service, but we had to get everything done for the second service and—"

"I'm feeling fine. Now, I want you to close your eyes and come with me." Mildred took her aunt by the hand.

"You want me to do what? Baby, I am tired and hungry. I just want to set this body down and get me a cold jar of water..."

Aunt Rose turned to go into the kitchen.

"Aunt Rose," Mildred repeated. "Close your eyes and come with me."

"But—"

179

"Okay. Since you won't follow my instructions, I guess I'll just have to cover your eyes." Mildred put her hands over her aunt's eyes and led her toward the dining room.

"Now look," she instructed.

The dining room table was set with Aunt Rose's best china, placed on a white-lace tablecloth. A platter of sliced ham covered with pineapple slices was placed off center. Next to it was a roasted hen. Collard greens, fried corn, candied sweet potatoes, macaroni and cheese, dressing, and potato salad filled up the rest of the space. In the center of the table were a pecan pie and a vase of red roses. Propped against the vase was a tarnished silver-framed picture of a young Aunt Rose standing arm-in-arm with another woman who smiled broadly at the camera.

Aunt Rose's gaze was locked on the table.

"This is a Crayton, Tennessee birthday dinner." Mildred said. " I fixed all of the foods that you were used to having in Crayton. What do you think?" She hugged her aunt. "Happy Birthday!"

Mildred felt Aunt Rose's knees buckle. "Whoa, let me get you into a chair."

"I need some ice water," Aunt Rose said in a strange voice.

"I thought you'd be surprised, but I didn't think you'd faint..."

"Mercy, Jesus," her Aunt Rose whispered. "Lord, have mercy. I need some water," she repeated.

Mildred looked at her aunt's face and saw tears coursing down her cheeks.

She ran into the kitchen and grabbed a jar from the dish rack and filled it with ice. She quickly ran tap water over the ice and hurried back into the dining room.

Aunt Rose was leaning on the dining room table, clutching a handful of tablecloth.

"Help me to the bathroom," she whispered.

Aunt Rose leaned heavily on Mildred's arm as the two walked down the hall.

Mildred gently lifted her hat off as Aunt Rose leaned over the toilet.

She caressed Aunt Rose's back as she splashed cold water on her face.

"What's the matter? Did I do something wrong, Aunt Rose?" Mildred's voice trembled.

Aunt Rose patted her niece's hand and held it.

Slowly the two walked back into the dining room.

Aunt Rose stared intently at the picture on the table.

Mildred tried to hand her the glass of water, but she seemed not to notice Mildred or the water. She fingered the lace on the tablecloth. "Where did you find this?" she asked softly.

"I found it in the box with the picture. I wanted to do something special for your fiftieth birthday so I looked in the box that was in your closet. I hoped I would find something in there that would remind you of Crayton, but all I found were two pictures and this lace tablecloth. I thought you said that you didn't have a good tablecloth," Mildred continued. "We could have used it when Reverend Giles came over. This one had stains on it, so I had it cleaned. Most of them came out. Why do you keep it in a box, Aunt Rose? It almost looks as if someone made it."

Aunt Rose was uncharacteristically silent as she sipped the ice water and stared at the tablecloth.

After draining the glass, she sat it down. She reached down and took her black pumps off and staggered into the living room.

"I didn't mean to upset you, Aunt Rose," Mildred said, realizing that she had done something wrong. "I shouldn't have looked in the box without your permission."

"That's okay, baby. I was just a little shocked, that's all. I haven't seen that tablecloth in almost 20 years. I wasn't ready to see it. It just hit me on an empty stomach."

Aunt Rose sat in her rocking chair and began to hum.

"I don't think having an empty stomach would make you cry."

Aunt Rose continued to rock and to softly sing.

Some glad morning, when this life is over, I'll fly away.
To a home on God's celestial shore, I'll fly away.
I'll fly away oh glory, I'll fly away. When I die,
Hallelujah, by and by, I'll fly away.

"That was your mother's favorite song. Did I ever tell you that?"

She looked out of the window, but her eyes seemed to be focused on something else. "When Greater Love sang that song today, I closed my eyes and I was back in Sweet Water Baptist Church listening to Millie sing that song."

"God is so good. He was lettin' me know then, while the choir was singing that song, that today was the day. He was preparing me."

She wiped her eyes with the backs of her hands. "Thank you, Master," she whispered.

"Today is what day? Your birthday?"

Aunt Rose turned and regarded Mildred. "No, baby. Today is *your* day. "Go into that box and bring me the other picture. I want to talk to you."

When Mildred returned with the photograph, she found her aunt still humming and rocking. She looked at the photograph in her hand. It was a small, slightly blurred, black-and-white picture of a man and a woman. They stood in front of a small wooden house with the strangest looking roof that Mildred had ever seen. The roof seemed to hang over each side of the house.

The man had on a pair of overalls and a straw hat. He had a stern, serious expression on his face. The woman beside him was wearing a light-colored, long-sleeved blouse and a full, dark skirt. Her hair was loose and curled. She leaned against the man, but unlike him, she was smiling. Her smile looked as if she was carrying a secret.

Mildred went back to the dining room table and retrieved the other photograph. Both pictures seemed to have been taken the same day.

The woman had on the same outfit, but was now standing next to Aunt Rose, their arms intertwined. Aunt Rose had on a long dress with a round collar. Her hair was put up in a bun. Both women were standing in front of the same, wooden house. This time the woman was grinning and Aunt Rose was smiling.

Mildred brought both pictures to her aunt.

"Aunt Rose, whose house is this? Was this your house?" she asked. She handed the pictures to her aunt and sat down on the floor in front of the rocking chair.

Aunt Rose took the pictures. "No, baby. That wasn't my house." She studied the pictures and smiled. "This was your parents' house."

"My parents?"

Mildred snatched the pictures back.

"My parents? You said that my parents died in a fire..."

"They did, child, they did. This picture was taken before the fire."

"But who are these people? Why are they standing in front of my parents' house?"

Aunt Rose reached down and tenderly placed her hand on Mildred's cheek. She cupped her face and turned it so that Mildred looked directly at her. "Those are your parents. That's Mildred and L.C. Walker. Your parents," she repeated.

"My parents?"

Mildred stared at the photograph incredulously. Her eyes filled with tears.

"How could you have had pictures of my parents and never have told me?" She turned to her aunt. She looked back at the pictures. "These are my parents? My mother and father? Mine?"

She tried to focus on the photograph in front of her, but her teary eyes wouldn't let her.

"I can't believe you had these pictures and never told me."

"Baby, I couldn't show you the pictures without telling you the whole story. You weren't near ready to hear it..."

Aunt Rose closed her eyes and massaged her temples. "And I wasn't ready to reach back and get it," she whispered.

Mildred looked from one picture to the other. Her mother and father. "Mother," she whispered. The words sounded strange on her tongue. "Mama." Mama sounded better.

She looked into the slightly blurred face. This was her mother. Hers. She studied the eyes, ears, nose, and smile. The eyes were tilted at the corners. She had a wonderful smile. She was beautiful. She was the most beautiful woman that Mildred had ever seen.

She stared at the man—her father. He was tall. She couldn't tell much about his face because his hat cast a shadow over his features. His eyes were deep set. He seemed to have a slight cleft in his chin. Aunt Rose had always told Mildred that she had a slight cleft in her chin just like her father.

Mildred put her head on her aunt's knee and began to cry.

"It's okay, baby." Her aunt patted her hair. "It's okay." She continued to sing.

Just a few more weary days and then, I'll fly away.

Mildred clung to her aunt's knee and grieved for the parents she never knew.

To a land where joy shall never end, I'll fly away.

"Baby, go and wash your face. I'll tell you more when you come back."

Twenty-One

MILDRED SAT ON THE FLOOR at Aunt Rose's knee as she began the story.

"So my name was *Rosemary Mildred Walker?*" she asked. "My mother named me after you?"

"Millie and I were best friends for as long as I can remember. I introduced her to your father."

"You changed my name?"

"I didn't really *change* it. I just switched it around to Mildred Rosemary Walker. Mildred's name deserved to be first."

"What was my father like?"

"He was a proud man. L.C. believed that black people were put here to do more than sharecrop. He wanted a better life, not just for him, but for you and your children. He tried to make a difference..." her voiced trailed off.

Mildred looked at her father's picture again.

"Tell me about the fire," she said.

185

"Lord," Aunt Rose closed her eyes and rocked. "Lord, Lord," she whispered.

"You don't have to tell it now." Mildred stood up and kissed her aunt.

"No, now is the time. I knew this day was coming. You're 18 now and you have a right to know." Aunt Rose stood up and slowly paced the floor with her hands clasped together. Her lips moved softly.

Mildred couldn't hear the words.

Mildred got up, took her aunt's hand, and led her to the sofa. She put her arms around Aunt Rose's shoulder. "You can talk about it, Aunt Rose. It's just you and me. I love you."

Aunt Rose leaned into Mildred's shoulder and began.

She spoke of the beauty of Tennessee. The view from her front porch of magnolia trees in bloom. The sweet smell of the honeysuckle bushes outside her bedroom window. The heady perfume of roses and mint. The flowers, the smells, the trees, the people.

"Millie, it's a special feeling walking on the ground that your ancestors walked upon. Rocking on your front porch at night and looking at the stars.

"I had never known anybody like Millie. She didn't bow down to anyone. She did washing for white folks. She wasn't afraid to look them right in their eyes. She made it seem like *they* were doing her a favor by bringing their washing to her—not the other way around. They never tried to cheat her or correct her when she told them how much she charged. I think they kind of respected her.

"L.C. was something else. All the women wanted him. He was quiet, but he was proud. He carried himself like a king. No one wanted to mess with him. He was like a leader in the church and in our crowd. People came to him all the time for advice and stuff. They just seemed to like to be around him...

"Being around the two of them made me feel more alive than I've ever felt in my life."

"Then I met Caleb Hawkins and everything stood still. I can still remember the first time that I saw him. I was working as a cook, and he came in and asked for a cup of coffee. Alice worked the front counter and she was out. So I wiped my face, straightened my apron, and brewed him a fresh pot.

"While the coffee was brewing, I watched him. My hand was shaking so bad when I brought him that cup. I knew he could see it. I spilled some of it on him. But he didn't say a word. He just took that cup of coffee from me and said, 'Thank you, Miss.' When he looked at me and said 'Thank you, Miss,' I knew that he was the one.

"I went into the back and watched him drink that cup of coffee, and I fell in love with him right then and there.

"He and L.C. became friends and they would get together and talk about voting and colored rights, and stuff like that.

"That kind of talk always frightened me. We would hear talk of blacks being killed or lynched for less than that. Baby, I was such a coward. I didn't want to vote. I just wanted Caleb. I was a foolish young woman who couldn't see past my own wants."

"You must have really loved him," Mildred said.

"That night, after the celebration party, Millie and I followed L.C. and Caleb up to the courthouse."

Aunt Rose described the wreckage that she and Mildred found inside.

"You mean you and my mother hid inside the courthouse while the police walked around?"

"L.C. and Caleb were the brave ones. They were inside the courthouse when the sheriff and his deputy came in. By the time Millie and I got there, the sheriff was leaving."

"I can't believe you and my mother followed them up there in the middle of the night. Weren't you afraid?"

"Yes, I was," Aunt Rose said. "But your mother had enough courage for the both of us. Her mind was set on going up there to make sure that L.C. was okay. Your mother loved L.C., baby. She would do anything for him. L.C. tried to hide it, but everybody knew that he adored Millie.

"Walking back to Sweet Water from the courthouse was the first time that Caleb and I really had the chance to talk about the future. I told him that I loved him," she whispered. "I'm so glad that I got the chance to tell him that." Aunt Rose closed her eyes.

Mildred was silent. But her mind was racing. She was anxious and numb at the same time. She wanted to hear more, but she was afraid. She didn't want to hear the ending. If Aunt Rose stopped now, her mother and father would still be alive. She wanted them to stay that way.

"Do you want to stop now?" she asked.

"No, baby, you need to know everything. This is your history.

"When we got to the church, Lew was talking loud. I hated him. There was a lot of confusion. Caleb kept telling me to run. He said that he would catch up with me. I started to run."

Aunt Rose stood up.

"I was running and smiling. I was thinking about Caleb. I thanked God for him. I was thinking about our wedding. I was smiling," she repeated.

"Then I heard a loud boom, and I stopped and turned around. I looked back and I couldn't see anything, but I could smell something. I backtracked a few steps, trying to figure out what the noise was and what was that awful smell..."

Standing in the middle of the floor, Aunt Rose's eyes were closed, but her fists were moving.

Mildred stared at her through tears in her eyes. Her aunt was running back to Caleb.

"The smell got stronger. It was in my eyes and in my mouth. My eyes began to burn and my mouth had a bitter taste. I felt the smoke covering me as I ran back to the church. Then I saw the flames. They were shooting up into the sky, and smoke was pouring out of the sides of the church, through the broken windows, and from the roof. It even looked like smoke was coming from underneath the church. The ground felt hot. I tried to get close, but it was too hot. Every breath I took felt hot. My eyes were burning, and I couldn't see. All I could do was smell that awful smell.

"Fire!" her aunt screamed.

"Fire!" she screamed again.

"I ran and left them behind. They should have run and left me behind. I wasn't trying to help anybody vote. I wasn't trying to get people registered. I just wanted Caleb!"

Mildred closed her eyes and she could see the fire. Instinctively, she knew what the awful smell was. It was the smell of burning flesh. The smell of death. She started to tremble uncontrollably. Her parents were gone. They had left her. She wrapped her arms around her body and began to rock back and forth, like a child.

"Fire!" Aunt Rose kept screaming.

Mildred put her hands over her ears to shut out the words.

"No!" she whispered.

"Fire..." Aunt Rose moaned.

Mildred felt her stomach turn. Her throat began to burn from the bile that found its way upward. She got up and stumbled, crawling on her hands and knees toward the bathroom.

Aunt Rose clutched her leg as she tried to pass.

"...Got to go..." Mildred moaned.

Aunt Rose held on.

Mildred's stomach emptied itself on the floor. She folded her body into a ball and sobbed.

Aunt Rose held on.

"I'm falling," she whispered.

Aunt Rose held on.

Twenty-Two

CHICAGO, ILLINOIS, 1984

"LOOK AT THE TWO OF THEM TOGETHER," Mildred whispered.

"Why are you whispering?"

O'Kanta came behind her and looked through the kitchen curtains into the backyard, where Aunt Rose and Chapman Jackson were strolling. Aunt Rose talked while Chapman jotted in a notebook.

"I can't believe those two."

Mildred continued to look out the window.

"What's so hard to believe?"

O'Kanta rinsed the chicken wings in the sink. "They have a lot in common. They're both from Tennessee, they love the blues, and..." he stopped.

"And what?"

"And... I don't know."

He spread the wings out on wax paper and began to season them.

"That's what I mean," Mildred continued. "I don't think they have that much in common. I can't ever remember Aunt Rose dating."

190

"Really?" O'Kanta began to sing.

"...*I don't want you to cook my bread...*"

"Never. I remember men from church trying to talk to her. But she wouldn't have any of it. Now look at her..."

"...*I don't want you to make my bed...*"

"Are you listening to me?"

"Hmmm?" O'Kanta looked up. "I'm listening, love. I just like to sing while I cook. Maybe she wanted to make sure that you were taken care of before she committed herself. Now as for her coming over here, I think Chap is laying his groundwork."

"Groundwork for what? Is he serious about her? I hope he's not stringing her along and playing with her feelings. I'm not going to have any of that."

O'Kanta peeked over Mildred's shoulder again.

"Relax, love, relax. They're going to be okay. He's never invited a woman over here that I know of. And," O'Kanta put his arms around Mildred, "between you and me, he asked me to go with him downtown to pick up a couple of suits. Said he wanted to have them ready for his next visit to Wisdom Seat."

"Really?"

"Really." O'Kanta kissed her forehead and cheek.

"Now, what do you think?" He pointed to the meat. "I think this should do it. "We've got chicken, steak, and hamburgers."

"What? No ribs?" Mildred teased. "It's not a true barbecue without ribs."

"Do you mean these ribs?" He began to tickle her.

"Stop!" Mildred laughed and tried to wiggle free. "Stop!"

"Give me a kiss first."

"You already kissed me!"

"Ah, but you didn't kiss *me*."

Mildred and O'Kanta embraced.

"...*I just wanna make...*" O'Kanta sang.

"We're not going to get much barbecuing done that way," Chappie said.

Chapman and Aunt Rose were at the window.

O'Kanta raised the kitchen window higher and spoke through the screen. "I'm all ready. I'm waiting for the grill to heat up. Were you giving Aunt Rose a tour?"

"Rose is going to help me with my garden."

Chapman gestured toward the large backyard. "She's giving me tips on what to plant."

"Aunt Rose loves to garden," Mildred said. "I know she's always missed the garden she used to have in Crayton. What have y'all decided to plant?"

"We'll start with greens, tomatoes, cabbage, peppers, and squash," Aunt Rose said. "I don't know about this Chicago dirt, though. We'll just have to see."

"The grill should be good and hot now," O'Kanta said. "I'll put the wings on, and the steaks and hamburgers should be ready in no time. Is my assistant ready?" He winked at Mildred.

"Ready." Mildred picked up the tray of chicken wings and followed O'Kanta outside.

Aunt Rose and Chapman sat down on the lawn chairs.

"Will the owners of this building let Chappie plant a garden back here?" Mildred asked as O'Kanta placed the wings on the grill.

"Chap owns this building. He also owns a couple of houses that he's renting out. He said that if he ever settled down that he would sell this building to me and move into one of his houses."

"Oh."

Mildred looked over at the lawn table. Chapman returned with two glasses of lemonade.

"I see," she said.

* * *

"Well, well, well," Chapman said as he looked at the table. Corn-on-the-cob, potato salad, cabbage and okra, and two lemon meringue pies surrounded platters of chicken, steaks, and hamburgers.

"It's been a long time since my table has looked this fine. A long time," he repeated.

He held out Aunt Rose's chair as she sat down.

They all joined hands.

"Lord, thank You for blessing us with this fine day," Chapman said. "Thank You for blessing us with the fellowship of Rose and Mildred," he continued. "Thank You for this food we're about to receive. Bless the hands that prepared it. May it nourish out bodies and strengthen us for the delight of Your service. We also ask for blessings for those who are less fortunate. All these things we ask in Jesus's name. Amen."

"Amen!"

"Well, O'Kanta, next week is the primary. How we doin'?" Aunt Rose asked as she fixed Mildred's plate.

"I think we're doing pretty good. If we have a good turnout, we just may make history."

"I can't believe that it's finally coming to an end," Mildred said. "All of the rallies, debates, speeches, campaigning, and it all comes down to one night.

"My supervisor told all of the tellers that we can no longer wear Williams' campaign buttons at work. She said that it was upsetting some of the customers."

"But you've always worn campaign buttons!" Aunt Rose protested.

"I know. Now things are different. I don't even talk about the campaign unless I'm alone in the break room with other Williams' supporters. I feel like I'm walking on eggshells at work."

"Clarence showed me a leaflet that was put in several lockers down at the Sanitation Department," Aunt Rose said. "It had a picture of Raymond Williams with huge lips, eating a slice of watermelon. Underneath the picture it said... What did it say Millie?" she turned to her niece.

"Something like, 'Don't let State Street become Soul Street. Don't elect a monkey for mayor of Chicago.' It was horrible. I couldn't believe it."

"There's a lot of fear going around," O'Kanta said. "People don't know what to expect. But it sure feels good to know that for every ten people that are afraid of change, there one person who's willing to embrace it."

"You think they'll try to hurt him?" Aunt Rose asked.

"The entire world is watching this election," O'Kanta answered. "It's national news now. I think he'll be all right."

"How's Tom Carroll's campaign going?" He turned to Chapman.

"He's holding his own, he's holding his own." Chapman began to butter an ear of corn. "This food is delicious," he said to no one in particular.

Mildred laughed and passed Chapman the bowl of cabbage and okra. "What I like to see are all of the types of people who come to the rallies."

"Yes," Aunt Rose agreed.

"When you look around you, there are people in three-piece suits, jeans, and house dresses. White, black, Hispanic..."

"Old and young," Aunt Rose added.

"I like to see the new faces coming down to the center," O'Kanta said. "Our GED classes have doubled, and more people are now registering to vote than ever before. We registered two busloads of students from Illinois State last week. We're planning on adding job-training classes. We've recruited two teachers from Malcolm X College who have agreed to volunteer."

"I'm meeting so many people from my neighborhood," Mildred said. "Several told me that they don't think that Raymond Williams will win, but they'll vote for him anyway."

"We'll take those votes," O'Kanta said. "We're going to elect him one neighborhood at a time. Now, let's get serious for a moment. I need to ask you all a very important question." He paused until he had everyone's attention.

"How is the barbecue?"

"Excellent, excellent," Chapman answered. "My compliments to the cooks." He nodded to O'Kanta and smiled at Rose. "But I'm saving room for that lemon meringue pie."

"It is good," Aunt Rose agreed. "But what happened to the ribs? Greater Foods have 'em on sale for $1.59 a pound."

"Yeah, what happened to the ribs?" Mildred asked innocently.

"Let me tell you what kind of man I am," O'Kanta began.

"Tell 'em," Chappie suggested.

"I'm the kind of man who's not just concerned with how a woman looks on the outside."

"Uh huh," Chappie agreed.

"I'm concerned with how she feels on the inside," O'Kanta continued. "I don't want to see your digestive system struggling to digest all of that pork."

"He turned me around, that's for sure," Chapman said. "My cholesterol was over 200. I had high blood pressure, and the doctor said I was a borderline diabetic. But 'Kanta changed my diet and I feel like a new man." He pounded his chest.

"What's your cholesterol?" he asked Aunt Rose.

"Uh oh," Mildred replied.

"My cholesterol is fine," Aunt Rose snapped.

"Chappie and I have a surprise for you two after dinner," O'Kanta interrupted.

"Humph," Aunt Rose sniffed.

"What is it?" Mildred wanted to know.

"I'll give you a clue. She was born in Georgia, although we claim her in Tennessee. Her first name begins with 'I'," O'Kanta said.

"Rose, you should know her," Chappie broke in. "The name of her band was called 'Raisin Cain.'"

"Ida Cox? You've got an album by Ida Cox?" Rose exclaimed. "I don't know how long it's been since I've heard one of her songs. Which album do you have?"

"Who is Ida Cox, Aunt Rose?"

"She's the 'Queen of the Blues' in my book," Chappie said.

"She was a blues singer ahead of her time," Rose added.

"She was singing about racism and women's rights way back in the forties."

"That she did," Chappie agreed.

"Have you got the one with 'Four Day Creep' on it?" Rose asked.

"I just might," Chappie said with a wink.

"'Four Day Creep?'" Mildred said.

"Don't worry none, daughter," Chappie answered. "We've got something for you, too. 'Kanta told me that you're a big Koko Taylor fan."

"She's the only woman that still sings the Mississippi Blues," O'Kanta said.

"Where did you find Ida Cox?" Rose asked.

"From a buddy of mine who has a stand on Maxwell Street. He keeps an eye out for blues albums for me."

"My, my, my. Ida Cox." Rose took a bite of chicken. "Almost makes me forget about barbecue ribs."

* * *

Mildred and O'Kanta sat on the floor going through Chapman's Jackson blues albums. Rose and Chapman relaxed on the couch. Two hours had gone by. Chapman refused to play Ida Cox right away.

"You've got to build up to Ida," he said. "I can't just throw her at you right off the bat. We'll build up to her slowly."

Rose sang along with Ida Cox on "Four Day Creep."

"...When you lose your money, don't lose your mind
When you lose your money, don't lose your mind
When you lose your good man, please don't mess with mine..."
"...I'm gonna buy me a bulldog to watch my man while he sleeps
I'm gonna buy me a bulldog to watch my man while he sleeps
Men are so doggone crooked, afraid he might make a four day creep..."

"Now that's the blues," Chapman said as he raised his finger in the air. "That's the blues," he repeated.

"Listen to this next one. Rose do you know 'Take Him Off My Mind'?"
Rose stood and began to sing.

"...I've cried and I've worried, all night I lays and groan
I've cried and I've worried, all night I lays and groan
I used to weigh two hundred, and now I'm down to skin and bones.
It's all about my man, who has always kicked and dogged me raun;
It's all about my man, who's kicked and dogged me raun;
I've tried my best to kill him, but when I do my love comes down..."

Chapman leaned back and watched Rose with fascination.

After the song ended, Rose stood waiting in preparation for the next song.

O'Kanta put on a record and held out his hand to Mildred.

"May I?" he asked.

The sounds of Koko Taylor filled the living room.

"...So you see, I'd rather go blind
Than to see you walk away from me
So you see, I love you so much
And most of all, most of all I just don't wanna lose you..."

Mildred and O'Kanta began to dance.

"Chap, are you going to let the lady stand there alone?" O'Kanta asked.

Chapman rose from the couch and tentatively approached Rose.

Mildred watched the indecision on her aunt's face.

"I don't mind if I do," Rose said simply.

"...So you see, I'd rather go blind
Than to see you walk away from me
So you see, I love you so much
And most of all, most of all I just don't wanna lose you..."

Twenty-Three

MILDRED AND AUNT ROSE HELD HANDS as they entered Oakridge Cemetery. Aunt Rose carried a bouquet of flowers in her left hand, while Mildred carried a lawn chair under her right arm. She and her aunt had been making this trip for as long as she could remember.

Walter Lee of the West Side Livery Cab Service brought them out a couple of times a year and waited to carry them home. After Walter Lee retired, he continued to bring them out at no charge—although he said that he wouldn't mind taking a dessert back home with him.

"Anything you care to fix will be fine with me," he said to Aunt Rose each time she called to let him know that they needed a ride. "I'm partial to sweet potato pie," he'd add. "But anything you care to fix will be just fine."

Mildred always brought a sweet potato pie, plastic knife, and plate. Walter liked to snack on a piece while he waited.

Mildred and her aunt walked through the cemetery in silence. Miss Roberta's grave was located at the end of a winding trail. Mildred looked at the familiar headstones along the way.

Patricia Hendrix
Born 1917–Died 1983
Wife of Theodore Hendrix
Beloved mother of Arthur, Barbara, and Sharon

Eldridge Ford
Born 1909–Died 1971
In Loving Memory

David K. Kennedy
Rachel Kennedy
Born 1970–Died 1970
May You Rest in God's Arms

When they reached Miss Roberta's grave, Aunt Rose and Mildred stopped and said a short prayer.

"Well, well, well, Miss Roberta," Aunt Rose said to the headstone. "I guess you thought we wouldn't be coming to see you at all this year."

Mildred removed last year's flower arrangement of carnations and replaced it with the yellow roses. After opening the lawn chair for her aunt, she knelt down and began to clean the area around Miss Roberta's gravestone.

"I've got a lot to catch you up on," Aunt Rose began.

"Yes," Mildred said to herself. "There is a lot to catch up on."

She sat down on the ground beside Aunt Rose, hugging her knees.

"You see, Millie met this man on the El, and don't ask me why she stopped to talk to him, but it's a good thing that she did," Aunt Rose began.

"Had six months passed so quickly?" She twirled last year's artificial carnations between her finger. *"Was it only six months ago that O'Kanta walked into the El car and sat down beside her? What would have happened if he had chosen another car? Another seat? Another girl to talk to?"*

"...Went down to the center and heard that young boy speak. You would have thought I was back in Sweet Water Baptist Church..."

"Yes, O'Kanta had a way of speaking. Aunt Rose said that he put her in the mind of L.C. when he spoke. But where did that leave her?"

"...Joseph Matthews is working with us! So are the Dillons, the Millers, the Westbrooks, the Smiths, the Coopers, even Miss Esther Patillo is going around wearing a Raymond Williams button. She says that she'll vote for him, but I don't know, because you know how Esther is..."

Her life was exciting now. Each day brought a new event. Speeches to hear, rallies to participate in, debates to watch. After the primary, there was the general election. O'Kanta said that the movement should not stop if Williams is not elected. He said that it was important for people to understand and be involved in the total electoral process, but it was all going by too fast. The days were flying through Mildred's fingers. She didn't want it to stop. She had something to say and people were listening. Her neighbors stopped her as she waited for the bus and asked, 'How's our man doin'?'

People wanted her opinion. She was important; she was somebody. She volunteered for the center, worked the rallies...

"Miss Roberta, you should have seen Raymond Williams standing in the pulpit of Wisdom Seat. You should have been there to hear him for yourself. I sure can't do him justice..."

Mildred got up and wandered a few steps from Roberta's grave.

After the excitement, the rallies, the speeches, then what? What happened when it was all over? What would she have to say, to do, to give? She would return to being the Mildred Johnson who was not seen, not heard, not noticed.

She'd be like one of those wind-up toys that had slowly wound down.

She walked back to her aunt.

Aunt Rose sat in the lawn chair with her head down and her hands clasped.

Mildred looked at the headstone.

Roberta Brown

Born 1892– Died 1960

Beloved friend and devoted Christian

Her memories of Miss Roberta were fuzzy. Aunt Rose told her that without Miss Roberta she would never have been able to survive Chicago. The cultural differences between the North and the South were too great.

"Baby," Aunt Rose said, "these people up here laughed at the way I walked and the way I talked. I didn't know how to get around and was too afraid to ask for help. I was afraid of everything and everybody. Those El cars frightened me. When the doors opened in front of me for the first time, I just stood there. I didn't know if I was supposed to wait for somebody to tell me to come on board or what. I just stood there waiting and watched the doors close in my face. There was so much noise at night that I couldn't sleep. It was a relief to hear you cry at night, cause at least that was a sound that I could understand."

Miss Roberta had never married and had no children. She had adopted Rose Johnson and Millie and claimed them as her own.

"And if any two people ever needed 'claiming,'" Aunt Rose said, "it was you and me. Baby, when my Aunt Dee died in that car crash, I was left alone in this city that seemed ready to eat me up. Miss Roberta was my rock. God rest her soul."

When Miss Roberta died of a heart attack, she had left her entire estate to Rose Johnson. Aunt Rose said that she had no idea what to do with the money. She knew that she would tithe to the church, but did not have a clue as to what to do with the rest.

"To tell you the truth, baby, I was afraid of all that money," Rose recalled. "Lord knows I didn't deserve it. It should have been me giving money to *her* for all that she gave to me."

201

She had talked with Reverend Giles, who convinced her that she should invest it in real estate. Reverend Giles went with Rose to Independence Bank on Chicago's West Side and walked her through the process of home ownership.

"Millie, I couldn't believe it. Me owning something after renting all of my life. If it hadn't been for Reverend Giles, I wouldn't have even known what to charge for rent. Flossie, Reverend Giles, and me drove around until we found this two-flat.

"Reverend Giles told me, 'Sister Rose, this is income-producing property. You won't have to worry about making your mortgage.'"

After all of these years, the Matthews family had no idea that Aunt Rose owned the building. They paid their rent to Walker Realty Company at the post office box each month.

"Baby, you ready?" Aunt Rose's voice broke into Mildred's thoughts.

"Uh huh."

Mildred picked up the lawn chair, and she and her aunt walked back to Walter's car.

It was a quiet ride home from the cemetery.

"Are you hungry?" Mildred asked as she opened the door.

"No, baby."

"You want to watch some television?"

"Not now. I need to be by myself for a spell. I'll be out after a while." Aunt Rose went into her bedroom and shut the door.

Mildred sat in Aunt Rose's rocking chair and looked out the window. Rocking always relaxed her. The creak of the rockers on the wooden floor was soothing.

How could one person have the power to change her life? She and O'Kanta had not discussed the future. When the election was over, would he lose interest? Would she return to "Unstained Mildred Walker?" If he walked out of her life, would it all end? Would he carry her new life with him onto the next girl? The next election?

* * *

202

"Millie, baby!" Aunt Rose's voice was in Mildred's ear.

"Millie! Wake up, baby. If you sleep too long, you won't be able to sleep at all tonight."

Mildred opened her eyes slowly.

"I didn't mean to go to sleep. What time is it?"

"Eight o'clock. Are you hungry?"

"Not really."

"Good, me neither. Come on in the kitchen. I made us some hot chocolate."

Aunt Rose opened the refrigerator and got out the whipped cream.

Mildred sat down and sighed heavily.

"What's the matter with you?"

"I don't know. I guess going to visit Miss Roberta kind of made me sad."

Aunt Rose took a sip of her hot chocolate.

"You know, I was a little down myself when we left, but after talking with Miss Roberta, I knew I had to come in here and spend some time on my knees. Now, I'm feeling much better."

"Oh."

"I talked to Mildred, L.C., and Caleb," Aunt Rose continued. "We laughed together and we cried."

Mildred's eyes opened wider, "Huh?"

"Drink your hot chocolate now while it's hot."

"You talked to who?"

"I just told you."

"I know, but..."

"Are you going to drink it?"

Mildred obediently took a sip.

"Now, I want you to tell me why you were sad."

"I told you..."

"I mean I want to know all of it."

"I don't know."

Mildred stirred her hot chocolate. "I've just got a lot on my mind, that's all."

"O'Kanta?"

"He's part of it. But that's not all of it. I don't know if I can even explain it. Aunt Rose, I just don't know who I am anymore. I mean, is this the new me? The one who goes with you and knocks on doors and talks about Raymond Williams? Is it the real me? When the election is over, will I have anything to say? Will O'Kanta still want to be with me when I don't have anything to say? I'm not sure that *I* would even want to be with me," she finished quietly.

Aunt Rose took her hand and held it.

"Yes, baby, this is the real you. I know it and O'Kanta knows it, but, bless your heart, you don't know it yet.

"When I was talking with Miss Roberta today, I was telling her about you. How you've come into your own. How you've claimed your heritage and how proud Mildred and L.C. would be of you. But baby, Mildred and L.C. were proud of you before you were knocking on doors. I was too.

"Then Miss Roberta turned the tables on me. She told me that I..."

Rose's hand shook as she tried to take a sip of hot chocolate. She started again, "You see, I made a promise to Mildred and L.C. on that Friday night as I rode the Greyhound bus to Chicago. You were such a good baby and slept most of the way. I looked down at you as the bus passed through town after town. I promised them during that trip that I would raise you the best way that I knew how. I would teach you to love God and to love your neighbor. I promised them that their death would not be in vain and that I would never let you forget them or the sacrifice that they made for you that night.

"I also told them that when the time came, that I would let you go."

"What do you mean 'let me go', Aunt Rose?" Mildred's voice rose loudly. "I don't want to go anywhere..."

"Ssh, ssh," Aunt Rose said as she squeezed Mildred's hand. "Baby, there are a lot of ways to hold onto people. Some are good and some not so good. When we left Crayton, I held onto you so tight and wouldn't let anybody in. But God sent me Miss Roberta. So when I relaxed and let her in, her friendship was a blessing to both of us. Can you imagine where we would be today if I had refused to let her into our lives?

"The Lord reminded me what a blessing I received when I relaxed, depended on Him, and let someone into our lives. Where would we be without the Reverend and Flossie Giles, our church family, our neighbors and friends?"

"Yes, you're right," Mildred agreed.

"But I have not always let people in. Over the years, there were several gentlemen callers that came my way. Aunt Dee sent some by—and we won't talk about those. Miss Roberta tried to introduce me to a gentleman or two, and even Flossie Giles wanted me to meet a couple of her relatives. But I told them all that I couldn't even think about courtin' because I had to raise you. But baby, I lied. Miss Roberta knew it. I was using you as an excuse because I was holding on to the past and that was not good.

"I was holding on to Caleb, you see. I compared each man to Caleb, and of course none ever measured up to him. It was Caleb or nobody. He was my first love and when he was gone, it was like Rose was gone. I was just an empty shell. But God reminded me that whenever I trusted Him, and opened my heart and my hands, that He blessed me. Then I looked at where He brought me from. If I had stayed in that church back in Crayton for five more minutes, I wouldn't be here today. And what would have happened to you? Who would tell you the story? Caleb pushed me out that door. You could say that he was letting me go. Now I've got to let him go. Look at where God's brought you. Baby, I know how you're feeling and it's my fault."

"No, Aunt Rose," Mildred broke in.

Aunt Rose raised her hand for silence. "It is my fault. I've sat here and watched you pour all of yourself into O'Kanta and this election and I didn't try to stop you. But I won't sit here and let you make the same mistake that I made. It's time for you to open your heart and your hands."

205

"What do you mean, Aunt Rose?"

"I talked to Mildred and I talked to L.C. I apologized to them for holding you back. I told them that we were coming."

"Aunt Rose, what are you talking about? Where are we going?"

"Haven't you heard anything that I said? We're going to Crayton."

"Crayton? Crayton, Tennessee?" Mildred stood up.

"You said that you would never go back there, Aunt Rose. You said that—"

"I know, I know, and that was right for me then, but now it's time for us to go home. I've got to go and say good-bye to Caleb and you've got to go and say hello to Mildred and L.C. I'm taking you back for a visit. We're taking a trip."

"To Crayton? But Aunt Rose, what about O'Kanta and the election? We're just going to up and leave? How long will we stay? What about O'Kanta?" she repeated.

In her agitation, she knocked her cup of hot chocolate over.

Aunt Rose got up to get a cloth to wipe it up.

"We're leaving after the primary."

"But what about Raymond Williams?" Mildred asked. "What about O'Kanta?"

"Baby, Raymond Williams will do fine without me and you. We've done all we can for him. Now we've got to work on us."

Rose walked over to her niece and grabbed both of her hands.

"I want to show you where you were born. I want to show you the restaurant where I worked. I want to visit the place where Sweet Water Baptist Church used to stand. It don't matter if none of these places are there. The ground is still there, the spirit is there, and your history is there. Do you want to go?"

Mildred nodded. "But what about O'Kanta?"

"Baby, if God sent you O'Kanta, he's not going anywhere. He'll be the same man when we return. But you," she cupped her niece's face, "you'll be different."

"But what about you, Aunt Rose? What about Caleb?"

"I'm going to tell him good-bye," Aunt Rose said. "But before I tell him good-bye, I'm going to introduce him to you."

"Oh, Aunt Rose! I can't believe I'm going to finally see Crayton, Tennessee. This is so exciting! How long will we stay? What should I pack?"

"I don't know how long we'll stay, but we'll know when it's time to come home. Are you hungry? You feel like running over to Chicken Shack and getting us something to eat?"

"I'm too excited to eat."

Mildred grabbed her aunt's hands. "Aunt Rose, you always know what to do. Whenever I'm confused, upset, angry, or sad—you always have the answer. What would I do without you?"

Mildred hugged Aunt Rose. "Where would I be?" She leaned on her aunt's shoulder and began to cry. "Where would I be?" she whispered.

"Now, now," Aunt Rose patted her back. "Where would any of us be without the Lord's grace and mercy? Where would any of us be?" She lovingly rubbed Mildred's head and kissed her softly on the cheek.

Twenty-Four

CHICAGO, ILLINOIS, 1985

"THIS IS IT, AUNT ROSE." Mildred squeezed her aunt's hand. "This is it!"

"I know, baby, I know. Lord have mercy. We really did it, didn't we?"

Mildred looked around her. Posters of Raymond Williams covered every wall of the center. Newspaper clippings, pamphlets, and brochures were posted everywhere. Red and white helium-filled balloons hung in mid-air, and tables were covered with tee shirts, campaign buttons, baseball caps, and bumper stickers. Raymond Williams' famous grin beamed out from eight-by-ten glossies and campaign buttons. Yet another table was laden with hats, whistles, and party favors.

Aaron, the owner of Ray's Liquors, where the center was housed, donated a case of Korbel champagne. O'Kanta said that no matter what the outcome of the primary, everyone was going to celebrate.

Gospel music blared from the speakers, and the air was filled with a nervous excitement. Supporters streamed in and out, questioning whether any results had come in. Several people gathered in groups, hotly debating the campaign. Others huddled close to the television set, watching vote tallies as they came across the screen.

"What time is O'Kanta coming back?" Aunt Rose asked.

"I don't know. He and a few of the guys were driving the seniors to the polls. He should be back soon."

"Reverend Giles and Flossie said that they would come by after the prayer service," Aunt Rose said.

"I'm glad they decided to open Wisdom Seat to the community to pray for peace tonight," Mildred answered.

"I feel like dancing myself," Aunt Rose exclaimed.

"Well, I brought you a dancing partner." O'Kanta's voice surprised them both.

Aunt Rose and Mildred turned around to face O'Kanta and Chapman Jackson.

"Chappie!" Mildred hugged him. "I'm so glad to see you here. Did you come to celebrate with us?"

Chapman nervously twirled his fedora between his fingers.

"I decided to come where my heart is," he said to Mildred, but looked straight at Aunt Rose.

"I've been waiting for you," Aunt Rose said.

"I'm here," Chapman answered.

They continued to stare at each other.

Chappie leaned forward and kissed Aunt Rose's cheek.

She took his hat.

"Do you want me to go and get your pocketbook?" Mildred asked.

Rose glared at Mildred.

"Any results in yet?" Chapman asked.

"Some of the precincts are just beginning to turn in their votes. Let's go sit down and watch the news," Aunt Rose suggested. She and Chapman walked to the front of the center and sat down next to each other in front of the television.

O'Kanta took Mildred's hand and led her into the inner office.

He sat down on the edge of the office desk and pulled Mildred onto his lap.

"I've been thinking about you all day," he whispered. "Everyone around me was talking about the election, but all I could do was nod or shake my head. I feel like I'm winning and losing at the same time."

Mildred caressed O'Kanta's face. She slipped off the rubber band that held his dreadlocks and wrapped a handful of his hair around her fingers. She squeezed the soft, spongy dreadlocks.

O'Kanta took her hand and kissed each finger. "When are you leaving?"

Mildred pressed his hand against her cheek. "You know we're leaving in the morning," she reminded him.

"Who's going to be here to motivate me, to encourage me? Who's going to be here to *love* me?"

Mildred kissed him. "I'm coming back," she whispered.

O'Kanta held her close.

"Hey! Hey!"

Shouts, screams, and whoops of jubilation erupted outside the door. Mildred and O'Kanta ran out into cheers and the noisy sound of party favors. A crowd of supporters gathered around the television.

"*Again, with a third of the precincts reporting, Parker and Carroll are neck and neck in a dead heat, with Williams trailing. However, the votes have not been turned in from the south and west sides of Chicago. Sources report that a high voter turnout in those areas could put Raymond Williams over the top. There is a possibility that Congressman Raymond Williams could be the first African American elected mayor of Chicago. Stay tuned to CBS for continuous election coverage...*"

"O'Kanta can you believe it!" Mildred squeezed his hand. "Can you! Where's Aunt Rose?"

"Up there with Chap."

Chapman Jackson had his arm around Aunt Rose and seemed to be in the midst of a serious discussion.

"I wonder what they're talking about," Mildred said.

"He's probably begging and pleading his case for her to stay like I

210

did with you. Chappie told me last night that the South can woo and court a woman just like a man. He's afraid that Rose won't want to come back to Chicago."

O'Kanta heard his name being called.

He excused himself, quickly kissed Mildred on the cheek, and hurried away.

Mildred debated whether or not she should go over and sit with her aunt, who appeared engrossed in conversation with Chappie.

"Hello, Mildred," a voice distracted her.

Mildred turned into the shy smile of Charles Gilbert.

"Why, Charles Gilbert, it's good to see you."

Charles Gilbert nodded. "I brought some students with me from my art class."

Mildred shook hands with several of the students. "I want to thank you and your class for all of the posters and flyers. Please help yourself to some coffee and cookies."

"Well, Mildred," Charles Gilbert cleared his throat. "I hear you're leaving for Tennessee tomorrow morning," he addressed the floor.

"Yeah. We're going back to Crayton for a little while. It's been a long time since my aunt has been home."

"Well, uh, have a good trip."

"Thank you, Charles Gilbert."

Charles Gilbert looked up. "Just *Charles* is fine with me," he said.

"Thank you, Charles." Mildred smiled at him and extended her hand.

"Well, I'd better get back to my friends," he said.

Mildred watched him walk away.

"Was that Charles Gilbert just now?" Aunt Rose asked.

"Yeah. He brought some of his friends who painted the posters. Where's Chappie?"

"I left him over there talking to Esther Patillo."

"Mrs. Patillo's here? I didn't see her come in. Did she vote for Raymond Williams?"

211

"Claims she did. She walked over and took Mr. Jackson a saucer full of *your* cookies. I left her with him sharing her personal testimony."

"Aunt Rose! How could you? He's looking over here right now!"

"Is he?" Aunt Rose looked over at Chapman. "Well let's wave to him."

Mildred and Aunt Rose smiled as they waved.

"Hello! Hello! How are you all doing?" Reverend Giles's voiced boomed, parting the crowd as he entered the center. "Bless you son! Who's in charge here?"

Mildred and Aunt Rose hurried over.

"Good evening, Reverend," Aunt Rose hugged Reverend Giles. "Flossie, I'm so glad you all could make it."

"We just stopped by for a minute. The reverend wanted to have a short prayer here at the center before we headed home," Flossie answered.

"That's an excellent idea. Mildred go and find O'Kanta so he can get the microphone and..."

"There's no need for that," Reverend Giles interrupted. "May I have everyone's attention? Can someone please turn that music down? Who's in charge here?"

"Can we all pause for a minute?" O'Kanta said. "Reverend Giles is here to lead us in prayer."

A hush fell over the Center.

Reverend Giles began. "God is in His holy temple. Let all the Earth be silent before Him! Let us bow our heads for a moment. The Bible says that where two or more are gathered that the Lord is with them. Father God, we thank You for this gathering of Your people. We come together in thanksgiving. We thank You for all that You've done in our lives. We come together as many, but we are all on one accord."

"Yes, we are!" Dwayne said.

"We come before You and pray that after tonight, no matter the outcome, that we will continue to be of one accord. We pray tonight that Your will be done.

"We hope and pray that it is Your will for Raymond Williams to govern this city and lead Your people."

"Yes, Sir!" someone said.

"But if that is not Your will, we ask you to give us patience as we wait upon You. Oh we can be a stiff-necked people sometimes, but we're so grateful that You love us in spite of ourselves. We ask your blessings upon this gathering here of Your people. Please bless our city on this election night and every night."

"Bless us, Lord!" Aunt Rose said.

"We thank You that here, in 1985, we have the opportunity to vote. Father, some of us remember the time when we neither had the right nor the privilege."

"Tell it!" someone shouted. "Tell it!"

"Amen," Aunt Rose whispered. "Amen."

"You've truly brought us a long way. We thank You for the hills and we thank You for the valleys, too. We thank You for the rough side of the mountain. Because Lord, we realize how difficult it would be to try and climb a slick mountain. We thank You for the nooks and the crannies that allowed us to get a grip. We're thanking You tonight, Lord."

"Yes, sir," Chapman Jackson said. "Yes, sir."

"We thank You for the work that the people are doing at this center. Thank You for placing them in our community. Bless them for the challenges that lie ahead. Equip them with all that they will need."

"Please," Mildred whispered. "Please."

"Lord, we don't know what the future holds, but we are leaning and depending upon You. The songwriter says, 'My hope is built on nothing less than Jesus's blood and righteousness. I dare not trust the sweetest frame, but wholly lean on Jesus's name. On Christ the solid rock I stand, all other ground is sinking sand...'

"Bless everyone under the sound of my voice, and we ask a special blessing upon our children. They hold the keys to our future. Lord, we just can't thank You enough for all that you've done. We thank you most of all for your precious son, Jesus Christ, and it is in His name, the name that is both strong and sufficient, that we ask this prayer. Amen."

"Amen!"

Mildred, Aunt Rose, Flossie, and Reverend Giles, all embraced each other.

"Well, well, well," Reverend Giles rocked back and forth on his heels, "headed off in the morning, are you? I know of one somebody is going to be mighty heartbroken when you're gone," he winked at Mildred. "Do you know who that somebody is?"

"Is that my baby over there?" Flossie asked.

"Yes. Charles Gilbert came over here especially to wish Mildred a safe trip," Aunt Rose confided.

"Aunt Rose!"

"He did, huh? That's my boy!" Reverend strolled briskly in Charles Gilbert's direction.

"Don't you all worry about anything. We'll go by the house and keep an eye out for you," Flossie said.

"Flossie Mae. What would I do without you?" Aunt Rose hugged her.

"Oh, I don't know. I'd say you're doing okay. Isn't that Mr. Jackson over there?" Flossie looked at Rose with a twinkle in her eye.

"Yes," Mildred answered.

"Rose Johnson! Are you blushing?" Flossie laughed and hugged Aunt Rose again. "Well, let me get over there and rescue my child."

Mildred looked in Charles Gilbert's direction. Reverend Giles appeared to be having a church service with Charles and his friends.

"Here's an update!" someone shouted. All eyes turned to the television.

"*With 76 percent of the votes in, Congressman Raymond Williams has a slight lead. The majority of the votes that are yet to be counted are from the south and west sides, which are a stronghold for the congressman. There's talk of a concession speech later tonight from Parker Reynolds...*"

Cheers erupted throughout the center.

"Hey, O'Kanta!" Dwayne yelled out. "Do we pop the cork yet?"

"How about waiting until 90 percent of the votes are in?" he yelled back.

Mildred looked around at the many faces that filled the center. This was her community, and it was laughing, crying, shouting, and dancing. This was her family. Her eyes rested on O'Kanta, who was talking with two groups and writing something on the board. Mildred was sure that he was organizing teams in preparation for a grassroots general election campaign. She couldn't tear her eyes away from him. She wanted to remember the way he smiled at her, the way he tugged on his beard, his smell of incense and musk, the way he touched her, the sound of his voice when he whispered her name.

She felt Aunt Rose's hand slide into hers. "It's all right, baby. It's all right to miss him."

"Aunt Rose?"

"Yes, baby?"

"I'm ready to go home."

Aunt Rose hugged Mildred tightly. "Let's go, baby. We'll just sneak on out. I never liked good-byes either."

* * *

Mildred carefully poured the Mogen David wine into the lead crystal glasses that once belonged to her Great Aunt Delores. She took a glass over to Aunt Rose.

"What shall we toast to?" she asked.

"The movement?" Aunt Rose suggested. "Raymond Williams? O'Kanta?"

"Chappie?" Mildred countered. "Crayton?"

"To you," Aunt Rose said.

"And you," Mildred answered.

Both women stared solemnly at each other as they turned their glasses up. Mildred walked over to the record player and started the record.

"*I've been from Spain to Tokyo, from Africa and O-h-i-o,*" B.B. King sang. "*I never tried to make the news, I'm just a man who plays the blues.*"

215

Mildred started out with her shuffle.

"I take my loving everywhere, I come back and they still care...
One love ahead, one love behind, one in my arms, one on my mind...
but there's one thing they know – I never make my move too soon..."

She turned to Aunt Rose who, never moving from one spot, broke into her shimmy. Taking her hand off her hip, she put the tip of her index finger to her tongue and touched the floor with it, whispering, "Caldonia, why is your head so hard?"

POST-PRIMARY MORNING, CHICAGO, 1985

MILDRED AND AUNT ROSE STOOD on the platform of the Grey-hound Bus Station waiting for Number 57 that would take them to Crayton, Tennessee.

"Aunt Rose, are you sure you want to take the local?" Mildred asked. "The local stops at a slew of places."

"I know that it stops at a lot of places, baby. I need to pass through all of the stops that I went through when I brought you here. I prayed at every one of those stops and I want to thank God as I pass back through each and every one. I need to thank Him for bringing me out and for answering my prayers. You were such a good baby. Hardly cried at all. I cried enough for the both of us. I cradled you in my arms, and I promised you that everything was going to be all right. I promised you," Aunt Rose whispered. "And I tried...I tried to keep my promise."

"You did more than keep your promise, Aunt Rose," Mildred replied, her voice on the edge of tears. "You did a whole lot more than that."

"*Now boarding at Gate 8, Number 57 leaving from Chicago and stopping at Homewood; Kankakee; Champaign; Mattoon; Effingham; Centralia; Carbondale; Fulton, Kentucky; Newberg; Crayton; and Memphis.*" The string of stops was announced over the loud speaker.

Number 57 pulled up to the platform. Mildred and Aunt Rose were the first to board.

The doors opened.

Mildred took her aunt's arm.

Aunt Rose's knees buckled on the first step.

"Are you all visiting or going back home?" the driver asked.

Aunt Rose made a choking sound.

Mildred spoke for her.

"We're going home," she said, gently helping her aunt up the stairs.

She led Aunt Rose to a seat near the front of the bus and put her arms around her.

Aunt Rose turned her face into Mildred's neck and began to sob.

"It's going to be okay, Aunt Rose," Mildred whispered. "We're going home."

She looked out of the window as the sun's early morning rays sparkled on the skyscrapers of downtown Chicago. The rose-gold sky seemed to glow in the early morning hours.

She nudged her aunt. "Is the sky this pretty in Crayton?"

Aunt Rose raised her head up, blew her nose, and looked out of the window and up at the sky.

"It's prettier," she said and leaned back into the cradle of Mildred's arms. "I'll show you."

Dear _____:

Some Glad Morning brought me reading pleasure. Knowing your tastes, I thought it might do the same for you. Why not ask for it at your local bookstore or order it directly from the publisher at AS/IS Press at www.irenejsteele.com?

Sincerely,